Living in a
Star's Light

A novel based on
the life of Miss Lotta Crabtree

Steve Lindahl

Living in a Star's Light

A novel based on the life of Miss Lotta Crabtree

Steve Lindahl

Dedication

I dedicate this novel to the theater people I have known during the years I spent in school, community and professional theater groups. They taught me ways to understand and appreciate the characters they portrayed, a skill I believe has helped me in my writing. They also taught me the joy of music and dance. Although Lotta Crabtree was unique and one of the most famous performers of her time, she shared many qualities with every player who has ever stepped on a stage.

Chapter One

Dancing and Fishing

Little Lotta Crabtree spun on the stage in Mart Taylor's Saloon, her hair flying out, her toes tapping and her legs crossing and uncrossing faster than a hummingbird's wings. She modified her dance a bit by flipping her skirt with her hands, as well as her legs, the white frills of her bloomers covering her calves and knees. Her shoes click-clacked loudly on the wood, her dance a traditional leggy jig to an old Irish tune.

She had about a year over Walter Cain's five and a half. He stood close to the edge of the stage, staring like he was watching lightning.

Lotta's dark green dress had a long skirt with white stripes running up and down. She wore a top with short puffy sleeves and a loose neckline, showing off her pale-white shoulders and arms. Her body was thin, while her face was round. Her dark red, shoulder-length curls bounced when she moved. Walter hadn't met many girls his own age since there were few children living in the gold camps. But today Lotta was here, the prettiest girl he'd ever seen.

Still, there was more to her than the pace of her dancing. On stage, she could be anything she wanted, from a rough and tumble camp girl to an eloquent society lady, all while keeping the innocence of her young age.

Walter and his pa, Oliver Cain, stayed in the saloon long enough to meet Lotta following the show. Actually, they stayed the entire night because Oliver was too drunk to walk his son back to the bunkhouse. They slept on the floor. Walter didn't know it at the time, but it was a good thing his pa had overindulged not only because Oliver's drunken state gave Walter a chance to meet and hug Lotta, but because his pa, who dozed in a corner, didn't toss his gold onto the stage as all the other miners had. They ate well the following week.

* * *

Oliver was not a terrible pa, but bad luck ran in the family. Walter knew the history. His grandmother died bringing his pa into the world. His grandfather took care of Oliver for eleven years before the old man coughed himself to death in the slums of Five Points. Oliver told Walter his grandfather had died of consumption, but he also said they never called for a doctor.

When Walter's ma disappeared, Oliver decided he would raise Walter on his own. He wasn't married to the woman and didn't know for sure the boy was his, but if Oliver's own pa could take care of a baby, he could as well. They spent a couple of years in New York on Mulberry Street where Oliver made enough as a bare-knuckle boxer to keep a roof over their heads, and Walter fed and clothed. Then, in 1848, James Wilson Marshall struck gold at Sutter's Mill. The California Gold Rush was on and Oliver set off hoping his luck would change.

It didn't.

He hadn't struck it rich, so he and Walter slept in some rough conditions—sometimes outside or in caves or ravines, but mostly in sheds that passed for bunkhouses, along with too many other miners who generally snored and smelled. There was one nice thing, though. Walter's best friend Frank and his pa traveled, panned, and bunked with them, so there was always someone to talk to.

Walter and Frank established a routine for a couple of years, one that helped keep them alive. While their fathers went to the creeks, the boys went to the fishing lake. Even if there was no luck finding gold, they still had to eat. The boys had to help with the cooking, too, but that wasn't why Walter had brought a frying pan with him that day.

"You plannin' on cooking up here?" Frank asked as they approached their favorite fishing lake.

"Nope, just fishing," Walter told him. "But I've got a plan for something much better."

Frank grinned and walked a little closer to Walter.

"My pa cooked a coon last night," Walter explained, smiling as if he had just found the gold his pa had been dreaming about. "This here pan's filled with grease."

"So?"

"Grease for Lotta."

"Heard she was coming this way. You gonna watch her with me, ain't you?" Frank rarely missed a show, especially when Lotta was the one dancing. "But why would she want your coon grease?"

"I'm gonna watch her fall." Walter laughed at the look on Frank's face. He knew his friend wouldn't like his idea. "They're setting up a platform and I'm gonna grease it. She'll be slipping like a hound running on ice."

Frank still seemed a bit put off. "Why would you want to hurt Lotta?"

"Don't be stupid. She's too quick on her feet to actually fall. She'll just stumble. It'll be fun and maybe bring her down a bit. Remember, she gets to live in that fancy boarding house in Coulterville, the one her ma owns, while we have to sleep in a shed."

"Your pa will be mad. Mine too."

"Maybe or maybe not." Walter leaned in toward his friend and spoke quietly. "Maybe they're getting tired of her. She acts so high and mighty. She's just a kid, like us, yet she gets all that gold for tapping her feet. If she had to spend her days panning or fishing, she'd know how hard it is for the rest of us to get something to eat. I think my pa would like that."

"Fishing ain't so hard," Frank told him, but Walter hadn't felt a tug on his line for a while, like the fish had something to say about this, too.

Each boy had a stick with a string tied and wound around it. The strings had store-bought hooks. They'd long since learned how fish could wiggle off homemade ones. The boys could release some string to cast their hooks into the lake then wind the string around the sticks by spinning, although they usually backed up to pull a fish in because winding was slow. Both Walter and Frank were good at this process. Their fathers had taught them well.

They had caught six small whitefish, five by Frank. Walter wasn't having a good day. Yet, six was enough to feed the four of them. They strung the fish but decided to keep fishing. It was still early and if they caught extra, they might trade for a little gold.

"I got something," Frank shouted, trembling, almost losing his grip on his stick.

"What is it?" Walter jumped to see, tossing his own stick as he stood.

Frank moved from the shore and back-peddled as fast as he could. Meanwhile, Walter stuck by the bank, so he could grab the line when the fish was close and pull it up on land. They worked well as a team. But this time, when Walter pulled on the string, he jumped back, dropping the catch into the water.

"Blazes!" Walter yelled, "It's a snake." He grabbed a sturdy stick and again stepped toward the lake. "Move back further. You get it on land, and I'll hit it."

Frank managed to get the serpent up without hooking on the bushes overhanging the lake, which took some moving about. The snake was gray with yellow stripes.

Once on land, the snake twisted and wiggled, like one of Lotta's dances. Walter took a swing but missed. The serpent was squirming over toward Frank, who kept backing up. Walter took another swing and hit it, narrowly missing its head. The ground was soft, so the stick didn't seem to slow the thing down. "Pull it across that stone," Walter said, indicating a flat rock with a nod of his head.

Frank moved to his right. The snake had no choice but to follow. He edged it up on the rock, but the snake wriggled off. Frank moved again, pulling the string in the opposite direction. This time the snake tried to cross the stone. Walter swung, again and again, the skull-crunching under Walter's blows.

When he was sure the snake was dead, Walter used the tangled string to tie it with the rest of their catch. It was time to head home. Their fathers would be looking forward to the show that night and were likely to get home early. Walter hoped the platform would be in place, so he could grease it before they started the cooking fire.

Building supplies were scarce in the camps, which meant the temporary stage had to be built out of material borrowed from the housing. This was another reason why Walter was angry. The men took boards from the wall by his pa's bunk. It was embarrassing to have their things out where everyone could see and, if it rained, all their stuff would get soaked. Once again, Lotta was getting everything while Walter had nothing. The men put the platform near the creek, which was a distance from where the tents and shacks were. That was good since the boys needed to get to it without getting caught.

When they reached the platform, they hid behind a cluster of apple trees and studied the area, looking for a chance to apply the grease.

"What now?" Frank asked after they'd been there a few moments.

"We wait. Last thing I want is for my pa to catch me."

"Me neither. I don't want to get caught by nobody."

Lotta's ma showed up while they were watching. She was short and looked a lot like Lotta. She checked over the place where the show was to take place. Walter didn't expect any problems from the lady since he hadn't applied the grease yet. But she did find a loose board. She had a hammer with her, so she nailed it tight.

After Lotta's ma left, they continued to stare at the platform and were about to step from behind the trees when another lady arrived. She sat on the platform and began knitting something. Walter had seen her around the camp but didn't know her name. She probably lived in one of the tents. The ladies from there were always looking for an outside place to sit, a place with plenty of light—where they could work without being disturbed. If her husband was home, she might be trying to get away from him as well.

Frank asked. "Should we tell her somebody's looking for her?"

"Do you know someone who *might* be looking?" Walter felt his chest tighten.

"I don't," Frank told him.

"She wouldn't believe two kids like us anyway."

They were quiet for a while, until Frank suggested, "We could annoy her until she chases after us. Maybe throw pebbles?"

"Or," Walter said, pausing as he thought his plan through. "We could scare her off with the snake. It's still hanging on the fishing string."

"There's an idea," Frank told his friend. "Where are the fish?"

"They're on the tree with two trunks. You stay here. I'll get the snake."

When Walter returned, he told Frank to grab a handful of pebbles.

Frank moved near the lady and started tossing them at the end of the platform.

"What are you doing, boy?" the woman shouted. She sat on the platform but turned to face Frank.

"Nothing." Frank replied.

The woman crossed her arms and leaned toward Frank. "Go do *nothing* someplace else. You could hurt me throwing stones like that."

While the woman's back was turned, Walter stepped into the field. He moved toward the platform, avoiding sticks that might snap under his feet. He half covered the snake with leaves, then ran the string along the side of the platform. He would kneel back there, out of sight, while he pulled the dead serpent across the grass.

When Walter was in place, he waved to Frank who looked at the snake, yelled "Aaaagh!" then turned and ran. The woman jumped, spun around, then shook her head. Walter could tell she knew the snake was a joke, but she grabbed the material she'd been knitting and walked off toward the tent area anyway.

Frank circled back to Walter, laughing like a miner who just discovered a mother lode. "What now?" he asked.

"Now we grease the boards," Walter was eager to complete the prank. He left the snake and went back for the coon pan he'd left behind the apple trees.

He had just turned and stepped toward the platform when he heard, "Walter!" He spun around to see his pa approaching from the direction of the creek. Frank must have seen him sooner, because he took off toward the bunkhouse.

"Why are you here so early?" Walter asked. He tried to hide the pan behind his back without getting grease on his clothes.

"We stopped," his pa told him, "so we can finish eating in time to see Lotta dance. What's that behind your back. Is that the cook pan? You had the same idea, didn't you? Are there fish for dinner?"

Walter nodded. "Six whitefish and a snake," he said.

"A snake, you say. What kind?"

"It's got yellow stripes." The snake was lying on the ground near them. Walter wondered if he should show it to his pa but decided he would get in trouble for playing games when he was supposed to be fishing.

"You cut off the head?"

"Mashed it with a stick."

"Not good enough. If the thing still has fangs, you got to watch out. Where's it at?"

There was no choice left. Walter took his pa to the spot where he'd left the snake.

Oliver picked up the dead serpent by the attached string. "Blazes, boy! You know better than this. The head's still half there and even if there ain't any poison left you don't leave food on the ground. Where's *your* head at?" He brushed off a few ants. "But it's a decent size and should make a good dinner."

"Frank caught it," Walter admitted.

"Good for Frank. We'll clean it and cook it. This plus the fish should be plenty."

Walter considered admitting Frank had also caught most of the fish but decided he'd given his friend enough credit for one day.

Cyrus, Frank's pa, and Oliver brought a couple of blankets to see Lotta. They were able to lay them out close to the platform because they were earlier than most of the other miners.

"You two sit here and save our place," Oliver told his son. "We're going to get something. We'll be back soon."

Miners kept showing up, but the boys managed to keep the men off the blankets. It was annoying but having something to do made the time go faster.

Their fathers smelled of whiskey when they returned, and they were both carrying flasks. Walter shook his head at Frank, but they were used to this behavior.

Finally, Lotta's ma walked out from one of the sheds near the stage and stepped up on the platform. "While Lotta's getting ready I wanted to come out here to thank you, boys. We love being among miners. You know how to have fun and so do we." Some of the men whistled and one shouted something obscene. Lotta's ma shook a finger at him then laughed and shouted, "Here she is, the one and only Lotta Crabtree!" She began the applause. The men joined her, as Lotta came out of the shed and skipped up onto the platform.

Lotta had a banjo with her and began playing "Camptown Races," but after one time through the chorus, she handed the instrument to Jake Wallace and started dancing. As Jake continued the song, she began a jig. She tapped her heels twelve times then hopped and crossed her legs back and forth until Walter felt himself going cross-eyed. Before long Lotta was kicking her heels up and tossing her petticoats side to side. This was no average Irish jig. Lotta was high stepping.

Her light blue, long-sleeved top with a white-collar brought out the shine in her eyes. Her checkered skirt with light and dark blue squares lifted like a sail as she turned round-and-round. Her red hair was pulled back, but so many strands were loose, swinging by the side of her head as she moved.

"Thank God we didn't grease the stage," Walter said to Frank. "Why'd you let me even *think* about doing that?"

"Me?" Frank shouted, but Walter didn't turn to look at his friend. They both had their eyes on the girl bouncing in front.

Their fathers couldn't hear what they were talking about, because the drunken men were attempting to sing, but just yelling along with the music. "Doo Dah! Doo Dah!" they screamed. Somebody threw a leather purse, probably loaded with gold pieces. Walter's pa joined in by tossing a watch he'd won in a poker game. Walter saw him do it but didn't say anything. The boys were into the music every bit as much as their fathers were.

"Camptown ladies sing this song," Frank and Walter belted out together, rocking back and forth to the beat of Lotta's swaying body.

When Lotta finished her first song, she slowed way down and started "I've left the snow-clad hills." Walter sat down. He was having trouble breathing. He'd seen Lotta dance two years before, but she was even prettier now. And when she sang soft and mellow, she looked right at him. He couldn't help but dream about such a wonderful girl.

When Lotta left the stage, Walter lay back on the blanket and closed his eyes.

He thought about panning for gold. His pa had taken him by the creek a few times, so he knew what to do. He painted a picture in his head of Lotta waiting for him. She was dressed in the same blue blouse and skirt she'd been wearing when she danced. She twirled toward him like she'd done on stage, sending her blue checkered skirt and clean white petticoats spinning through his head like white-capped waves. He dug loose dirt on the bank then shook it through a strainer into his pa's pan and dumped the remaining worthless stones. Then he stepped back to the creek with Lotta close behind, her warm breath on his neck as he filled the pan with water. Walter swished the mixture until a dozen nuggets appeared, each bigger than his pinkie finger. Lotta sighed, saying, "You did it, Walter. We're rich."

There were other daydreams as well, of walking with Lotta to the fishing lake, holding her hand as Frank followed with the poles, of living in Lotta's beautiful boarding house with her cooking his meals while he counted their gold, and of Lotta lying beside him at night, outside on a blanket, counting the stars.

Walter had always felt a strange mixture of emotions when Lotta was around. Sometimes he was so jealous of the money she had and the exciting life she led, he could explode with anger. But other times he just wanted to talk to her, to watch her, and to be near her. Around Lotta, Walter was as unpredictable as a grizzly bear.

That's when Walter felt a hand on his shoulder, shaking him. "Open your eyes," Frank said in a low voice. "She's coming!"

Walter jolted up and stared. It was Lotta, all right. She'd changed out of her dancing dress into a loose brown dress with a white apron. She no longer had the layer of petticoats fluffing out, but her legs were still covered with bloomers. Her dress was long, but since he was sitting, he could see her ankles when she took a step.

He stood, noticing she was slightly shorter than he was, even though she was a year or so older.

"Hello, Walter," Lotta said. "Do you remember me?"

He couldn't believe what he was hearing. Did he remember Lotta? Of course, he remembered. Everyone knew Lotta Crabtree. He couldn't think of what to say, so he did the only thing he was capable of doing. He nodded his head.

"Good. My ma pointed you out to me. You've changed so much; I wouldn't have recognized you if she hadn't. I met you a couple of years ago at Mart Taylor's Saloon. You and your pa slept on the floor that night and were there the next morning. I thought that seemed like fun. We're always moving from camp to camp. Even when I'm in Coulterville I'm dancing at the saloon. I never get a chance to do any of the things other children do."

Walter nodded his head again.

Frank reached his hand out to Lotta. "I'm Frank, Walter's partner."

Lotta said, "Nice to meet you, Frank." She did not, however, shake his hand, so he dropped it to his side. She turned back to Walter. "Why does a boy like you need a partner?" she asked.

"We're more like friends than partners," Walter told her. "We do everything together."

"Everything?"

"Yup," Frank said.

"That sounds nice. I don't have friends, 'cause I'm always traveling. You two doing anything tomorrow? If so, I'd like to come along. I don't have to leave until afternoon."

"We go fishing almost every day," Frank said.

Walter added. "I can make a pole for you, show you how to use it."

"That would be very nice," Lotta told him. "I'll be here tomorrow, first thing in the morning and I'll bring vittles."

This time both Frank and Walter could do nothing but nod.

Their fathers continued to wobble a bit from drinking but still worked that evening with the men who tore down the platform and rebuilt the wall of the bunkhouse. So, the next morning there was nothing but an empty field when Walter and Frank went. They looked around for only a moment until Lotta came into sight. She was wearing the same brown dress she'd had on the day before and carrying a picnic basket. She walked up to them with a bright smile and greeted them with a "Good Morning" which had a delightful sing-song tone to it.

Lotta opened the basket so the boys could peek inside. She had packed ham, a few hard-boiled eggs, a loaf of white bread, three baked potatoes, and a tub of what appeared to be butter. Walter hadn't eaten this well since the Christmas dinner they'd attended at the town church and they'd had to walk miles for that.

This is what it's like to be rich, he thought, as he felt his stomach harden.

"Ma prepared this," Lotta told them. "She said if I was to get me a sweetheart, I had to bring good food."

"A sweetheart?" Frank gasped, his eyes bulging.

"I mean Walter, Frank. Ma says he's well-looking, for a young boy."

Walter stared at Lotta, his mouth open, but no words coming out.

"Take it easy, both of you," Lotta said. "I'm just horsing around. Let's go fishing."

She's teasing, Walter thought. *I should have known. Lotta thinks she's too good for the likes of me. She's got all that food packed in her fancy basket, showing off her money like she's the governor. I bet she's never gone to bed hungry, not one day in her life.*

Frank had the old can they always used for worms, so finding bait was the first task. The boys took Lotta to a pile of leaves the wind had blown against a cluster of boulders.

"What now?" she asked.

"You get on your knees and dig through the wet muck at the bottom of the pile," Walter told her. "If we find worms, we put them in the can. And when we have enough, we put them on the hooks and start to catch fish."

Walter stood silently when Lotta didn't hesitate. She got down, brushed aside the dry leaves then started to dig through the wet layer. The boys let Lotta do all the digging. She glanced up at them once, as if to ask if they were going to help, but when they didn't, she kept running her fingers through the muck. Within a couple of minutes, she found a half dozen fat worms and plopped them in the can Frank was holding.

"What next?" she asked, as she stood up and brushed off her dress as well as she could with filthy hands.

"We check under stones," Walter told her.

Frank handed her the can and they all moved to some smaller rocks beside the leaf pile. Walter and Frank dug their fingers under one of the stones and flipped it over. Sure enough, there were two more worms. Lotta picked them up and dropped them in the can. The boys turned four more stones over until they had at least twelve worms.

"Now we fish," Walter said. He had to struggle to keep from laughing because Lotta had scratched her face with her dirty fingers and now had a brown streak from the arch of her nose to her cheek near her right nostril. Somehow the smudge made her seem prettier than before. Maybe because the dirt mark made her seem like a real friend, someone capable of looking a bit foolish, instead of some rich girl trying to see how poor people live.

Frank helped bait Lotta's hook the way he liked, pushing the wire through the worm's body the long way, instead of piercing its body sideways then wrapping it around and doing it again, the way Walter liked. Lotta watched him intently.

"You have to be sure he's on there good or the fish will pull him off before you can hook one."

"I see," Lotta said.

Lotta was watching Frank's fingers, while Walter was watching Lotta's face. Behind the small smudge were round cheeks, deep black eyes, and the hint of a smile. He loved to watch her dance. The way she moved was so wonderful. But there was something just as special about seeing her standing still, trying to learn something she didn't know.

Walter tied a short stick to Lotta's line. "This is called a float. You toss it away from shore along with the hook and the string that runs between. The hook will drop straight down from the floating wood. When you see the float get pulled under the water, you got a fish."

Lotta nodded.

He did the same with his own. Frank didn't tie a float on his line because he liked to walk along the shore, pulling the line in the water as he went. This left Lotta and Walter where they could talk alone.

"You know you're lucky to have each other," Lotta said.

She was looking out over the lake while she spoke, but Frank was the only other person she'd seen him with. She had to mean him and Frank.

Lotta turned toward him. She looked down and said, "I would give anything to have someone like him." Then she slowly moved her gaze up to his eyes and added, "Or you."

Walter stepped back and almost tripped on a stone.

"You know what most days are like for me?" Lotta asked.

"I figure you dance a lot," Walter told her, then he laughed and added, "And eat the kind of food you have in that basket."

She smiled and shook her head. "I practice dancing most of the time I'm not performing. And when I'm not dancing, I hang out with my ma, because I don't know anyone else. There's Ashworth, my brother, but he's so little and my ma has another baby on the way. Fishing with you is the most fun I've had in a long time. I've talked to you only twice before today, yet you're the closest friend I have."

Closest friend? Walter thought. He tried to respond, but the words caught in his throat, so he told her, "I have chores to do—gathering wood for the cooking fire and cooking our meals. I don't fish all the time and when I do, it isn't just fun. We don't eat if I don't catch anything."

"Your pa gets gold. Can't he buy supper?"

"If I have bad luck fishing and Pa has bad luck panning, we go to bed hungry. My pa is a good man and will give me what he's got, but sometimes he's got nothing."

"Nothing to eat?"

"That's right."

"I can send you enough to eat. I can have meals sent up here every day. All I ask is for you to be my friend, maybe visit me a few times in town."

Walter's eyes narrowed as he leaned closer to Lotta. "So, the little rich girl is showing off again. Well here's the truth. I'm not your friend. We don't want your charity, Miss Lotta. My pa would never accept handouts. He's gonna hit it big one of these days and we'll be throwing more gold than you can imagine at every dancer and singer who isn't you. You better believe that."

Lotta didn't reply. Walter saw her eyes start to tear up before she turned to watch Frank come back along the bank of the lake with a decent size catfish and a few whitefish.

They spent the rest of the day fishing quietly. Frank grabbed a potato and some ham out of Lotta's basket, but the other two didn't eat. They walked home in silence.

Chapter Two

San Francisco

For six more years, Oliver and Cyrus worked together, promising to share whatever they found. They told Walter they were more like brothers than friends, but that changed when Walter's pa finally found a creek capable of producing a profitable amount of gold.

Oliver and Cyrus had gone separate ways that day, so Oliver was alone when he made the strike. Instead of sharing his good news, Oliver staked his claim and filed the paperwork the following day. He worked at the creek every day, which he needed to do to turn the claim from unpatented to patented.

It didn't take long for Cyrus to become suspicious. He followed Oliver and learned his "brother" had betrayed him, at least that's how he saw it.

Walter and Frank were watching when Cyrus approached Oliver. Frank's pa was breathing hard, glaring at Walter's pa. "We've *always* shared what we had."

"It was easy back then. We didn't have nothing *to* share," Oliver answered. He paused for a moment, then added. "We never spoke about this. Never said we *would* share when the day came. Now here it is and what I found is mine."

"You want to take it all? Every last speck of gold dust?"

"Yup."

Frank took a step away from Walter, which surprised him. Frank was taking his pa's side. Even though Walter understood why, he felt his shoulders tighten.

Walter watched as Cyrus moved in, his eyes wide and nostrils flaring. He was a stocky man, much bigger than Walter's pa. With a sudden sharp move, Cyrus threw a punch to Oliver's face and knocked him to the ground. Oliver scrambled to his feet. Cyrus circled him and threw a few more wild punches. Using his experience as a bare-knuckle brawler, Oliver managed to weave and duck, avoiding each swing.

When Oliver finally threw one of his own, it landed on Cyrus' nose, causing him to stagger back. Cyrus shook his head then advanced again. He swung at Oliver with his left fist, missed, but managed to wrap his arm around Oliver's neck. He pulled him close and started throwing punches to his midsection. After multiple strikes to Oliver's stomach, Cyrus tossed Oliver back.

Oliver landed on the ground. While Oliver struggled back up, Cyrus grabbed a thick stick. He used it to push Oliver against a tree, holding the limb to his neck, pushing hard enough to keep him from breathing. When Oliver fell to the ground, Walter rushed to his pa, fearing he was dead. Oliver breathed sharply then sputtered out a bloody cough. Walter felt tears welling up as the tension released. "Pa, I know you held back. You could have killed Cyrus with one punch." Oliver held his hand against Walter's face and nodded. "Thank you Pa, thank you for not killing my friend's pa."

Frank and his pa left that day, without saying another word. Walter would miss his friend but didn't have much time to think about it. He was too busy.

Walter recruited a couple of men to help get his pa back to his bunk in the shed and that's where Oliver stayed for a week. The first few days, Walter had to remain by his side, feeding him by hand and emptying the bucket he used for a chamber-pot. After Oliver had recovered enough to walk to the latrine, Walter was able to get back to the claim to do a little panning. The claim was still producing, so they had money to pay for food. After a week had passed, Oliver limped out to the creek and joined his son in working the claim. A couple of weeks after he started, things seemed to be getting back to normal.

"I'm proud of you, son," Oliver told Walter. "You behaved like a man, took care of me, worked the claim. I couldn't ask for anything more." He put his hand on Walter's shoulder and squeezed. "I'm thinking we need to celebrate, and you need to learn what a man does for fun. So I say we leave the camp for a week and make a trip to San Francisco. What do you think?"

"What about the claim?" Walter asked.

"Just a week, I'm saying. It should be OK. And if it isn't, well...whoever jumps this claim will have to deal with me."

"I don't know." Walter bit his lip and twisted the pan he was holding.

"I've been thinking about this for a long time," Oliver said. "Life is different up here. There are things you miss out on, living here with a bunch of old men."

"I had Frank."

"Yup, you did, but you don't now. Besides, Frank wasn't enough. We're going to San Francisco and you, boy, will have the best time of your life."

They rode the coach to the city. The trip took them a day, rocking back and forth along the rough roads, passing through forests and fields. When they reached San Francisco, Oliver took his son straight to the Niantic Hotel, where they could get a room. The building was made from an abandoned ship, one of the ones that had been left floating in the harbor after the crew had all headed to the camps to seek their fortunes in gold. The investors ran it aground then hired a crew to move it to Montgomery St.

The hull of the boat was still intact, with a two-story structure protruding up from the deck. They were staying in one of the rooms on the second floor, with a window that looked out over the bow of the boat and onto the street below. They bought sardines and bread at a general store next to the hotel, ate until they were stuffed, then went to bed and slept long into the morning.

The following day Oliver took his son on a walk through the city, exploring the port first. "This place is like a dream," Walter told his pa when they first saw the ships tied to the piers.

"Same way I felt when I first landed here," Oliver replied, "and now the dream's come true."

They walked out on a pier, to get a closer look at the rigging on one of the ships. The majestic vessel was more than a hundred feet long. It had three masts, with horizontal yards, but the sails weren't up since it was in port. Walter was curious about some openings in the side of the ship, above the waterline. Walter wasn't sure if these were for people to look out from below deck or if they were for cannons. They started to walk closer, to study the ship more, but a crew member told them to go back to the street.

"You think I'll ever sail on one of those?" Walter asked, glancing at his father then turning back to look at the ships.

"You rode a steamer when we first came here."

"But I don't remember. I was too young. And I'd rather ride one of the sailing ships with the tall masts."

"Things are starting to go right for us. We've got a good claim and that means plenty of money to do whatever we dream of doing." Oliver turned away from the water and pulled on Walter's arm. "Come along now and think about that later. There's plenty more to show you in the city."

Although they could see tall buildings toward the center of town, the shops near the ports were a mixture of single-family homes, boarding houses, and shops in one-story buildings. They looked at some of the small stores and boarding houses, then stopped at a coffee house for a meal. Walter had a chicken sandwich while Oliver had eggs and bacon. They both had coffee. It was afternoon when they left the restaurant and headed back toward the hotel.

Walter bumped into his father as he passed the hotel's doorway. He fully expected his pa to make a quick right through the doors, but he hadn't. Walter stood at the front of the Niantic and pointed to the building as his pa strode on. His father's eyes began to glaze over, and his lips smacked.

Oliver entered a saloon, three buildings away from the Niantic. Walter trotted up behind him and walked in through the open doors. Red and green glass beads strung down from the arched doorway clacked when they collided.

"I'm going to buy you a whiskey," Oliver told his son, "and we'll see where we go from there."

Walter had tried his pa's liquor on a day when Oliver was too drunk to know the difference. It tasted horrible. Yet, his pa was trying to show him the ways of a man and Walter was grateful. He decided he would drink the whiskey and make as if he enjoyed it. He might even take a second glass if his pa offered him one.

The room smelled like stale sweat and fish. *From the sailors,* Walter thought. The saloon was too close to the ocean to have many other customers, unless, like Walter and his pa, they were staying at the local hotels.

Oliver led his son to an empty table and, when they were seated, ordered two whiskeys.

There were women in the room, too. Oliver didn't seem surprised. However, Walter was shocked. He wasn't used to women like these. They were dressed differently from the ladies in the camp, in short skirts with their tops pulled down so their bare shoulders showed. They were younger than most of the camp women, although there were a few older ladies mixed in. Also, the ladies seemed happy. The women at the camp were always working and generally scowling when they were at it. These ladies were constantly giggling, whispering to each other, and smiling at the men.

Walter noticed one girl who was about thirteen, his age. Her light brown hair was down to her mid-back and fixed in curls like Lotta's had been when Walter had last seen her dancing at the camp, sometime after their fishing day. Walter sneaked off rather than speaking to Lotta, figuring she was still mad at him for his harsh words.

Although this girl reminded him of Lotta, she was dressed in clothes Lotta would never wear in public. The girl had on what appeared to be a white, cotton nightgown. One of her shoulders was covered, but she had her gown pulled off the other, exposing more skin than any of the other women.

She wore white stockings and black shoes. She seemed to notice Walter looking at her and responded by smiling, staring back, and lifting her skirt with her right hand, to reveal her pale thighs and the garters attached to the tops of her stockings. Walter snapped his eyes away and stared up at the ceiling. He began to whistle an off-key tune, but he still could hear her laughing.

"Wait here," Oliver said. "I may be a while."

Walter watched his pa as he approached the young woman. They spoke for a while, then she led Oliver to a staircase to the right of the bar. They walked up the stairs together. Walter watched until they were both out of sight.

The bartender returned with the whiskeys. He set one at Oliver's place and one in front of Walter.

The liquor smelled worse than the sweat of the people in the room, but Walter was determined to drink his. He took a sip, just a small one, and choked a bit. He glanced around the room to see if anyone had noticed, but the men closest to him were involved in a card game. There was another cluster of men by the bar. They were talking and didn't seem to be watching.

Another girl, one with pinned up dark hair, was glancing at him every so often. She had been talking to the one who took his pa upstairs. Her flimsy green dress accented her small waist, with a loose skirt and top. Her shoulders were bare, like the other women in the saloon, and once, when one of the gamblers raised his eyes, she looked at the man and started to lift her skirt, the way the first girl had. But when his attention turned back to his cards, she let it fall.

Walter tried another sip of whiskey. He knew what to expect now, so he didn't choke and, after he swallowed, he took another. He didn't drink fast but kept going. When his pa and the girl came back down, he was close to half done. Everything in the room seemed a bit rocky, like a fish on dry land, once it was worn out from flipping about.

"This is Tabby," Oliver told his son, as he pulled an empty chair to their table so Tabby could sit.

"Good to meet you, Walter," the girl said, then she turned her attention to Oliver and asked, "Are you gonna buy me a drink?"

"Not now," he told her. "Maybe when you're done with Walter."

Walter held his breath for a moment. He wasn't sure what *"done with"* meant.

"Your pa asked me to spend some time with you," Tabby told him, "to go over a few things."

"Things?"

Tabby smiled. "Yup. I understand there aren't many girls in the camps, are there?"

"There's one my age, but she's mean as a skunk."

"Is she?" Tabby paused, then smiled and winked at Walter. "Well, I'm here now and I'm your age. You don't think I'm a skunk, do you?"

Walter shook his head.

Tabby stood, then took Walter's hand and pulled him to his feet. He was wobbling a bit until Tabby took his arm and pulled it around her shoulder. She put her arm around his waist. She was a little taller than he was, but not by much.

"You don't drink much, do you?" Tabby asked.

"No, but my pa thinks I should."

"Does he? Well...he looks out for you. He's a good pa."

"He says thirteen is old enough to act like a man."

"Are you thirteen?"

He nodded.

"Then I guess I am a little older than you. I'm fourteen, which is what your pa said you were." She frowned at Oliver, who simply shrugged his shoulders.

Walter got his bearings once he took a few steps, but he kept his arm around Tabby's shoulder. It felt good to be close to her. "Lotta Crabtree is a friend of mine," he said when they were halfway up the stairs. "I met her at the camp."

"Did you? She's got a show going on here in town," Tabby told him. "It's supposed to be good. Maybe we can go sometime."

Walter smiled. "I'd like that."

There was a hall at the top of the stairs. Tabby led him to the third door on the left, opened it and brought Walter inside. There was a bed in the room, with a crumpled blanket on it and a single bureau, with a mirror on the wall behind it. There was also a vase with flowers on the bureau, a mix of yellow, orange, and purple. Walter didn't know what type they were, but he'd seen similar ones growing wild.

"Take a seat here," Tabby said when she brought Walter to the bed. She lit a kerosene lamp on the bureau then stepped back to close the door. Once they were alone she turned to him and asked. "Have you ever seen a girl naked?"

Walter nodded. The camp ladies had a tin tub for bathing. They kept it outside during the warm weather, so he and Frank had snuck a peak a few times. That wasn't much to brag about, but Tabby didn't ask for details.

"That's good," she said, as she took off her shoes. "You're about to see another." She lifted her skirt and put her foot up on the bed next to him, exposing her right leg. Then she untied her garter, rolled down the stocking, and took it off. She repeated the routine for her left stocking. After that, she took a step back, paused for a moment, stared at Walter, then pulled her white chemise over her head in one motion. She had nothing on under the gown. "I hope you like what you see," she said, as she turned slowly. When she was facing him again, she added, "Now it's your turn."

The whiskey wasn't bothering him as much now, so he stood and undressed as quickly as he could. "Now lie on the bed," Tabby told him, "on your back. I'll take care of the rest."

Walter climbed on the bed. He lay there for a moment, staring at a mark on the wood ceiling.

"Give me a little room," Tabby told him, speaking in a soft voice.

He shifted toward the center of the bed then stared at the ceiling again, his arms rigid at his side. He started to turn his head to look at Tabby but worried that staring might be the wrong thing to do. Instead, he closed his eyes.

She touched his stomach, lightly. It tickled a little and he almost moved his arms to take her hand but didn't. He sucked in a deep breath and held himself perfectly still. He tried to think about the spot on the ceiling, this time without opening his eyes to look at it. She moved her hand to his private parts and when that happened, he couldn't think of anything but her touch. His body seemed to swirl and the bed spun as his heart raced.

"I'm getting on the bed with you now," she whispered, pulling her hand away from him. Her beautiful voice seemed to echo in his mind, "with you now" floating through his head like a butterfly over a misty meadow.

He felt her weight beside him, then over him as she pulled herself up and straddled his body. He opened his eyes, unable to resist looking any longer. There she was, leaning over him, her long hair dangling, framing her face. Her eyes sparkling, her smile as soft as a flower petal, her breasts swaying softly.

It took all his will not to touch her, but he didn't give in. He lay still, muscles tensed, as Tabby lowered herself, reaching between their bodies to guide him with her hand. She made his body into a part of her, with a magic Walter had never known before. She took complete control and he was thrilled to let her have it. When they were done, they separated, struggled up, and sat on the bed for a moment, side by side without touching.

"What next?" Walter asked, still breathing hard.

"We get dressed, go downstairs, and you finish your whiskey." She stood and reached for her stockings, but he didn't move, so she added, "That's all for now."

"Now?"

"Your pa, he's paying me to teach you what you should know. You did fine, but there's other things I need to show you. He said he'll bring you back tomorrow. And the next day, too."

He looked at the clothes he'd left in a pile, then turned back to her. He ran his right hand through his hair before he spoke. "Can I ask you one more thing?"

"Sure."

"What did you do with my pa when he was up here with you?"

Tabby sighed and bent forward slightly. "Walter, that's the first thing you did wrong all night," she said. "I don't talk about any of my men and you shouldn't ask. It's wrong and could get me in a lot of trouble."

Walter didn't know what to say to that. He wasn't even sure what he thought about it. So, he stood and dressed. When he was done, Tabby led him back to his pa.

"Good tail, right?" Oliver asked his son. He had finished Walter's drink as well as his own and was probably on his second or third. His words were slightly slurred. When Walter didn't answer, Oliver asked again, in a different way. "You had a good time, didn't you?"

Walter looked at Tabby, who had taken a seat beside him. He said, "Yes."

Tabby smiled. "Now you gonna buy me a drink?" she asked Oliver.

"Hell, I'll buy you dinner," he said, laughing.

"Not here you won't," she answered, wrinkling her nose. "Food here isn't exactly fizzing."

"Then, have a whiskey with us. I just had two. Or was it three? I can't remember."

Tabby leaned toward Walter and touched his arm. "I believe I will if Walter will join me."

Oliver laughed again and signaled for the bartender.

That night, as he lay on the floor beside his pa's bunk, Walter thought about the experience. He was young, but not stupid. Tabby was a prostitute, a "tail" as his pa called her, which meant Tabby was paid to be with him. He was nothing more than a job to her. Yet he still liked her. He liked her smile and her laugh. He liked the way her skin felt against his. He liked her dreamy expression when she looked in his eyes, especially the way that look of hers seemed to get prettier after she'd had a couple of drinks. But most of all, he liked the way her deep dark eyes, round face, and long curls reminded him of Lotta.

The next afternoon, Walter anticipated his father would want to go back to the saloon. Sure enough, right after lunch, Walter found himself at the saloon's doorway again. Tabby smiled from her spot at the bar, as Walter and his father walked in. There was a difference this time, Oliver didn't spend time with Tabby. Instead, he went upstairs with the dark-haired girl, while Tabby and Walter went their own way. The other difference was that Walter had nothing to drink before he went to her room.

Tabby was dressed in dark blue this time, with stripes on the collar and above the hem of the skirt. As she had the day before, she dropped her outfit as soon as the door was shut.

She taught him a few other things to do with women and showed him a different position for what they'd done the day before. But what impressed Walter the most was what happened after the lesson was over. She didn't jump up to put her clothes on and when he stood to put his on, she touched his arm. "Let's sit here for a while. Is that all right with you?"

"Yup," he answered, relaxing a bit.

Tabby twisted on the bed, bringing her right leg up, as if she was going to sit cross-legged, but keeping her left foot on the floor. This way she could look at Walter as they talked. She was as comfortable naked as she was with her clothes on. He thought about mirroring her position but decided instead to simply turn his head.

"Tell me about yourself," Tabby said. Her tone was mild, sweet as if she really cared.

Walter didn't understand what she wanted to know or why she wanted to know it. "What?" he asked.

"Let's start with your ma. What happened to her?"

"All I know is she didn't want me, but Pa did. She left us when I was a baby. My pa doesn't like to talk about her, but I know she stayed in New York when we came out here. She might have been like you."

"Like me?"

"Yup. Getting paid to be with men."

Tabby raised one eyebrow. "I doubt it. If your ma worked the johns, she'd want to fix the baby problem before she got too fat. We lose money if we let ourselves get fat, especially if it's 'cause we're carrying. Even out here we have ways of dealing with that and she was in the big city where there are plenty of people who know how to help. Your ma chose to give you life, which means she had something going for her, something more than what I've got."

"You seem happy enough."

"I ain't complaining. I got beat up a couple times, but that comes with the job. My friends took care of those guys, so I'll never see them again—nobody will. And the girls are nice enough, always joking and laughing. Jahiel, the fella who owns this place, is easy going—for a pimp. He mostly ignores us and says as long as we keep bringing in money we won't get hurt. He brought me here a little more than a year ago. My pa ran out on us and my ma, well—I'll never see her again."

"I'm sorry."

"Nothing you did." She paused. "The girls taught me how to entertain a man, so that's what I do. If it wasn't for this place, I'd be dead." She moved closer to him and leaned her head on his shoulder. "Let's talk about you. How did you meet Lotta Crabtree?" Tabby smiled slightly.

Walter grimaced. He wasn't sure what he should tell her.

"That was true, right?" Tabby asked. "Lotta's a friend of yours?"

He shrugged. "Most of it was true." He went on to tell her the story of the day he spent fishing with Lotta and the way the day ended.

"That don't sound so bad. It was a long time ago and you were just a child. Go to one of her shows. Apologize. I bet she'll be glad to see you. I would if I was her."

"You think so?" Walter asked.

"Yup. But we better go. Your pa was waiting all this time."

Tabby's top had a few buttons to deal with, but she was still dressed before Walter. After he had his clothes on, she did something that surprised him. She took his arm and pulled him toward her. "Have you ever kissed a girl?" she asked.

He didn't answer but could feel himself shaking a bit.

"I don't let most men do this," she said. "To be honest, it isn't what they generally want to do. But in some ways, it's more intimate than anything else I've shown you."

She leaned forward and touched his lips with hers. He wrapped his arms around her and pulled her against his chest. He felt her slip her tongue into his mouth to touch his, causing a shiver to run up his spine. His eyes were closed, so he opened them, but only for a brief moment. When he saw she had her eyes shut, he closed his again.

Walter didn't separate from Tabby until he felt her pull away. "Now you've taught *me* something," she said. "My heart's pounding in a way I haven't felt before. You need to understand something. My body's for sale, but my soul is not and when your lips touch mine, you connect with my soul. I like you, Walter. I like the way you talk, the way you look, and the way you make me feel."

He still felt her kiss and brought his hand to his mouth as if he could catch the feeling, but he didn't say anything.

Tabby let out a long sigh, then said. "I understand if you want to skip tomorrow."

"Oh no! Please!"

Her eyes seemed to dance as she said, "Good. Don't tell your pa we kissed and don't tell him how long we talked, all right?"

Walter nodded.

"Go have a drink with your pa. I'm gonna stay up here for a while. I'll see you tomorrow."

When Oliver and Walter came to the saloon the following day, Tabby wasn't standing at her usual spot by the bar. The dark-haired girl, Tabby's friend, approached them. "I'm gonna take you both upstairs."

"Oh," Oliver crossed his arms. "Where's Tabby? I paid her, so she should be here."

"She is. We're to drop Walter off at her room. She's got something special planned."

Walter felt his knees weaken a bit but tried not to look too excited.

"All right," Oliver told her. "As long as she spends her time with my son. That's what we agreed to."

"She will, and I'll show you a good time as well."

He smiled. "Like yesterday."

She returned the smile saying, "Maybe even better."

Walter knocked on Tabby's door and entered after she called him in. She was standing to the side of the bureau and her appearance made his skin tingle. Her hair was parted in the middle with much of it pulled back, but with a layer of curls underneath. It must have taken her hours to do her hair that way. She had two chain earrings, each about two inches long with a small ball close to her ear and a larger ball dangling at the end. Her dress was elegant, with a wavy collar that wrapped around her neck and came down her front, hiding her buttons. The dress was cream color with blue and green flower prints and a stripe around the hem of the ankle-length skirt. She wore a dark green belt with it, tied in a wide bow.

Walter's skin tingled as he looked her up and down. He'd seen this dress before. He'd seen the total look before. The first day in San Francisco, when he'd walked the streets with his pa, there were posters all over the city of someone else wearing this dress, someone who had the same hairstyle and even the same earrings. Tabby was taller and had light brown hair rather than red, but otherwise, she was a dead ringer for Lotta Crabtree.

"Sit down," Tabby said, indicating the bed. After Walter did as he was told, she began to dance. There was no music and Tabby didn't kick her legs as high or move as quickly as the original, but she sure looked good.

Tabby laughed as she finished the dance. "What do you think?"

"How?" was all Walter could say. His eyes were wide and his mouth open.

When Tabby finally stopped laughing, she smiled, stepped forward and kissed him on the forehead. "I know Lotta, too," she said. "She used to dance here before she became such a big star. I went to the theater last night and met her after her show. She remembers you well. When I told her what I had in mind, she loved the idea. This is her dress. I had to let the hem out because she's such a short thing, but other than that it fits well."

"She remembers me?"

"Yup. And she isn't mad at all. She even helped me with my hair. I told her I was gonna bundle up tight in this dress and everything else she wears, even her corset. I told her I would teach you how to take it off a woman. That way you'll know what to do if you two ever meet again."

"What did she say to that?"

"She laughed, said there was no chance of that ever happening, but I wasn't sure she was being honest. I think she likes you. She remembers what you said, but that was years ago."

Walter wasn't sure how he felt about all this. He was happy Lotta still remembered him and had forgiven his burst of anger. She had been haughty back then, yet she was trying to help. He should have let her. He worried more about what Lotta must think of Tabby teaching him how to be with a woman.

And what about Tabby? She'd told him she liked him, but today she seemed more concerned with what Lotta thought than her own feelings.

This was all so confusing. Walter was thankful he and his pa were headed back to Coulterville in the morning.

Tabby took his hand and helped him stand, then she put her arms around his shoulders and kissed him like she had the day before. "Tell me I'm pretty," she said.

"You're the most pretty thing I've ever seen, Tabby. Prettier than gold in the pan."

"Nice words, Walter. Tell them to me again but call me Lotta. Today, for you, I'm Lotta."

Chapter Three

Fights

Walter and Oliver sat in the coach, rocking to and fro down the long road back. After a while, Oliver looked up at Walter's face.

"What you lookin' all mad at boy?"

"Nothin' Pa." Walter did not look up at his father, wishing to not show him he had been sulking over leaving Tabby.

"Aww, shucks. You all stuck up on that Tabby whore aren't you?"

Walter perked up. "No Pa."

Oliver clucked his tongue and spat out the window. "See son, she weren't any friend of yours. She was tail, I tol' ya before, just tail selling herself for what she can get. She would have taken us both on at the same time if I had pay enough for her. You weren't nothing to her but the chance to earn my gold."

Walter's eyes shot back out the window.

"I'm just trying to save you from..." Oliver stared at the floor of the coach for a moment then looked up. "Never mind, son. Never mind."

Walter could tell his pa was thinking about his ma, probably thinking how much Tabby was like her. He never told Walter he loved the woman but he probably did, even though she'd left him—handed Walter over and walked away.

They rode the rest of the long and rugged way home in silence, arriving way after dark. When they reached the camp Walter and Oliver went straight to the bunkhouse. They sneaked in around the snoring men and settled into their beds.

In the morning, as they were about to cook breakfast, Abner Johnson showed. Abner was the claims officer and a friend of Cyrus. Walter couldn't think of a single reason the man would be up this early that didn't come with trouble.

"What do you want, Abner?" Oliver asked, stopping the man in his tracks.

"There seems to be an issue with your paperwork."

"There can't be. It's patented."

"Remember how I mentioned Cyrus when you were filing. I knew the two of you had been working together. Well...I put a note on the paperwork concerning that issue. Now Cyrus is back and saying the claim is his. I'm leaning toward granting it to him since you should have straightened the issue before you filed."

"To Hell with your note. That claim is mine."

"That's up to me, not you, Oliver. And you know it. Cyrus and Frank are back in camp. You were the one who was away when this came up. I've ruled that you have no rights until the legal issues are straight and I've told Cyrus he can work the claim. It seems fair since you already pulled plenty of gold from that spot."

Oliver jumped to his feet. "I wasn't gone ten days and you know it."

"That's not what I heard."

Oliver threw a punch, hitting Abner in the face and knocking him to the ground.

A wobbly Abner stood, rubbed his face, and dusted himself off. "That settles it. I was gonna come up with a plan for the two of you to share the stake. That's over. I could have you locked up for attacking an officer, but I'm not gonna do that for Walter's sake. I'm also not gonna require you pay back the gold you've already taken. Other than those two rulings, I'm deciding in favor of Cyrus. As of this moment, the claim is his. You and your boy better stay away from Cyrus and Frank."

Abner nodded toward Walter, then turned and walked.

Walter was standing beside the cooking fire. He kicked dirt on the small twigs that he'd just managed to set to burning. His hands were trembling so badly he couldn't cook breakfast. He looked at his pa, who was staring at Abner as the man headed back toward town, where he had his office.

Oliver was breathing loudly, his nostrils flaring. He looked like a pit-fighting dog. Walter was worried Oliver would do something he'd regret and end up spending more time recovering in bed, as he had the last time he and Cyrus had fought. Or worse than that, fight him without holding back and possibly do some serious damage to Cyrus. His fears seemed real as Oliver turned and ran, in the opposite direction from where Abner Johnson had walked.

Walter should have followed but didn't react quickly enough. He saw his pa run up the path to the woods but lost him when he went over a ridge. Walter stepped into the forest. He didn't know where to go next. It was possible his pa was headed for the claim even though Abner had said they should not go there. If Walter headed that way and was wrong, he'd not only miss his pa, he'd create more problems by disobeying the claims officer.

Walter walked through the forest slowly, wandering in random directions, feeling the need to keep moving even if he didn't know where he was going. After what seemed like hours, he ended up at the fishing spot where he and Frank used to go. He tossed a few stones into the water, then sat on the shore and watched the breeze blow small ripples in the surface.

Life is hard, harder than I thought it could be. I'll be trapped in the camp for years to come. This lake used to give me a chance to figure things out. Now, all I can think about is the port in San Francisco, the big waves, the tall ships, and Tabby. I had no idea how much it would hurt to be away from her. I think I've fallen in love with a prostitute and I don't have Frank to talk to anymore.

As Walter kept thinking, he remembered how Oliver and Cyrus used to get drunk. He felt bad when he and Frank had to take care of them, but their fathers liked each other back then. They shared their whiskey, shared their fun, and probably shared women who came into the camp to make a little extra money. *Like Tabby,* Walter thought.

Frank used to join him every day at this lake, talking about what they would do when they struck it rich. Walter always said he would find a wife, have kids and start a real life. The dreams Frank talked about were simpler than Walter's. He imagined himself catching the biggest fish anyone had ever seen or shooting a gigantic bear. Walter wasn't sure whose dreams were more dangerous. A bear can kill you with one strike of its paw, but a woman can kill your heart.

"Walter." He recognized Frank's voice, calling from behind. "I thought you might be here."

Walter turned to see his old friend.

Frank came and stood beside him, staring out across the water. "I have some bad news."

Walter's chest ached like he'd just been punched. "Give me a little more time," he said, crossing his arms.

Walter looked at a tree that had fallen into the lake years ago. The trunk and many of its branches remained solid, although it no longer had leaves. Frank often walked out on it because fish bred in it.

"Remember the day that tree fell?" Walter asked.

"Yup. You were so funny, the way you went out on it, slipped and landed in the water, face down. I had to pull you out."

"I never thanked you for that. I was so tangled up in that mess, I might have drowned if you didn't help."

"Is that why you haven't stepped on it since then?"

Walter nodded. "I learned something that day. You can't think when your mind is scared."

"I'm sorry I laughed," Frank said. "I couldn't help it." Frank breathed, his shoulders lifting. "Listen, Walter, let me tell you about your pa."

Walter shrugged but ignored Frank's request. "I might have been mad at the time, but not now. We were always doing something crazy, but you would come through. You were a good friend—still are."

"You have to know about your pa."

Walter looked up over the water. His eyes caught the flash of something moving in the distance. He sighed quietly.

"He brought a gun to the claim, used it to threaten my pa." Walter knew this was not the truth. Oliver didn't need a gun to kill Frank's Pa. He could have done it with his own two hands. But this was neither here nor there. Walter allowed Frank to keep speaking his lie.

"Your pa was waving the gun in the air and shot it once. I don't think he would have killed either of us, but my pa didn't know, so he took a run at him. They wrestled and the gun went off. Your pa is dead. Mine sent me here to tell you."

Walter gulped air then went limp. He was with his pa before he left. His eyes were glued to him until he lost sight of him going over the ridge. He didn't take the gun from the lockbox he kept under his cot. He knew if anything Cyrus was the one with the gun. Cyrus probably drew when he saw Oliver approaching. Oliver might have rushed the man or Cyrus might have just shot out of pure meaness. Same ending, Oliver was dead. How he got that way really didn't matter.

"Did he send you to say he is sorry?" Walter asked as he bent forward and shivered. *Dead?* He wondered. *Pa is dead?*

"That's not what my pa said. He told me to warn you to stay away from the claim. He says it's ours now and no son of Oliver Cain is gonna take it from us."

Walter pressed his fist to his lips. "You told me, so leave me alone. I won't go to the claim, 'cause I don't want to see you or your pa ever again."

Frank stared at Walter and held his head high. "I hafta say something else."

"More?" Walter tried to stand, but his knees were weak. He sat back down, then hung his head, wiped a few tears from his cheeks and kept talking. "My pa, he helped me make decisions. He kept me safe without a wife to help him. He pointed the way even when he wasn't doing the right things himself. And I needed that. I needed someone who cared even when he was too drunk to show it. What is the sense of being alive if there's no one to share things with?"

"You're right," Frank told him, touching Walter's shoulder, "so let me speak." When Walter didn't argue, Frank continued. "My pa's a drunk, just like yours." He paused then added, "was." Frank sat next to Walter and crossed his legs. "I don't care about him or the gold. Let's run off, you and me. We can make it on our own. We're the ones who've been finding food for years, cooking it as well, all while taking care of my pa and yours every time they drank too much."

Frank had always been the best friend anyone could have, but Walter hadn't expected Frank to choose him over his own pa. If Walter agreed to run off with him, it meant he didn't have to face life alone. Still, it didn't stop the grief.

"I want to see him first," Walter told Frank. "I want to see his body, to say goodbye."

"If my pa catches you near the claim, he'll kill you. He's already killed once, so he has nothing to lose. Besides your pa is probably under the ground by now, since my pa has to get rid of the body before anyone comes by.

"Hiding a body means digging a hole deep enough the animals won't get to it, so I figure we've got time. Let's you and me go there. Let's sneak up on him. We're good at being quiet in the woods. Let me at least see his body laid to rest."

* * *

When they made their way back to the claim, they found it was easier approaching Cyrus then they thought it would be. He was working hard, digging a deep grave. Walter and Frank watched from a safe distance, behind a cluster of small trees.

Oliver was on his back. He looked like he was sleeping, without snoring or moving at all. Walter could see his pa's brown hair and the dark tanned skin on his arms, face, and neck, but no blood. He was also too far off to see his pa's mouth, nose, or eyes. Walter wished he could see his eyes, to know if death brought the same haze as whiskey.

Walter had never gone to hear the preachers who moved about from camp to camp. And since his father didn't talk to him about stuff like that, he didn't know much about religion or God. Still, he understood death from watching birds and animals. What he said quietly to himself might have been a kind of prayer, but it was directed to his pa rather than any god Walter understood.

"Life wasn't easy with you," Walter spoke as softly as possible. "But I'll miss you anyway. Maybe the way you made life hard, made me strong enough to make it on my own. I hope so because Frank and I are going off. We'll have each other and hopefully Tabby will help us as well. If nothing else, I thank you for introducing her to me. It wasn't the easiest way you chose, but you did it and that's a good thing. Now I've seen you and said my goodbyes, so I'm off. If there's a heaven, I hope you make it there."

"We can go now," Walter whispered loud enough for Frank to hear, "let's get out of this camp."

"That's what I was thinking"

Walter stood and started to step away from the claim. Frank followed. They didn't speak again until they were far enough from Frank's pa they couldn't be heard. That's when Walter said, "I know someone in San Francisco who can help us. She likes me. She told me she did. Let's go there."

"I can't think of anywhere I'd rather go," Frank said, as they headed back to the bunkhouse to grab what little they owned.

Chapter Four

On Their Own

Walter and Frank walked the road the stagecoach had taken, the one Walter and his pa had ridden, barely a full day before. At first, the land on either side was open fields with a few scattered evergreen trees. When they entered a wooded area, their path continued to be clear of small branches. Tall pine trees grew along the sides of the road, but few vines or small brush. The canopy over the open path allowed plenty of light to see, but not enough for bushes to grow.

Walking gave Walter a chance to see more of the forest than during the coach ride. There were small animals, squirrels standing at attention, watching them while they passed by then returning to their business when no danger appeared apparent.

At one point Walter and Frank reached a small creek. There was a tiny bridge made from some old boards positioned side by side and held in place by some stakes on either side. Walter wondered if the bridge might wash away in heavy rain. It was there for the coach to use, but it made it easy for the boys to keep their feet dry.

A few dark clouds appeared as the sun began to set. They left the forest and entered another grassland sparsely populated by scrawny pine trees. Frank shrugged, then turned to Walter. "We need to find shelter for the night. I'd rather be in the forest than in a field."

"What if there's lightning?"

"We could stay away from the tall trees and hope for the best. In the field we'd be the tallest things out there."

"Maybe, but maybe we could find a gulley." Walter squinted as he surveyed the field. "Over there." He pointed. "That area looks like it's got a few hills and valleys. There are also rocks. Maybe we could find a dry place beside a boulder."

"Or we might find a bear."

"We won't know unless we try." Walter set out at a fast pace and Frank followed.

They found what Walter was hoping for, a cluster of boulders halfway down a hill. The stones were large enough to provide partial shelter. There were no bears, but they had to chase a snake away and found what looked like an abandoned groundhog hole. Frank thought the snake was a rattler, but it didn't make any noise. Whatever it was, Walter was sure it wouldn't come back. "It's more scared than we are," he told his friend.

"Not so sure about that," Frank replied in a quiet voice.

Before they settled in for the night, they ate some jerky and potatoes they'd brought with them.

Although Walter slept well, Frank woke with bags under his eyes. He didn't complain, but Walter thought he'd had a restless night. The only rain Walter felt overnight was a light sprinkle which didn't bother him much. The wind wasn't very gusty, so the stone kept it off him.

The next day was much like the first. They walked up and down hills, through fields and wooded areas, all while following the stagecoach road. The only creeks to cross were small ones they could jump over, which made the walk easier. They ran out of jerky for dinner that night, so they had to be satisfied with a single potato each. Since the sky was clear they walked until it was too dark to continue and slept in another field, this time with no shelter.

They made it to San Francisco on the third day, late in the afternoon. They headed straight for the saloon where Tabby worked. Tabby's dark-haired friend approached them. "Are you looking for Tabby?" she asked.

"Yup. Is she upstairs?"

"She's not here anymore. The boss, he sold her contract."

Walter tilted his head and stared at the girl. "Contract?"

She leaned toward him and whispered, "You don't know how things work here, do you?"

"I guess not."

"I'm not supposed to talk about the business, but I know you were Tabby's friend."

"I thought I was." He paused before asking, "What's your name?"

"Ru," she told him, then turning slightly she added, "I know you're Walter, but who is this fella' here?"

"Name's Frank," Walter said. Frank smiled at her as Walter continued. "So, Ru, what can you tell us?"

Ru glanced back at the bar, then smiled at both Walter and Frank. "Most of the girls here are under contract. I mean the white ones. The Mexicans and Indians were forced, but we came here for money. I lived with Tabby and her ma and pa in Montana. They took me in when I had no place to go and treated me like kin. When her pa took off and it looked like her ma would lose her home, we needed to find quick money. Jahiel, the owner of this place, was in Montana looking for girls. Tabby approached him first and he offered her money if she'd sign on, but it wasn't enough to save her ma's farm. I signed up, too. She got more money since she's a couple years younger than me and prettier, but together we had enough. We both agreed to come to San Francisco and to sell our bodies, she for seven years and me for five. It was our choice and we both signed the contracts. Jahiel hasn't been bad to us. He protects us when the clients get rough. He also lets us keep some of what we make, depending on how many drinks we push. But Tabby's at another brothel now. All she'll get is room and board. We've been in California for a year and a half, so she'll be working for another five and a half years."

"What do we do now?" Frank asked Walter.

Ru spoke up before Walter could answer. "I wouldn't try to visit her, not unless you have money to pay for her. Odell, her new boss, can be rough. You might get beat up and she definitely would."

Walter rolled his eyes. "I don't think Frank was asking about Tabby." Ru shook her head and started to turn away but brought her gaze back when Walter added. "But I'd like to know. Is there any way we can help?"

"Not unless you have the money to buy out her contract. Though you shouldn't worry too much. Tabby's tough and very good at what she does."

"I know that," Walter said, looking down as he spoke.

"I don't mean giving a screw, if that's what you're thinking. Any of us can do that. Tabby is great because she knows how to talk to men, how to get them to think she cares for them."

Walter's head jerked back involuntarily. Ru seemed to notice his reaction.

"I'm sorry," she continued. "I didn't mean you. You're different. For one thing, you're our age. You're also innocent and I mean that in a good way. Tabby told me she likes you and said you're a friend. That's why I'm talking to you."

"We've got to do something," Walter told her.

"She'll be all right. She's already had dozens of marriage proposals, none from men rich enough to buy her, but one of those will come. She'll end up on a farm somewhere, raising chickens, hogs, and children, which is what all the women aim to do back in Montana. Me, I'll probably stay here even after my contract is done. I'll die here, selling a poke to any miner or sailor who wants one, until my body wears out."

No one spoke for a moment, until Frank said, "Like I asked before, what do we do now?"

Walter shrugged. "I don't know."

Ru glanced at the bar, then back at the boys. "You can stay in my room tonight and maybe I can sneak some food up for you. But you got to go now. Come back when the place is empty."

"What about tomorrow?" Frank asked.

"You are a greedy little one," Ru said. "I'll tell you this. You can both stay for a few nights, to give you time to find a place of your own. But you can't be up there when I'm working and you can't live here permanently, understand?"

They both nodded. Ru smiled, then walked back to the bar and sidled up to a man who was standing there.

It was raining when Walter and Frank stepped out of the saloon. They found a porch with a roof, in front of a watch repair shop.

"The people here have enough watches for a repair shop?" Frank asked, tilting his head as he spoke.

"Shhh," Walter whispered. "This place looks closed, but the owner probably lives in the back. We don't want anyone to hear us."

Frank nodded. "You're right," he said quietly.

They sat on a bench to the right of the shop door and watched the rain come down. They didn't speak for a minute or two until Frank said, "It was nice of Ru to offer us a place to stay, but she said a few days, so we still have to figure out what to do next."

"We need jobs. I figure all we're good at is fishing, cooking, and recognizing gold. Everyone in San Francisco knows gold so that's no good. And fishing is different here than it was at the camp. The men go out on large boats and fish in the ocean, with nets. All you and I know is how to fish in a lake with a hook and string."

"I guess that leaves cooking," Frank said. "But we've always cooked on a campfire. I don't know much about stoves."

"Still, look at all the restaurants and saloons in this area. So many men live in shacks or canvas houses with no kitchens. They have to eat out all the time. I'm certain someone needs a cook. We'll try in the morning."

The watch repair shop was down the street from the saloon, so the boys could keep their eyes on it while they sat and waited for the time when Ru said they could return. The rain died off as the evening dragged on. It was gone when the men lingering in front of the saloon went their various ways.

Walter and Frank went back to the saloon. They found the door locked, so they knocked. Ru answered and waved them in. The bartender was cleaning up and a few of the other prostitutes were sitting at a couple of tables, giggling and talking. Ru brought them to an empty table and suggested they sit. She went to the bar and brought back a couple of plates of chicken and beans. "Here you go," she said.

"You're sure you're not gonna get in trouble?" Walter asked.

"No, I've told them you're Tabby's friends. We all miss her and want to do right by her, so this food is on the house. If you stay another night or two, I'll have to pay for whatever you eat, and I'd appreciate you paying me back when you get settled."

The fried chicken was a little cold but tasted good anyway. The beans were cold and soggy, but the boys offered no complaints. When they were done, Ru led them to the back of the saloon, opened a door, stepped outside, and gestured for them to follow. Walter was afraid she was going back on her offer to let them sleep there that night, but instead she stepped to an outhouse and went in.

After they each took a turn, Ru led the boys back inside and upstairs to her room. Her place was like the room where Tabby had lived before her contract was sold. Like Tabby's, it was simple, almost barren with no window. However, Ru's room had one significant difference, something that made Walter's skin tingle as soon as he saw it. On the wall next to the mirror, there was a poster of Lotta Crabtree, the one where she was wearing the dress Tabby had borrowed before their last time together.

"You're gonna have to sleep on the floor," Ru told them, bringing Walter back from his trance. "Sorry I can't do better than that, but at least you'll be dry and warm. I borrowed a couple extra blankets." Ru removed her shoes, then undid some buttons on her blouse and slipped it over her head. She began to fold the blouse but stopped when she noticed Frank staring.

"You can stay here a few nights," she said, "but if you want anything else, you have to pay. And only during working hours. Understand?" He nodded.

She stepped to her bureau and placed the blouse on top. After that, she stayed facing the wall as she took off her skirt and stockings.

She pulled on a cotton chemise, turned and slipped into her bed. She nodded toward a kerosene lamp. "Turn that off when you're ready."

The boys stripped to their undershirts and drawers. After Frank turned off the lamp, they both lay on the floor and pulled their blankets over their bodies.

Ru's room was pitch dark. Walter lay on his back, staring up, seeing nothing. He was tired, so despite the hard floor, he started to doze. He shook his head, wanting to think about the poster before he fell asleep. The darkness helped him keep the picture in his mind. The image seemed to flip back and forth between Lotta and Tabby—both women dressed in that same dress, both with their hair curled and pulled back, both wearing those long, chain earrings.

Then the image seemed to split in two. Now it was Lotta *and* Tabby, still dressed exactly the same. He tried to blink, but the pictures didn't go away, even when he closed his eyes. The two women started to move and soon Tabby and Lotta were dancing side by side, both staring at him, their bodies perfectly matched, their legs moving in identical patterns.

The image vanished as Walter sat up, his lips trembling and his hands clammy.

"Are you all right?" Frank asked, his voice cracking slightly. Walter could tell Frank was also sitting up, although it was too dark to see his friend.

"Just a dream," Walter told him. "It was nothing."

Ru cleared her throat. "You both either stay quiet or get out of my room. Ya hear me?"

Walter and Frank answered like they were one person. "We won't make a sound," they said, their words as together as the legs in his dream.

Walter added "Goodnight," which he knew was a mistake when he heard Ru flop back on her bed then turn over and grunt. It took him a while to fall asleep, but he made sure he was quiet the entire time.

If he thought of Lotta and Tabby again that night, he didn't remember it the next day.

Chapter Five

Looking for Work

Ru told the boys her saloon didn't need cooks since the owner did most of the cooking and the girls filled in when he wasn't there. After a breakfast of bread and coffee, Walter and Frank headed out to try some of the other restaurants in town.

They were not well received, which Walter believed was due to their age. When the few owners who were willing to listen heard they had come from the camps, they immediately asked if the boys had experience with cookstoves. Walter tried lying but wasn't very good at it, so he went back to admitting he'd always cooked on an open fire, like most of the miners.

At a makeshift restaurant outside a canvas house, a woman offered some good advice. "You say you cooked coon, squirrel, and fish?" she asked.

"Yup," Walter answered.

"Lots of fish," Frank put in.

"That was most of what we ate," Walter continued. "We also traded fish and other meat for vegetables and potatoes, so we have experience there too."

"If you cooked those animals, you had to clean them, right?" she asked, ignoring his last comment.

Walter nodded.

"I think you'd be better off trying one of the butchers. They're always looking for hard workers."

Her advice turned out to be good. The first place they tried had need of a boy to clean the work area. Frank took the position. The pay wasn't much, but the butcher agreed to let him have some meat trimmings each day.

They found an old hotel in Chinatown, an easy walking distance from the butcher shop. It was similar to the bunkhouse they'd slept in back at the camp, a wooden structure with a single narrow, but long, room. This one, however, had bunks lining the walls, three high. Two were available in one location. Walter took the top bed, Frank the middle one. Another of the residents, someone they hadn't met, was to sleep on the bottom. They were to keep their possessions on shelves at the foot of the three-layer bed.

The hotel owner said he would hold those two bunks for them, but they couldn't stay overnight until they could pay. Frank's job started the next day, which meant they had to impose on Ru one more time.

That evening, at the saloon, Ru brought them each a plate of pork and yams. She offered whiskey or beer to drink, seeming more generous than she had the night before. Ru also appeared somewhat nervous, blinking rapidly and rubbing the back of her neck. Walter wondered what was going on but decided not to ask. Ru would tell in her own time if she wanted to.

Ru sat down next to them. "Frank got a job at the butcher on Sutter Street," Walter told her, "And we found a place to stay, a hotel in Chinatown."

"Really? They speak English there?"

"Yup. At least the owner does. He said a few of the residents do as well. I'm sure we'll get by just fine."

Ru looked at Frank and asked, "When do you start work?"

"Tomorrow."

"I'm glad things worked out for you today, but as I said before, you're welcome to stay tonight and tomorrow night if you'd like. It's possible the butcher won't pay you until the end of the week. If you have a problem at the hotel just let me know and I can put you up."

Walter smiled. "Thanks."

"You're a friend of Tabby's and I'm always willing to help her friends." She looked toward the bar as she spoke.

"Are you waiting for someone?" Walter asked. "You seem nervous."

"No, I'm not waiting for anyone."

"Come on, Ru. Tell us what's bothering you. We're friends of yours, too."

Ru glanced around the bar then leaned closer to Frank and Walter. "Jahiel doesn't want us talking about this," she whispered. "He says we'll stir up trouble with Odell, but I think he feels guilty over selling Tabby's contract." She looked around again, before continuing. "A Chinese prostitute we know spoke to Tabby earlier today. I knew her new pimp would be a rough master, but he's worse than I thought. He's got her doing twice as many men as she did in the saloon. He told her she needs to, because he's getting no money from drinks. He's even put her in situations where she does two at once. Men get mean in situations like that, when talk is limited and they're showing off. She's been hit a couple times and Odell doesn't care about anything except money. It's rough times for her."

Walter felt his body tense. "What can we do?" he asked, his voice cracking.

"Nothing. If there was, we would have done it already."

"There's got to be something." He pounded his fist on the table.

Ru covered Walter's hand with hers and squeezed. "Odell's got her contract. She's his for the next five years."

No one spoke for a minute until Ru reached for Walter's beer, took a swig, sat up straight, and said, "I'm glad things worked out for you two today, but as I said before, you're welcome to stay tonight and tomorrow night if you need to."

"Thank you," Walter said and in a low voice added, "We'll keep thinking and I'm sure we'll come up with something to help Tabby." He stood up. "I mean that. We will think of something we can do."

"That's right," Frank said. "Walter and me, we're pretty good at figuring things out."

Ru leaned toward Walter and hugged him, then turned to Frank and kissed him on his cheek.

The following morning Walter got up early, dressed, left Ru and Frank still asleep, and walked out of the saloon. He had skipped breakfast and was dressed in the same clothes he'd worn for days. He was supposed to be job hunting, but all he could think of was Tabby. Instead, he headed toward Chinatown and the hotel they would soon call home, hoping there might be a few English-speaking men there who would know something about Odell's brothel.

He found one, a dock worker named Guan Wu, who had been in California for five years. "Ah Toy is woman you need talk to," Guan Wu said in his broken English. "She have girls in Sacramento, but still run house here. She in San Francisco now."

Walter went to see Ah Toy, to speak to her about Tabby's situation. The woman was welcoming but refused to help. "Odell's chickens are often hurt and angry. They no longer good for ji nu."

"Ji nu?" Walter asked.

"Tail." Ah Toy grinned then added, "whore, like me."

"Her name is Tabby. She's more than what she does."

"What her last name?"

"I don't know."

Ah Toy's voice rose as she asked, "You not know her last name, but say you are a good friend?"

"I'll tell you something about Tabby. Everyone likes her. The people she works with consider her a friend, even her old boss does."

"Then why sell her?"

"I don't know. Maybe he likes money more."

"If she a good ji nu, men will always like her more than money."

Walter took in a deep breath, exhaled slowly, then spoke in a calm tone. "She is gentle and cares about other people."

"Good."

"Better than good," Walter told Ah Toy. "I would say perfect. Someone who does not deserve to be treated like she is."

"She sign a contract to prostitute. This the life she chose. I chose the same life after my husband died and it was good for me. I am happy and my girls are happy. They have good lives. I cannot help everyone, but I help my own."

"That's why I came to you. People say you're a good woman. I'm asking you to help one more woman, one innocent woman. She signed the contract to save her ma's home."

Ah Toy shook her head. "You can call a ji nu many things, but not innocent. This Tabby friend of yours, she knew her ma needed money. It good to respect one's parents, but one must pay price. It wrong of her to ask me to pay. I did not sign the contract."

"I could pay you back," Walter suggested.

"No. No. No. You could not pay me back for years. That is not good business."

The conversation lasted long enough for Walter and Ah Toy to finish the tea she served, but Ah Toy did not give in or make any practical suggestions, except one. "You should make money while you wait," she told him. "Tabby will grow old fast with Odell. When she is no longer a good ji nu, he will sell low."

There was a horrible thought—wait until Tabby was beaten and scarred so badly, no one would spend money on her. Walter apologized for interrupting Ah Toy's day and left her brothel, clenching his hands as he walked. He wanted to hit someone, preferably Odell, but he knew nothing would come of that. He'd heard from Ru that the man had a private army, which would probably kill him and leave Tabby working out her contract, a much slower and more painful way of dying.

Walter had a couple of hours before he was to meet Ru and Frank at the saloon, so he went to the docks to see if he could find Guan Wu. He hoped the man could name another person who might be able to help Tabby. He didn't see Guan Wu, but he spoke with a supervisor and managed to land a job.

When Walter returned to the saloon and they sat down for another meal he told Ru, "I met with Ah Toy." He turned to Frank and said, "She's a Chinese madam, runs a number of brothels here and in Sacramento."

"She's got connections in China," Ru added, as she offered the boys dried fish, potatoes, and beer. "She brings young girls in from over there, but once they're here she treats them well and protects them from the Chinese gangs."

Walter didn't think those girls came to California by choice, but rather than saying anything he looked down at his plate. He didn't know what kind of fish it was and didn't like any fish dried, yet he was hungry and very grateful for another dinner. "I hoped I'd convince her to buy Tabby's contract, but no luck."

"That's what you did today?" Frank asked, tapping his foot as he spoke.

"Not all I did," Walter told him. "I got me a job at the docks, unloading cargo. You won't be the only one making money. I start tomorrow. How did your day go?"

"It was all right—smelly and messy, but not hard work." Frank turned to Ru. "I didn't get paid today, like you said might happen. We'll have to stay on your floor one more night."

"If you don't mind," Walter added.

"I don't," Ru said. "Tell me about Ah Toy."

"She's a small woman with bound feet, so she shuffles when she walks. She wears her hair in an odd way, some pulled back and some pulled to the side, but she's pretty and must have been beautiful in her day. She seems proud."

"What did she say about Tabby?"

Walter looked away from Ru. "She said no."

"That's all?"

He looked back into her eyes. "She said she never buys contracts from Odell, said his girls are worn out and angry. To her this was a business decision. She said she treats her own girls well and can't worry about what others do. I can see why she's rich."

Ru leaned back in her chair and smiled. "So, you both have jobs now."

"We'll still come and visit," Frank told her.

"Good," Ru said, grinning. "I want you to do that and maybe, when you have a little money saved, you can buy yourself a poke." She winked at him as his ears turned red. "But tonight, it's time to celebrate. I'd like to take you boys out. Lotta Crabtree is appearing at the American Theatre and Lola Montez is supposed to be with her this week."

"Won't that be working hours?" Walter asked.

"I told all my regulars I'd be out and one of the girls is covering for me by the bar."

"So, you've been planning this?"

This time Ru winked at Walter. "Maybe."

"Who is Lola Montez?" Frank asked.

"You don't know?" Ru asked them both.

Frank and Walter both shook their heads.

"I'm surprised. She's a dancer and was Lotta's neighbor some years back. She's famous for her spider dance, which sounds strange, but is very funny. She puts fake spiders up her skirt. While she's dancing, she begins to scratch and pretends the spiders are bothering her as she's trying to dance. She has to lift her skirt, of course, to get rid of those blasted spiders. The higher she lifts it, the more the men enjoy the show. She's the one who taught Lotta to entertain while she's dancing. Lotta had plenty of talent, but without Lola, she wouldn't know how to use it."

"I bet you gave her a few hints yourself, didn't you?" Frank asked.

Ru laughed at that. "Yup. Tabby and I both did. We're entertainers, too. Not so much difference as you would think. But enough of this. You two got to bathe and get dressed. I borrowed clothes from one of my rich men, but first, there's a tub out back."

They had to heat water on the stove and carry it outside. That took some time. When the tub was full, Ru suggested Walter go first. "The butcher shop filth on Frank will ruin the water," she told them.

Frank dropped his chin slightly, so Walter said, "Hard work ain't nothing to be ashamed of. You go first."

Frank stripped and got in the water. Ru helped him scrub his back, which Walter thought was her way of saying she was sorry for calling Frank dirty. But when Frank was putting his old clothes back on and Walter was in the tub, she scrubbed his back as well.

There was no privacy. Anyone who needed to use the privy passed the tub. Although Ru was there to make sure no one gave them a hard time, the men shook their heads and the women giggled. When Walter was done, he also dressed in his old clothes. After they were ready, Ru led them back to her room to show them the clothes they would wear to the show.

"San Francisco has its society," Ru said, as Walter and Frank started to dress in the clothing she had laid out for them. "It's mostly based on money." She looked at Walter. "Ah Toy could be there tonight, but most of the audience will be people who had money before they came here."

"Then why come?" Frank asked.

"To make more, of course." Ru rolled her eyes. "These are the men who brought their families, who are here to set up shops, work for the mining companies, or even get involved in politics. They have to entertain their wives, so they throw parties, attend dances, and go to the theater. In exchange, the wives turn a blind eye to the time they spend with me and the other girls. Everybody wins. The women get highfalutin events, the men get some excitement in their lives, and we girls get to make a living."

"They sound like snobs," Walter said.

"Not all of them. Lotta's family, for example. They ran a bookstore in New York and were doing just fine, but her pa heard about the gold out here and wanted a part of it. He headed west without them, so Lotta's ma sold the store and followed. Mrs. Crabtree opened a boarding house and was doing well enough when Lotta began dancing. After that, the gold flowed to them and Mrs. Crabtree invested what Lotta made in real estate. They're rich now. Funny thing is Mr. Crabtree ended up with next to nothing. I heard he keeps going back to his wife, begging." Ru winked.

Walter looked down at his feet. "She never mentioned her pa," he said.

"Don't suppose she would. He didn't even bother meeting them at the pier when they arrived in San Francisco. Although, he did meet up with her ma long enough to make two brothers for Lotta." Ru chuckled and winked again. Walter was a little irritated by Ru's winks, especially now that she was talking about Lotta.

Walter and Frank were dressed, so Ru stood back and looked them over. Her eyes were bright and wide, and she seemed to be laughing. At first, Walter thought she was laughing at him. But when she said, "You both look so good!" He knew they did and felt proud.

He turned to Frank, who was wearing a brown suit with a long coat that almost reached his knees, a matching vest, white shirt, a dark tie, and a felt hat. Frank had on shiny, black shoes, almost as shiny as the ones Ru had given Walter.

Walter's outfit was similar, except his suit was gray. He stepped to Ru's mirror, and was pleased with what he saw, although he couldn't get back far enough to see his entire reflection.

Ru kept smiling, but what she did next, surprised Walter. She asked them to step into the hall while she changed. They obliged her. They considered going down to the saloon for a drink while they waited but didn't want to get laughed at by the customers who knew their usual torn and dirty clothes. When a couple of the saloon girls passed them they prepared themselves to be laughed at. The girls didn't giggle this time. Instead they smiled and one of them even looked down and blushed a bit.

Ru's door opened and Walter was almost as impressed as he had been on the day Tabby had dressed like Lotta. Ru had on a light blue, floor length gown that matched her eyes. The gown had an elaborate trim that reminded Walter of some patterns he'd seen in Indian blankets. The trim ran around the skirt about a foot off the floor and up her legs in the front. There was also a similar trim around the off-the-shoulder neckline and on her short sleeves.

What surprised Walter the most was not the look of the dress itself, but the way it changed Ru's lanky appearance. Something under the dress pushed up her breasts and something else gave her the appearance of having wide, lovely hips. This was also the first time Walter had ever seen her hair down. All this made Ru look great, not as good as Tabby or Lotta, but still very pretty. She spun around the way Tabby had when she was wearing Lotta's dress and Frank grabbed Walter's arm, making him think his friend might pass out.

Ru hugged Frank and kissed him first on his cheek then once lightly on his lips. "Let's go," she said after she stepped back. She didn't hug Walter, which made him feel like he was intruding on something between the two of them, especially after what Tabby had told him about kissing. He thought he might ask if they wanted to be alone but didn't. He was looking forward to seeing Lotta and besides, it would be a shame to waste the bath.

At the theater, they were surrounded by a huge crowd of rich people dressed in their finest. The line was long, but Walter didn't mind. He enjoyed looking at the people in the crowd. The clothes he and Frank wore were nice enough to fit in, especially since they were standing beside Ru, who was among the youngest and prettiest women in the audience. She didn't acknowledge any of the men they saw, but Walter could tell by a few surprised expressions, some of her men were in the crowd.

Their seats were on the lower level about halfway down the aisle. Frank sat on Ru's left and Walter sat on her right. Up front, there was a massive gold frame surrounding a red curtain as tall as a two-story building. Although they were seated off to one side, Walter thought they would still have a clear view of the stage. He was proven right once the curtain was raised and Lola Montez entered from the back of the theater, dancing down an aisle and up onto the stage.

The spider dance was exactly what Ru had described, but not what Walter had imagined. Lola entered wearing a black shawl over a red dress. She threw the shawl off stage as she began her dance. The music had a Spanish flair and she moved to it well, spinning about, waving her arms, and tapping her feet. Her dress was short, reaching just below her knees and she did pull it up as she looked for the spiders. Yet she never lifted her petticoat, so the men in the audience never got a glance of the garters holding her white stockings up, just a tease. Despite what Ru had said, this wasn't anything like what the saloon customers got from Tabby or Ru.

Walter stared at Lola, trying to figure out how she was releasing those spiders. He saw her hand go to her waistband a couple of times, causing him to think there were strings tied there with bows Lola could release quickly. But that didn't explain all the spiders. It was almost like a magic act.

After Lola, Lotta was introduced as the San Francisco favorite and came out to dance her own solo. Her performance had changed a lot since the last time Walter had seen her. For one thing, she wasn't wearing a skirt. Instead, she was dressed as a working-class boy, in worn trousers and an old yellow shirt that reminded Walter of one he used to wear. *Could that be on purpose?* he wondered.

The shirt was covered with a ragged vest. Her sleeves were rolled up and she wore a cap. But when she began to move about, she walked with a sassy strut. She circled the stage, stopping a few times to look out over the audience. The Lotta Walter had known was still there, but she had changed in a way he hadn't thought possible. She was more confident and talented. She danced a jig to a song he recognized: *Geese in the Bog*. Her legs flew so fast, he could hardly see them.

After the dance, Lotta sat at the edge of the stage, between two of the gas footlights. The orchestra slowed the music as she scanned the audience until she seemed to look in a single direction. It might have been Walter's imagination since the theater was so full of people, but Lotta seemed to focus on him. She started to sing a beautiful, soft song:

> *BELIEVE me, if all those endearing young charms,*
>
> *Which I gaze on so fondly to-day,*
>
> *Were to change by to-morrow, and flee from my arms*
>
> *Like fairy-gifts, fading away!*
>
> *Thou wouldst still be ador'd as this moment thou art,*
>
> *Let thy loveliness fade as it will;*
>
> *And, around the dear ruin, each wish of my heart*
>
> *Would entwine itself verdantly still!**

Walter leaned over to Ru and whispered, "Did she ever sing that song when she was at your saloon?"

Ru leaned toward him and nodded then whispered, "She sings it so well."

A woman sitting in the row in front of them turned and glared but didn't say anything.

Lotta introduced another song, speaking with a cockney accent and started to sing about a young rower who worked on a river, ferrying people across and charming all the maidens. That one had nothing to do with Walter, but she sang it well.

After the English song, Lotta left the stage for a short time while the orchestra played. When she returned her long red hair was loose. She was dressed in a blue blouse and skirt similar to the outfit she had worn when she danced at the camp. Walter didn't think her clothes could be the same, but her look brought his memories back. She danced some more, flipping her skirt the way she had years ago. She still wore bloomers, so her dance wasn't as risqué as Lola's, but it sure made Walter's temperature rise.

After the intermission, Lotta and Lola danced a few numbers together, which seemed to thrill the audience. Walter couldn't keep his eyes off Lotta, even when Lola was out front. Maybe it was the age difference, but Lotta seemed to have much more energy than Lola. Her moves were cleaner. Lola slipped into the steps a bit slower than Lotta did and Lotta held positions with more strength. Lotta may have been Lola's student, but she'd passed her by.

When the show ended Walter and Frank stood up to file out with the rest of the audience, when Ru reached up and grabbed them both by the sleeves of their jackets. She tugged to indicate they should sit down, which they did.

"We're not leaving yet," she said.

"Why not?" Frank asked. "It was a wonderful show, but isn't it over?"

"Not for us." That's all Ru said. They sat there in silence until everyone else left the theater. Walter felt his stomach turn as he waited for Lotta to come from backstage, which had to be the reason they were sitting there. He was disappointed when Mary Ann Crabtree, Lotta's ma, walked out from behind the curtain, holding the hand of Lotta's youngest brother, George.

"Move to the aisle," Ru said, as she stood. Frank and Walter did as they were told, while Mary Ann walked toward them.

"Do you recognize me?" Mary Ann asked Walter.

"Yup."

"Good." She shifted from George's right side to his left and planted her feet firmly. "I understand our friend Tabby has a problem and we may have a solution."

Walter turned to Ru, who shrugged and smiled.

"Lotta wants to help and I've agreed, as long as you accept our demands."

"Demands?" Walter rubbed his forehead.

"We'll buy Tabby's contract from Odell and we won't use her as she's been used. We need someone to look after Ashworth and George while Lotta is performing and I'm attending to other business."

"Wonderful!" Walter smiled and even laughed a little. His eyes were wide open.

"And..." Mary Ann went on after waiting for Walter to calm down, "in exchange we want you to sign your own contract."

"What kind of a contract?"

"The same one Tabby signed."

Walter gasped.

Mary Ann paused again then continued saying, "Lotta and I were talking. We don't think it is fair that women and men are treated differently. You will agree to prostitute yourself for a period to end when Tabby's contract ends."

"Is that possible?" Walter asked.

Ru nodded. "There are male prostitutes, not as many as the girls, but they are around. A few work for Odell."

"Just like with Tabby, I won't be using you as your contract will state. I expect you to help with repairs to our house, with building scenery for Lotta's performances, and other tasks, such as delivering messages. If Lotta's show goes on tour, I'll expect you and Tabby to come along. But if either you or Tabby lets me down, I will be free to sell your contracts. Understand?"

Walter looked down, his chin touching his chest as he muttered, "Yes."

"And you will sign?"

He nodded, but said, "I think so."

"You do look handsome in those fine clothes. I will make sure you get clothes to suit your new position."

"You will own me for more than five years," Walter said.

"No," Mary Ann told him. "Lotta will own you. I have the paper here, but there's one more thing I want to make clear before you sign. If Lotta asks you to be her friend, don't tell her she's a rich snob."

Walter wondered what he would be getting into with this crazy situation. He didn't know much about Mary Ann, but Lotta seemed nice enough, at least the Lotta he'd kept in his head since the day they'd gone fishing. Still, one day together and a couple of times in her audience might not be enough to know the real Lotta. Yet hadn't she stared at him? Hadn't she sung that sweet song while looking right at him? He didn't know what to think about that.

What he did know was that Tabby was depending on him. He turned to Frank, who wasn't moving. His eyes were wide and his mouth open. Walter looked at Ru. She wasn't making a sound, yet seemed to be mouthing the word *please* over and over. Finally, he turned back to Mary Ann and took the paper. He could read, but not well. He signed it without even trying to understand what it said.

Mary Ann took the contract back, glanced down at it for a moment, then tucked the paper in a pocket in her skirt. She pulled a small bag out of the same pocket and handed it to Walter. "Here's your first week's pay, in advance. You and Frank have been in Ru's room long enough. Use this to get out. In the morning you can move your stuff to that Chinatown hotel I've heard about. Lotta and I will look into Tabby's situation while you're doing that. Come by our house in the afternoon. Hopefully, Tabby will be there before you. She'll be living with us."

Mary Ann started to step away, toward the stage and beyond that, the dressing rooms. Lotta and Lola were probably back there. After a few steps, Mary Ann turned and asked, "You do know how to use tools, right?"

"I can hammer a nail, read a ruler, and saw a board in a straight line. Anything else you need, I can learn."

"That's good enough for me," She turned back and left.

Walter looked in the bag as she walked away. It was gold dust, of course, what everyone used for money. There had to be at least an ounce in there, worth more than $20! He couldn't make that much working at the port for a week. Mary Ann was generous enough. That was certain.

Chapter Six

Starting to Heal

Lotta flung open the door as soon as Walter stepped foot on the porch. Her eyes were wide and her bright smile matched a white ribbon in her hair.

"Hello, Walter. I am glad you agreed to work for us."

Even though she was standing perfectly straight, her shoulders back and chest out, she seemed shorter than when she was on stage the day before.

The house was a cabin with a wood shingle roof and a wrap-around porch, facing three directions. Inside, was a living room with doors to four rooms. One had to be a small kitchen. The other three were probably bedrooms. The privy had to be in back, the way it always was in these communities. There were voices behind one of the doors, although he couldn't tell which one.

Lotta was pretty, dressed in a casual yellow dress with a pattern of white spots. It wasn't an outfit she might dance in, since there was no glimpse of a petticoat when she walked, but it was nicer than the brown dress she'd been wearing when she got on her knees to dig worms. Except for the strands pulled together by the ribbon, her red hair was loose and dangled over her shoulders.

Walter ran his fingers through his own hair while thinking of Lotta's. "I'm also glad, Miss Lotta. It is nice to see you again," he said coolly, looking around at the finery. "Thank you for what you did for Tabby."

"She's here, in her bedroom. She's been beaten and looks horrible, but there doesn't appear to be permanent damage. Ma had our doctor look her over. She's got two black eyes, a cut, and bruises on her forehead, and another gash beside her mouth. She's also got bruises on her stomach and legs. She'll need to rest for at least a week, so the first thing we'll have you doing is what she was going to do. You will take care of George and Ash."

"That's fine, Miss Lotta."

"Call me Lotta, Walter."

"Is that proper? You do own me."

"Is that bothering you?" Lotta ran her fingers through her hair. "Your contract was Ma's idea. She doesn't trust men and I can't blame her. Pa's treated her terribly since we came out west. She wanted something to hold over you and now she has it. She'll never sell it or use it like it's written. She knows I would hate her if she did anything like that."

"That's good to hear." Walter looked up at the ceiling, then back at Lotta. "Can I see Tabby?"

"She doesn't want you to see her like she is," Lotta said, her voice breaking. "What you did was wonderful, and Tabby knows it. Ma would not have bought Tabby's contract if you hadn't signed yours because she didn't want us to get a reputation for giving pure charity. This way she gets both you and Tabby to work for her and her reputation as a hard business-woman grows. Still, she won't sell or hold you to prostitution, but you had no way of knowing that. You risked everything for her. Tabby admires you for that and so do I."

"If I can't see Tabby, what can I do to help her?"

"I'll tell you what you *shouldn't* do. Don't do anything to hurt Odell. She's free of him and once she's better, we are going to give her a chance to start over. That's all that matters, so don't go near him."

"Then what do you want me to do?"

"There's a wood box attached to the back of the chicken coop with tools inside. A new pane of glass is in there, wrapped in newspaper. Ma wants you to replace a cracked pane in one of our windows. You know how to do that?"

"Never tried, but I imagine I can figure it out. Which window?"

"Just walk around the porch. You'll see it."

Walter walked out onto the porch and stood there for a moment, rubbing the back of his neck.

There were multiple windows, two in the main room where he'd just been talking with Lotta. They were close enough for him to see they weren't cracked. There was another one facing front that had to be in one of the bedrooms and there were others on either side. He would have to walk around the porch to see which pane was broken. Tabby was behind one of those windows, which was the problem. He could peer into all the bedrooms as he checked the glass, or he could just glance at them as he walked by and only look into the room with the cracked pane.

This had to be a test. If it wasn't, Lotta would have brought him to the broken window, instead of telling him to walk around the porch. This was her home. She had to know where it was. Yet Lotta had just told him two things: to stay away from Tabby and to wander the porch. What was more important to Lotta and her ma, Mary Ann—obeying orders or demonstrating that he cared enough about his friend to ignore orders?

He decided to get the glass before he checked the windows, which would give him time to think a little more. He wanted to know how Tabby was feeling, but truth be told, he couldn't add much to her care. Mary Ann and Lotta were giving her what she needed. He stepped off the porch and headed to the chicken coop. Raising chickens was a good idea. Eggs were scarce and went for a dollar each, as much as one night in the hotel where he and Frank would be staying. Mary Ann was shrewd all right.

He found the glass and brought it back to the porch, leaned it against the cabin wall then went back for tools. He found a hammer, pliers, and a small wooden box of assorted nails. He thought these were all he needed, but he wouldn't know for sure until he took the old pane out. He would see how it had been held in place and copy what had been done before.

He stood on the porch for another moment, looked to the right then the left, before deciding to check the right side first. As soon as he turned the corner, he saw the cracked pane. There was no need to look further.

Still, he wondered what was happening with Tabby. He thought back to the day she'd dressed up in Lotta's outfit. He remembered taking her earrings off, pulling the wire through the holes in her earlobes. She'd told him how most women don't care if their earrings stay on after they start kissing you, but some do, especially if the wire is long enough to catch on a man's ring or watch or even in his teeth. "Some men think that's funny," she told him. Walter imagined pulling on earrings would hurt.

When they had gotten to Tabby's corset, things had turned awkward. He had to untie her from the back. The lacing was in a bow, but he pulled on it wrong and ended up with a knot he had to work a bit before she could slip out of it. He felt bad for Lotta, who often had to wear fancy dresses on stage. Tabby didn't have that problem unless she played dress up for other men like she'd done for him.

The chemise had come off and he had finally faced her drawers. He trembled as he pulled them down and Tabby had to criticize him, saying, "Act like this is not new to you, Walter. Women like that." After she was naked, she sat on the bed, watching him. He could feel her eyes as he undressed in the light of the oil lamp that burned all day in that windowless room. He wanted to show her he was confident, so he faced her as he removed his clothes.

Walter had known Tabby wanted him to take the lead when she lay on her back and didn't reach out to him. He climbed over her but supported his weight with his arms so he wouldn't hurt her. He kissed her softly at first, on her lips, her neck, and her chest between her breasts. He felt her shiver slightly, then she pulled him back to kiss her lips again, this time harder.

When they were done, Walter lay on Tabby for a moment, enjoying the way her soft, smooth chest felt against his skin and the way the rhythm of her breathing seemed to dance with his. She wiggled a little, which he took to mean she was ready to separate. He pushed himself up, then rolled off and lay beside her.

She touched his chest, then brought her hand back and swiveled around so she could sit on the edge of the bed. She paused for a moment. He touched her back, massaging her neck gently until she moved to stand. She went for her chemise on the floor, bending over to pick it up. He watched for another brief moment then stood and stepped towards her. When she stood, he reached for her shoulders and turned her so she stood facing him, with her chemise crumbled in her hands between their bodies.

Walter leaned in and kissed her again. When he pulled back she smiled. She pulled the chemise on then picked up the drawers she'd been wearing. "They're open here," she told him, showing him the crotch. "That way the fine ladies don't have to go through all this every time they use the privy. It also means that after you've known Lotta for a while and don't have a strong desire to feel her skin against yours, you can be more direct."

Walter felt his jaw grow tight. "I told you Lotta is a friend, nothing more. It was nice of you to do all this, but you're the one I like that way, not her."

"Careful," Tabby told him. "You don't want to fall for someone like me. As your pa said, I'm a tail."

He had hated his pa at that moment.

Walter brought his thoughts back to the window and where he was standing. If he just walked a few paces toward the back of the house, he could catch a glance through another bedroom window. Maybe Tabby was there. Maybe he could see exactly what had happened to her.

Walter rocked in place a couple of times then looked around to be certain Mary Ann and Lotta weren't watching. He set the tools down and went further along the porch. When he was near the next window he moved in and stared through. Although the pane made everything blurry, he could see a bed, but no one was in it. Tabby had to be behind a window on the other side.

He picked up his tools to look like he was working, then walked with assurance. When he was near the first of the windows on that side, he slowed way down, so he could look in without anyone noticing. There were people in this room. Although this window was as blurry as the first, he could see Mary Ann glaring at him. Lotta was sitting on the bed her full head of red hair blocking his view of Tabby.

Mary Ann gestured for him to move to the front door. Walter got there before her, but a moment later she opened the door and sprung out at him. "So now you're peering through our windows?"

"Lotta told me to fix a cracked pane. I was looking for it."

"Don't lie to me, Walter. We could hear you walking around out here. The broken window is on the other side and you know it."

"I just..." His jaw started to tremble as he tried to speak. He paused for a moment then began again. "I need to see her."

"Working for me and Lotta means you do what we say, understand?"

"I care about her," Walter said, lifting his head.

Mary Ann sighed. "All right. It was my idea to tell you Tabby didn't want you to see her. Maybe I was wrong. Here's the thing. We've done what we had to do, and I don't want more trouble. You can see her if you promise, on your soul, you will not do anything against Odell and if you also promise not to ask Tabby or anyone else for the names of the men who beat her."

Walter sighed then said, "All right. I promise. But tell me this. Odell's a businessman, right? How does he make money if he lets his girls get beat up?"

"He makes *more* money when that happens. He charges a fine to any customer who beats a girl, then sends her regulars to others while she recovers. He doesn't lose any money since the men are still coming to his brothel and he also gets the fines. He's lost a few girls who were beat up too badly to recover, but when that happens Odell just drops the girl and buys another contract. That's why he bought Tabby. Like you said, Odell's a businessman. I had to pay double Tabby's worth to save her from that fate. Wouldn't have done it if she wasn't a friend of Lotta's."

Walter frowned and gave a little nod. He wanted to say something, but the words wouldn't come.

"I've put my faith in you," Mary Ann said glaring at Walter. "Most men are drunken, selfish pigs. We make our money, Lotta and I, from their need to be entertained, but there are few I'd trust to be alone with my daughter. You are one of the exceptions. Do *not* let me down."

She walked inside and Walter followed. At the door to Tabby's room, she stopped and said, "Wait here." He waited until the door opened and Mary Ann came out, followed by Lotta. They didn't say anything to him or even glance in his direction, but they left the door cracked. He went in.

Tabby was sitting up in bed, wearing a chemise he hadn't seen, probably one of Lotta's. The blankets were pulled up to her waist even though it was a warm day. Both her eyes were blackened. The right one was swelled so much she couldn't open it. There was a bruise on the center of her forehead and a gash over her swollen eye. There was another gash beside her mouth, also one on the right side of her face. Her hair was pulled back and seemed dirty. She probably hadn't bathed since the attack and smelled of old sweat, but it was hard to tell since there was a chamber-pot next to her bed with something in it.

"Not a pretty sight," she said, her arms wrapped around her stomach. "They kicked me after they were done punching. I've got bruises from my head to my feet, especially around my middle and my legs. There are also a few bite marks on my backside. It hurts to walk, so I've been in bed since I got here. I passed out while they were moving me. The doctor said I need to stay in place for at least a week. But at least I've still got my teeth." He thought she tried to wink at him after she spoke, but her face was so swollen it was hard to tell.

"They?" he asked.

"Mary Ann told me you promised not to ask their names and I won't tell you even if you do. I'm gonna be all right. I'm gonna heal. It's best to move on."

"What I'm trying to ask, and what I'm still wondering, is how many men?"

"Three." She paused. "You know what hurts the worst? I can't get their laughter out of my head. They thought it was all so funny, especially when I was lying on the floor too weak to move and one of them pissed all over me."

He reached out to her face, but she moved just enough to show she didn't want to be touched.

"What can I do?" he asked.

"You're giving up five years of your life. That's so much!"

"They told you about the contract?"

"Lotta did. They won't hold you to it, not how it's written. That's just the way Mary Ann is. She likes to make things equal between men and women when she can. But you'll still be working for her and Lotta as long as I am."

"I know. I kinda like that."

Tabby smiled a little, but the gesture seemed to hurt. She moved her lips down, back to the sad look she'd worn since he walked in the room. "There's one more thing I want you to know," she told him. "You, Ru, Mary Ann, and Lotta were gifts from God."

Walter took a step back.

"I did something I haven't done since I left Montana and my ma. I prayed—and God answered. I'm gonna change my life. God directed you to help me. He sent you to Ru, who sent you to Lotta, who sent you to Mary Ann, who had the money to buy my contract. If anyone of you hadn't been willing to help, I'd still be working for Odell. He'd put me with men who would attack me again and again until I was dead. The four of you saved my life with the guidance of God."

She winced as she struggled to sit tall. "You know St. Mary's, right?"

"Yup. It's the tall building with the clock tower."

Tabby spoke in a steady voice. "That's right and under that clock, it says: *Son, Observe the Time and Fly from Evil.* I may be a daughter rather than a son, but that's what I intend to do. I'm gonna pray regularly and not just to ask for things. I'm going to thank God every day for getting me away from that monster. But the most important thing is, I'm never selling my body again, never even going near those places again."

"Not even to see Ru?"

Tabby tilted her head slightly. "Maybe just to see Ru," she said. "I'll try to get her to come to me, but if I can't I'll go to the saloon. I couldn't stand losing her." Tabby cleared her throat before adding, "Or you." Walter smiled. He was about to say he felt the same way, but she spoke before he could think of the right words. "This reminds me. I could use help for something if you're willing. You read, don't you?"

"Not well. What do you have in mind?"

"I want to get a Bible and read it, but I don't know how. Can you teach me? Or at least read it to me?"

"I could try, but I bet Lotta reads real well. Her ma and pa ran a bookstore in New York before they came out this way. I'll ask her."

Tabby closed her good eye and leaned back. Walter watched her and shuffled his feet until she spoke again. "I'm feeling tired. I think I'll sleep now." She winced when she attempted to slide toward the foot of the bed. Walter went to help, pulling her blankets back so she could move easier. He could see Tabby's legs because Lotta's chemise was short on her. She had dark bruises circling both her thighs and another on her right calf. Her knees were bruised as well. He lifted her gently and placed her in a position where she could rest, then covered her again with the blankets.

Walter turned to leave without saying goodbye. When he opened the door, Mary Ann and Lotta were waiting for him. They entered before he could step out. Mary Ann turned to him and said, "Walter, before you finish the window, take the chamber-pot to the privy then bring it back. Don't rinse it. We don't have extra water."

The back door was through the kitchen. When Walter returned, after emptying the pot, Mary Ann was working in the kitchen, cutting onions for something she was cooking. "Hi ma'am," he said, as he passed through the kitchen. She didn't look up.

He went on to Tabby's room. Lotta was there. She put a finger to her lips, then nodded at Tabby, who was sleeping. Walter nodded back, set the pot down, then stepped out of the room. Lotta followed.

In the main room, she touched his arm and said, "I've got some dance steps I've been working on. I'd like to show 'em to you."

"I've got to fix the pane."

"That'll work. I love dancing on the porch."

Chapter Seven

Living Together

Lotta darted out the front door and Walter followed. When he reached the porch, he found her standing next to two young boys, each holding a store-bought fishing pole. The taller one had a couple of trout and a few whitefish hanging from a stringer. Seeing Lotta standing next to two boys with fishing poles reminded Walter of the day by the lake, the day he'd like to forget.

"These here are my brothers. The taller one is Ash. The other is George. Ash is nine and George is seven, quite a bit younger than me."

"Spoze we'll be eating fish tonight," Walter said. "It's good to meet both of you. I'll be working for your ma for a while. Looks like you two have had a good day. Maybe I will, too. I'm about to fix a crack in one of the windows."

George looked down and kept biting at his lip while Ashworth spoke. "That cracked window is in our room. When it's cold, I can feel the wind."

"I'll do the best I can."

Lotta grinned then opened the door. "Ma's in the kitchen. You ought to bring her those fish." When they were in the house, she turned to Walter and said, "They're fishing for our dinner, just like you used to. We do work around here, you know."

Walter was convinced Lotta would never forget what he'd said so many years ago. He sighed then went around the porch to look at the window again. Lotta followed.

After Walter studied the window he said, "The glass is held in place with wood strips nailed to the frame. The trick will be getting them off without snapping them. I'm going back to the toolbox for something thin enough to get under there and pry."

"I'll go with you." Lotta told him. After they stepped off the porch she started chattering about her latest show. "That show you saw at the American was just the beginning of a run there."

"With Lola?" Walter asked.

"No. She's moving on. There'll be other dancers, of course, but I'll be featured."

"That's good. You're better than she is."

"I don't know about that. She's got a thing, that spider dance of hers. The miners go crazy over it."

"So, get your own thing."

"That's what Ma wants from this run. She says since I'm short, I should always play a child."

"You like that idea?"

"I like anything that will work. Anyway, they have me playing this young girl fresh off the boat, whose ma died on the ship, so she's left alone. Seems this child has lots of spunk. She manages to steal some food and find a place to sleep that's outta the rain. She's discovered sleeping out there by a man who just hit it big in the mines. Turns out this rich man loves music and the girl can sing like all wrath. The man starts to dance, and she joins in. He has a banjo with him and plays a little, but he's not all that good, so she takes over and gets to show off. Of course, the rich guy adopts the girl after he falls in love with her music. It isn't all that different from some of the other shows they had me doing at the smaller theaters, but this one is set in the mines. They're trying to play off my experience going from camp to camp, but you know about that. What's important is I get to sing, play the banjo and try out a new dance I've learned call the soft-shoe."

"You think it's enough?" Walter noticed how Lotta's mouth opened as if she was going to reply, but she didn't, so he added, "There are others who play children, right?"

"Not like I do," Lotta told him as her expression turned to a slight grin.

"S'pose that's right." Walter smiled back.

They found a couple of knives in the toolbox and some chisels. Walter took one of each and they headed back to Lotta's house.

When they reached the porch, Walter went straight to work. He carefully removed the thin wood strips and the pieces of glass. The wood didn't split, and the glass didn't shatter. He reused most of the nails, but in different places so they would catch properly. Two were too bent to use. He replaced them with two from the box he'd found with the tools.

The only issue he had with the project was due to Lotta's curiosity. She leaned in to watch him work, so closely he could smell her hair. He didn't complain because he liked the way she smelled. Besides, she was the boss, she and her ma.

"You done?" Lotta asked.

Walter nodded as he gathered his tools.

"Good, 'cause I want to show you the dance I was talking about."

"I got to put these tools away," he told her.

"Put 'em away later."

Lotta stepped back and started to sing a gentle tune Walter didn't recognize, then she began to move to the music she was making. Holding her arms up, slightly bent, but always loose, they seemed to bounce as she danced. She crossed her feet, tapping with her left in front of her right then her right in front of her left. Floating, like a fallen leaf, gently blown by the wind across the surface of a lake. Her legs crossed a few times to move to her right then repeated the steps in reverse to move to her left. She spun one way then back the other, then finished with a couple of slaps to her thighs, taps to the porch, and one last move with her right foot behind her left and stopped with her arms outstretched toward him.

"Like it?" she said, letting loose a breath and smiling.

He'd seen Lotta dance before, but this was the only time she'd danced just for him. She was amazing. The yellow dress with the white spots clung to her legs like a flag blowing against a pole in a gusty wind. Yet her skirt did not affect the easy way she moved. This time there were no petticoats to show off and her legs were bare. She didn't flip the dress, as she had while she danced the jig when he first saw her perform, but he loved this even more. He was in awe of her naked calves.

"That was wonderful," he said. "Can you teach me?"

"I can try."

She pulled him next to her and told him to look at her feet. She explained how this dance was mainly on the balls of the feet.

Walter glanced down at his feet then asked, "Balls?"

"This part here, between the toes and the arch." Lotta stood on her left foot and held her right, so Walter could see where she was pointing. Her simple stance looked remarkable, holding her foot as if it was a treasure of gold. She seemed stable and strong, her dance muscles showing. "Moving on the balls of your feet makes you feel like a bird. And you hold your arms up when you're dancing the soft-shoe like you're sailing in the wind. See?" She spun around a couple of times with her arms waving softly. "You work your feet like this." She stood on her left foot while she moved her right forward, brushing the porch floor, then stepping firmly on it with a little tap. Then she moved her foot back, brushing the floor again, and repeated the step for the other side. "Try it," she told him. "Watch my steps."

Lotta held his hand as she moved through the first step at a very slow pace. He copied her, then she stood on her right and repeated the step with her left. He copied what she'd done again, then looked to her for approval.

"You did fine," Lotta told him. She dropped his hand and stood back to watch. "Now do it on your own." Walter could do the first step, with his right foot moving, but couldn't handle the left side. "You'll get it," Lotta told him, laughing a little. "Now you have to practice. I can't do that for you."

Lotta started to walk toward the front of the porch, looked back over her shoulder and smiled at Walter, moving her head to indicate she wanted him to follow. When she rounded the corner to the front side of the house, she sat on the steps and tapped a place beside her. He sat down and she slid close to him.

"That was fun," Walter told her.

"Great. I need someone to dance with here at home, someone I'm comfortable with rather than the guys at the theater. The dancer I work with most of the time over there is old. He's a good dancer, but I like the way you look."

"You do?"

"Yup. Dancing can be part of your job here." She put her hand on his knee. "It's important for a dancer to look good."

Walter cleared his throat then stood up. "I've got to get those tools away."

Lotta kept sitting. "We'll dance again tomorrow. Meanwhile, you practice and let me know if you have any questions."

He looked down at her. "Well," he said. "There is one thing."

"What's that?"

"Do you have a Bible?"

"A Bible?"

"Right. If you've got one." He leaned toward Lotta. "Tabby would like you to read it to her. She's turning to religion, thinks God got her away from Odell."

"Ma and I got her away," Lotta said, her eyes wide open and glaring. "Maybe God oughta read to her about me."

"I had something to do with it, too," Walter said, noticing God wasn't the only one she didn't credit. Lotta looked away without responding, so Walter continued. "She can't read and I'm not much better than she is, so it's up to you. You're her friend, right?"

"Spoze so."

Lotta stood up and faced Walter with her hands on her hips and her legs planted wide. "I'll find her a Bible and I'll read to her every day, if that's what she wants."

"Thank you."

She gestured toward the other side of the porch then flexed her fingers. "After you get those tools put away, you need to check out the shingles on the house and the chicken coop. If some need replacing you can work on that. And look in on Ash and George. You're supposed to be taking care of them while Tabby heals. I don't see you doing that."

Lotta started into the house but turned to add "They caught some fish. You need to clean those, so Ma can cook them. Do it before you check on the shingles." After she gave him his orders, she went into the house, closing the door loudly behind her.

Walter waited to give Lotta time to go to her room or wherever she planned to go. Then he entered the house where he found Ash and George playing dominoes. He asked them where the fish were, and Ash sent him to the kitchen. Mary Ann was still in there, cleaning up after she'd been cooking.

"Lotta told me to clean the fish the boys caught."

Mary Ann chuckled. "Glad to hear she's got you doing something other than dancing"

"I'm to do that, too."

"I see. Well, you gotta learn to do things in the proper order. I cleaned the fish already. They're in the icebox."

Walter felt his skin tingle, because this family was rich, real rich. He'd never met anyone who had an icebox and could afford the ice to put in it. Everyone he knew put their food in cellars and hoped it would stay fresh. Now here he was working for one of the richest families in San Francisco and he was going to have to get used to some surprises.

"I hate cleaning fish," Mary Ann told him. "Makes my hands smell. Next time get in here in time to do it or I'll come looking for you."

"Yes, ma'am," Walter said then he left the kitchen. He walked back through the main room where Ash and George were playing quietly. He could hear Tabby and Lotta talking in Tabby's room, but he couldn't make out anything they said.

He went back to the box behind the chicken coup. There he found a ladder tall enough to reach the roofs. He leaned it against the roof of the chicken coop and climbed it. The chicken coop's shingles were in good shape. So, he carried it to the house and climbed up the rungs until he reached the top. There were a couple of cracked shingles on the house. He went back to the toolbox and checked for replacements but didn't find any. He would have to ask where they got the others.

When Walter got back to the house and stepped inside, the smell of dinner rushed through him, bringing on a hunger like he hadn't eaten in a week. Everything was spread out on the table, fried fish, green beans, home fries, bread, and butter. There was also a pitcher of beer and mugs at all the place settings. The table was set for six. Ash and George were already seated, both chewing on biscuits.

"Help me get Tabby out here," Lotta said, waving for Walter to follow her. Her voice was light, and she seemed in a good mood again.

"She's eating with you?" he asked

"You and Tabby will both eat with us" She turned back to speak to him. "That's how we do things 'round here."

"But she's hurt. Shouldn't she stay in bed?" Walter asked.

Lotta shrugged. "She insisted. Says she needs to get up and move, even if it's just to the table."

"Spoze that's good," he said, as he stepped toward Lotta.

Walter noticed the smell of the chamber-pot as he and Lotta entered Tabby's room. He made a mental note to empty it after dinner. Tabby was sitting on the side of the bed, still dressed in Lotta's short, chemise.

"We'll get on either side and help her up," Lotta instructed.

"I think I can walk a little," Tabby told her.

"We'll support you just the same."

Walter took her right side, grabbing her arm with one hand close to her armpit and the other close to her elbow. Lotta held her the same way on her left side. They lifted at the same time to get her to her feet. Tabby's steps were tentative, but she was supporting most of her weight herself. When they had her in the main room, by the table, Ash pulled the chair out so she could sit. She winced a couple of times as she lowered herself. Once she was seated, Walter pushed the chair back in place.

"Thank you all," she said, smiling and glancing around at George, Ash, Mary Ann, Lotta, and Walter. "I'm still sore but doing much better."

Lotta nodded at Tabby then turned to Walter, who had taken the seat next to her and across from Tabby. "How did you do with the roofs?"

"I need to replace a couple of shingles, but I can't find any extras. Where do you get them?"

Mary Ann tilted her head back and turned toward Walter. "We make them. I'll show you tomorrow." She smiled. Everyone seemed happy, even Tabby, especially Tabby.

Walter picked up a bite of fish with his fork and popped it in his mouth as Tabby said, "Should we say grace?"

Mary Ann laughed. "Why not? Is that all right with you, Walter?"

He nodded and tried to swallow his mouthful as Tabby started to pray.

Give us grateful hearts,

O Father, for all thy mercies,

And make us mindful

Of the needs of others;

Through Jesus Christ our Lord.

Amen. **

When the meal was over Mary Ann told Walter he could go back to his hotel after he finished cleaning up.

Lotta shook her head as she put her hand on Walter's shoulder. "There is one other thing I'd like you to do before you go back to your place."

"What's that?" Walter asked.

"I need your help bathing Tabby." Lotta covered her mouth as she controlled a giggle.

Tabby grabbed hold of the table with both hands. "I don't think that's..."

"It don't matter what you think," Lotta told her, her eyes narrowing. "You stink and we gotta do something about it."

"It's just that..."

This time Mary Ann interrupted. "Tabby! You are to do what Lotta tells you to do. I don't mind a little Bible-thumping in this house. We can probably all use it, but we don't want you getting too prim on us. You're too beat up to reach around your own body. You need help. Walter will hold you up while Lotta uses a wet cloth This is what we want. We own your contract."

"Yes ma'am."

Walter shifted in his chair and leaned toward Mary Ann. "She's trying to say..."

"I don't care. Listen. I can only imagine what went on between you two before you got here, but you are here now and that means you do what we tell you to do. While Tabby's healing you will be her nurse. This is in addition to the other things you do. Lotta will work with you when whatever you're doing takes two people, but other than that you are in charge. Understand?"

Tabby and Walter both looked at each other and nodded. Walter kept watching her as she bowed her head and mumbled what appeared to be a prayer, which was too quiet for Walter to hear.

After Lotta and Walter helped Tabby back to her room and into her bed, Walter started cleaning up. He was worried Lotta or her ma might think he was stalling because the dishes took some time. He had to get water from the pump, heat it on the stove, which still had a small fire burning, then fill two tubs, one for washing and one for rinsing. Once he was set, most of the dishes were easy, but he had to use a knife to scrape the skillet Mary Ann had used to cook the fish. Pieces of fish were stuck to it. He dumped those outside, so he could keep the water clean. When everything was washed, dried, and put away, Walter went back to the main room where Lotta was waiting.

"I kept the dishwater if you want to use it for Tabby," Walter told her. He didn't want to waste time hauling in water if they didn't need to.

"Good. It should be clean enough and still warm."

"I put it back on the stove."

Once they were in Tabby's room, Lotta pulled the blankets off her. Then Walter held her body up as Lotta took off the gown. First, he had to raise her hips, so Lotta could get her nightclothes up to her waist, then, after Walter gently laid her back on the feather mattress, he started to pull her into a sitting position. "I can sit up on my own," Tabby told him, but when she tried, she couldn't sit and hold her arms up at the same time, so Walter had to help after all.

Walter thought he wouldn't be able to look away from Tabby's private parts, since his memories of the pleasure she'd given him were so clear. But it was her bruises he couldn't stop staring at, especially the black marks all over her stomach. How many times had those men punched and kicked her? How could anyone do this to such a wonderful, gentle woman? How could anyone be filled with such hate?

Lotta did the washing, while Walter helped turn Tabby's body and hold her so Lotta could reach all over. When they were done, they worked together to get Tabby into another one of Lotta's chemises. This one, like the first, stopped midway down her thighs.

"I'm going to send Walter to the store tomorrow, to get you some gowns that fit right, five of them."

Walter rolled his eyes at the thought of walking into a general store and buying women's chemises. That would not be his favorite thing to do.

Chapter Eight

Advice

On his way back to Chinatown that evening, Walter thought about his situation and blessed his good luck. He was staying with two women he loved, dancing with one and taking care of the other. He was well paid and well-fed. He enjoyed working as a handyman, switching from one task to another, especially when he was learning new skills. The work wasn't hard and kept his mind active. All in all, life was going well.

Frank was not at the hotel when Walter arrived, but Guan Wu was there. The dock worker asked Walter why he hadn't shown up for work that morning and was surprised to learn he'd found another job. "It easy for you. You young, yet you find a better job. It much harder for Chinese workers."

Walter looked down, rubbed his forehead then looked back at Guan Wu. "I'm working for someone I knew before I came to San Francisco." He paused and tapped his foot. "Did you see another white man here, my age, a little shorter than me?"

"No. You the only white man here. Can you find a better job for me?"

"I don't think she needs anyone else, but I can ask."

"She? You work for a woman?"

"Yes, two women. One is my age. The other is her ma."

"I will stay at the shipyard. I not want to work for a woman." Guan Wu bowed to Walter, then turned to talk to others. Although they were speaking Chinese, Walter was certain they were talking about him.

Frank had to be done with his work at the butcher shop, so he was probably at the saloon. Walter headed off in that direction. He knew the route they always walked. He would turn around if he found Frank along the way.

When Walter arrived, he started to enter the saloon, but noticed someone sitting on the porch of the watch repair shop. He headed that way to see if it was Frank, and it was. Frank was watching the saloon, waiting for the clients to go home, so he could visit Ru.

"I paid for a bed for you in Chinatown," Walter told his friend.

"I know."

Walter glanced up. "You plan to say here anyway?"

"If she'll let me." He shrugged then added, "I like her, Walter."

Walter nodded.

"You wouldn't understand. You've got Lotta and Tabby. For me, Ru is the only one."

"Did you tell her?"

"Not yet."

"You plan to?"

"Yup." Frank stood and paced in a circle, rubbing his hands. "It hurts," he muttered, just loud enough for Walter to hear, "like nothing I've felt before. The pain is worse than the time I had a fish-hook caught in my leg. I'm sitting here watching men going into the saloon all night, wondering which ones are there for her. But me? I've never been with her, Walter, never even kissed her."

"Never kissed her," Walter repeated in a soft voice, thinking of what Tabby had told him about the importance of a kiss.

"That's what I said." He took in a breath and let it out slowly. "I'm saving my money. In another couple of days I should have enough for an hour with her. I want to show her I'm a man. I want her to know I can do what those other men do, so she'll think right by me. Then maybe? Well, we'll see what happens after that."

Walter pressed his lips together. "I'm not sure that's the best plan."

"Really?"

"Yup. I think you should pay for her time, like you're planning, but you should forget about a poke. Tell her the money is for a kiss. Get that straight at the beginning. Then, before you kiss her, talk to her, tell her how much you like her. Don't push her. Don't tell her all your big plans, just talk about how you enjoy being with her and end with the kiss. Hold her tight and make it a long kiss."

"No poke?"

Walter shook his head. "Look, I'm no expert. I'm just telling you what I think. You and I, we grew up in the camps. This stuff is new to us and really exciting, but it isn't new to Ru. It's her job. You gotta decide what you want and go for it. If you want something with her that's long and lasting, you shouldn't be like every other man she's been with."

"Maybe you're right."

Walter grinned. "Does she know you're coming tonight?"

"No, but I was going to ask if I could stay."

"Why don't you wait. I'll give you some money. Between the two of us, you should have enough to buy time with her tomorrow. You can explain the situation, find out how she feels, before putting her on the spot. That's what I would do."

As they walked back to Chinatown together, they were both quiet. Walter wondered what Frank was thinking, in particular, if his friend thought of him as a busybody. Frank seemed to appreciate his advice, but it was impossible to know for sure. Walter kept hoping everything would work out well.

Chapter Nine

Shopping and Eavesdropping

"We're building a box set," Mary Ann told Walter as they ate breakfast. Walter had arrived in time to cook the meal, which was Hangtown Fry and sourdough bread. Again, Walter was impressed with what this family could afford. Hangtown Fry was an omelet with bacon and oysters. He couldn't think of a pricier choice for starting the day. The coffee wasn't cheap either, not a bit of chicory in it.

"Box set?" he asked, tilting his head as he spoke to look at Lotta.

"There will be a backdrop for the outside scenes," Lotta told him, "but when the story moves into the house of the rich man, the set will show the main room of his house."

"We'll build three walls by painting panels that can be hooked together," Mary Ann explained. "You'll help with that, after we show you how. With a set like this, the audience feels like they're looking through one wall of a room. When the scene changes, the side panels can be removed and the backdrop lowered in front of the remaining panels, so the scene looks like the outside again. The drop's lowered like the curtain, only toward the back of the stage instead of the front. It has to be painted, too."

Walter nodded. He took a small bite of the Hangtown Fry, swallowed then turned to Lotta and said, "You've come a long way since you were dancing on that makeshift stage in our camp."

"I have, but I miss some of it."

"We're making more money than ever before," her ma told her.

Lotta rubbed the back of her neck and answered in a softer voice. "I know and I like that. But sometimes I miss being so close to the audience and I miss the minstrel shows. The music was fun and the dancing smooth. Although, I don't miss the blackface makeup. That stuff was a mess. But other than that, the shows were easy. Now I have to wait for cues and do whatever I'm told to do. Can't sing what I'm in the mood to sing." She sighed.

"I never saw you in blackface," Walter said.

Lotta showed a little mischievous smile as she told him, "Just as well."

"You eating without me?" Walter heard Tabby's voice and turned to see her leaning against the door to her room.

"Help her," Mary Ann instructed Walter, but he was already on his feet and heading her way.

"Hi Tabby," Ash said. He and George had been talking to each other while Mary Ann and Lotta were explaining the work they had in mind for Walter.

"Hi boys," Tabby replied.

"We were letting you sleep," Lotta told her. "You feeling better?"

"About the same," she replied.

Walter had his arm around her waist. She leaned on his shoulder and started taking slow steps toward her chair.

"Don't forget to buy her some gowns today," Lotta told Walter. "Mine don't fit her right." He noticed she was looking at Tabby's bruised thighs.

"Take Ash and George with you," Mary Ann added. "They need to see a man buying women's things without dying of shame." She and Lotta both giggled at that.

Once she was sitting, Walter pushed Tabby's chair to the table. Then, as she bowed her head and closed her eyes, he considered how she was thanking God again, but hadn't offered any thanks to him for his help. The day before he'd been thinking how lucky he was to be working for the Crabtrees. He was starting to rethink his situation. Yes, he was given a variety of jobs to do, but most of them were women's work: cooking, cleaning, and today, babysitting and shopping for chemises. It hadn't bothered him until Mary Ann and Lotta had laughed at him. He was in for some embarrassing times. Combine that with Tabby deciding to put her newly discovered God over any feelings she had for him and Walter was going to get the short end of the horn.

Before he headed out the door with Ash and George, Walter cleaned the dishes and emptied the chamber-pots for Mary Ann, Lotta, George and Ash, as well as the one he'd emptied the day before, the one Tabby used.

Walking with Ash and George reminded Walter of the many days he and Frank had gone out to the fishing lake or into the woods to hunt for squirrel or coon. Frank was close to Walter's age while George was a couple of years younger than Ash, but Frank had always been shorter, so he'd seemed younger back then. Lotta had said Ash was nine and George was seven. Walter wished they were headed for something more exciting to young boys than a trip into the city to buy chemises for Tabby.

They found the store using the directions Lotta had given him. Walter went straight to the store clerk at the counter while Ash and George went for the glass bins of candy under the same counter, but off to the right.

"I work for the Crabtrees," Walter told the man. "Mary Ann sent me here to pick up some women's chemises, five of them."

"You need to speak to my wife." The clerk pointed toward a woman who was standing behind another counter, further into the store. "She can help you."

Walter saw two women in line, so he would have to wait. He leaned down to speak with Ash. "I have to speak to the lady over there. Will you and George be all right here while I get the stuff your ma wants?"

Ash nodded, but said, "Ma always buys us candy when she brings us here. So does Lotta." He looked back at the display. "I want the peppermint. George likes the chocolate."

"Is that true?" Walter asked, looking at the clerk.

He nodded.

"Then give them each one candy, whatever flavor they want. Put it on Mary Ann's tab."

Women's hats and dresses were on display in the clothing section, even a corset on what appeared to be a statue of a woman's midsection. Walter recognized the corset from the one Tabby had worn when she dressed up as Lotta.

Walter kept an eye on the boys as he waited in line. They had left the candy display and were now looking at some of the fishing rods. As long as they didn't wander out of Walter's sight, he was happy.

When Walter reached the woman behind the counter, he told her he needed five chemises for someone staying with Mary Ann and Lotta Crabtree. "They need to be longer than the ones Lotta wears."

"They're all the same length. I hemmed Lotta's, since she needed them shorter. It wasn't easy. I had to take the trim off, cut it back, then hem it and sew the trim back on. I can do that for these, but it's extra. How heavy is this woman?"

"She's about normal, maybe a little thin."

"How tall?"

"About my height."

"Here hold this in front of you." The woman handed him a white chemise. Walter glanced around to see if anyone was looking at him. There were no men in the store, other than the husband of the woman waiting on him. The two women who had been ahead of him in line were still browsing in the grocery section but didn't seem interested in what he was up to. Ash and George were still in view. They had moved on to look at a display of knives.

Walter did as he was told, holding the woman's gown against his body. He glanced again at Ash, who was looking back and grinning. This was even more embarrassing than he'd thought it would be.

"It's the right length. You say you want five?"

"Yup."

"I'll wrap them for you and put it on Mary Ann's tab."

Ash didn't say anything about the chemise on the walk home, not until they were stepping into the house when he smiled and looked at the package Walter was carrying, "I hope you share with Tabby." His smile turned to a laugh. Walter rolled his eyes but didn't reply.

Once inside, Walter headed straight to Tabby's room. He found Tabby sitting up and Lotta on the bed alongside her. "Here they are," he said, not wanting to use the word chemise in front of the women.

Lotta took the package. "At least you have something to wear now. Ma and I will buy you some skirts and blouses before you're ready to get outta bed. We couldn't trust Walter to pick those out." She looked at him and added, "Sorry."

Walter lifted his hands toward her, palms up. "No need to apologize. You're right."

"Sit by us," Lotta said to him, patting a place on the bed beside her. He walked around and sat on the other side. Lotta looked back at Tabby. "We'll buy you shoes as well and drawers, stockings, and garter belts if you want them."

Tabby shrugged and spoke in a quiet voice. "I should have brought my clothes from Odell's."

"We got you outta there," Lotta told her. "That's all that matters."

Tabby looked down and frowned.

"You need me to do anything else?" Walter asked Lotta.

She looked out the door of the bedroom. "You could sweep the cabin." Walter nodded then she added. "After that, you could clean the horse stalls."

"You have horses?"

"We have three. We need to get one for George soon. He's tired of riding double with Ash."

"I didn't see a barn out there."

"We keep them in our neighbor's barn. I'll show you where after you clean the floors. Taking care of the horses will be another one of your tasks, although Ma wants to keep feeding them. She says they like the person who feeds them. I think she just likes watching 'em eat. Me, I just like riding."

"You ride well?" Tabby asked Lotta.

"I grew up on a horse. We used to move our show from camp to camp and leave at night, right after we were done performing. I would sleep tied onto a saddle while one of the musicians held the reins and led my horse. I never fell off, not even once."

No one spoke for a short time. When Lotta shifted her weight and appeared ready to stand, Walter asked her, "What time would you like me to prepare lunch?"

"No need. We only eat together at breakfast and supper. We're all too busy for a sit down during the day. When we're hungry, we just grab a biscuit or something else we don't have to cook. Everyone takes care of themselves."

"Even Ash and George?"

"Ash takes care of George when he gets something for himself. But you should bring a biscuit for Tabby now. She can eat it when she's hungry."

"No," Tabby said, sitting up in the bed. "I need to walk a little bit each day, to loosen my muscles. I'll walk to the kitchen when I'm ready."

"You sure?" Walter asked.

Tabby nodded.

"Are you happy here?" Lotta asked Tabby. Walter noticed she didn't ask him the same question, but he shrugged it off. He was happy with the Crabtrees and very happy Lotta and Tabby got along so well. Lotta had to know that.

"I will be," Tabby told her, "once I start earning my keep, like Walter." She smiled at him.

"Your job is to get healthy," Lotta said.

Tabby reached over and touched Lotta's arm. "You and your ma have been so kind."

"Kind to me, too." Walter said. He didn't mention that making him sign the contract was mean.

"I'll be better soon and when I am, I'm going to be the best help you can imagine. You know what? When my contract is done here, I'm never going back to the saloon or any other place like that. I'm done with prostituting."

Tabby had told Walter her decision the day before. He still wondered if she would keep to it. She seemed determined enough.

"I'm not saying it wasn't fun at times. Most of the men were nice and wanted talk as much as anything else. The girls I worked with were great, especially Ru, and I enjoyed the liquor when I didn't drink too much. But I think God was sending me a message through this beating I took. Oh sure, I got hit a few times when I was working for Jahiel, but nothing serious. All that changed when he sold my contract. Bad men showed up at Odell's, men willing to pay for a chance to hurt us girls. Still, I couldn't even think about settling down when I was working the contract. Now, thanks to you both, and to your ma, Lotta, I can set my ways on a better path."

"You ever think about marriage?" Lotta asked her. Walter wanted to ask Tabby that very question but hadn't felt comfortable bringing it up with Lotta in the room.

"I can't while I'm working for you," Tabby answered. "But afterward? I do think about it and if I do marry, I'll be a loyal wife, good as you can get. I've had enough of the whiskey and the wild times."

"There's jobs at the theaters," Lotta said. "Which reminds me—Walter, you need to meet me at the theater in the morning, so I can show you what we need you to do there."

"What about breakfast?"

"We'll make our own."

Walter knew he'd have to eat something in the morning, too. He decided to take a biscuit or two with him when he headed home.

Lotta looked at Walter and started to tap her foot. "The broom is in a corner of the kitchen," she told him. "Why don't you get started. I want to talk to Tabby for a while."

Walter stood and walked out of the room. He closed the door but stopped there. Mary Ann and the boys weren't in the house, which meant no one was watching him. If he leaned a bit toward the door, who would know? He tried and discovered he could hear Lotta's voice. He moved away for a moment but was drawn back. They could be talking about him. Why else would Lotta ask him to leave?

Lotta's voice was clear. "This talk about marriage. What does it mean? Are you interested in Walter?"

Tabby said something he couldn't understand, so he put his ear directly on the wood panel."

Lotta spoke again. "It seems he's the only one available right?

"He's nice enough."

"That's what I thought."

"He seems to respect what you ask him to do," Tabby said. "I've been with too many men who think they have the right to push me around."

"They pay for that right, don't they?"

"Spoze so."

"Walter, he looks well, don't you think? Ma told me that once and I agree."

Walter dropped to one knee and pushed the side of his face against that door. He needed to hear every last bit of this talk.

"So, you're saying you like him, too?" Tabby asked.

"Not in that way. Not exactly." Lotta drew out her last words, as if she was thinking while she was speaking, then she continued at a faster pace. "I'm too busy to worry about things like that. Maybe what you've been through has made you believe it's time to settle down. I can understand that. Still, with me it's different. I live on the stage. It's sometimes lonely when I'm home, but dancing for people, that's a thrill

I can't give up. It's what I think about from the time I get up in the morning till I climb back under my covers at night."

There was another pause, then Tabby spoke again. "Maybe you're right. Maybe I think of marriage and children, because I don't have a life to give up."

"There are a lot worse things in life than living alone."

"Maybe you're right there, too," Tabby said in a soft voice.

"And there's other types of company. You have my friendship. I'm here to talk if that's what you need. Once you're healthy, I can set up a job for you working backstage."

"But on the other hand," Tabby told her, speaking stronger. "Walter may be a gift God has sent me. If I pass on him, there may not be anyone else."

"I doubt that. You're young and well looking."

"But I feel like I'm ready for more. Maybe children?"

"Did you ever get pregnant?"

"A couple times. I took care of that."

"Does it bother you"

"I think of it at times. I tell myself it was like dealing with a bad stomach-ache but in the back of my mind, I know there was life growing inside me. Don't get me wrong. I made the right decision. Like I said earlier, my men were nice enough, but they were old, dirty, and most of them were stupid. I didn't want a child who would grow up to be like one of them, whoring with somebody like me." They laughed. "Walter was different. He was innocent, pure. He didn't choose to come to me. Like I said, maybe a gift from God."

"More like a gift from his pa." Again, there was laughter, then Lotta continued. "There have been men in my life, too, and, like you, they weren't men I'd want to keep. While we're being honest, you should know I also think of Walter as someone I'd like to get close to. As I said before, I'm nowhere near ready for marriage, but that doesn't mean I wouldn't want to spend time with him."

"By time you mean a poke, don't you?"

More laughter.

"Spoze so. I don't have the experience you have, but that doesn't mean I don't have the desire. When I picture myself lying with a man, I want him to be someone I can trust. I think Walter could be the one. So—I guess this means we're both interested in the same fella."

"But you saved my life."

"Walter was part of that."

"Still, I work for you and if you say the word, I'll step aside."

"I won't say it. If I decide I want Walter, I'll need him to choose me over you or anyone else."

"Competition then?"

"I'm not afraid. How do you think I became San Francisco's Favorite?"

Once again laughter, but it stopped when Tabby said, "I doubt your skills are as important to a man as the ones I used to become the *saloon* favorite."

"Oh? Giving up on the Bible life already?"

"Not giving up, just thinking maybe it can wait."

Walter pulled away from the door and quietly moved to the kitchen to get the broom. He didn't want either of the girls to know he'd been eavesdropping.

While he swept, he thought about what he'd heard. Caring for Tabby while working for Lotta wasn't going to be as easy as it had been before he knew they both wanted something more. He had to make a choice: Lotta, Tabby, or no one. He was thirteen, way too young to be thinking of marriage and fatherhood and stuff like that. But what Lotta wanted was just as confining. It sounded like she wanted him to commit to working for her way past the date on his contract, maybe even forever. With Lotta it sounded like fatherhood would never come. In a way, that was a worse trap than having it forced on him too soon.

He wasn't any closer to a decision when Lotta came out of Tabby's room. "You about ready?" she asked.

"Just finished the inside, but I still have to do the porch."

"It can wait. Let's walk to the barn."

Walter put down the broom and followed. Walter was trying to understand how to handle what he had heard. He was having trouble focusing on what Lotta was saying. Trying to enter into the conversation he asked Lotta about her horses, but his mind wandered when it was his turn to listen to her answer. "We have three, one each for Ma, me and Ash. They're all mares. Ma doesn't like geldings because they lose their value if they can't breed and she doesn't like stallions because they're too hard to handle."

Walter nodded as he considered how exciting it was that two women wanted him. In the camp he'd had no one. This was all new to him.

"Spider is mine. She's all black, sleek as can be. I named her in honor of Lola's dance."

"Spider is yours," Walter replied. He walked a bit taller, as he replayed the way Lotta told Tabby about her feelings. He was the one she pictured when she thought of lying with a man. He was sure of that.

"You think Spider's a funny name?" Lotta asked.

"No. Why?"

"You're grinning."

"Sorry." He frowned. He needed to be more careful. "What about the other two?"

"Ma's is named Vespa and Ash's is Blink Bonny. They're both named after racehorses we like, British thoroughbreds. Someday I'm gonna buy us a racehorse, a great one."

He didn't want to lose the affections of either Tabby or Lotta, especially since he would be living with them both for the next few years. How could he keep close to both women as he won the heart of one?

"The funny thing is that Spider is a thoroughbred while Vespa and Blink Bonny are both quarter horses. Ma questioned that when I suggested their names, but I said *who cares?*"

"Yup. Who cares?" Walter wondered which one of those two could care for him the most. Tabby had made a living moving from one man to another while Lotta had made her fortune bouncing from one place to another. Neither of them seemed the type to settle down for a long time.

"Vespa is a dapple gray. Blink is a bay. They're not as pretty as Spider, but they're both good horses."

In the stable, Lotta stood outside Spider's stall, watching as Walter used the pitchfork to pick manure from the straw. He also put the wet straw the horse had pissed on in a wheelbarrow.

"They're all good riding horses," Lotta told him, "but Vespa and Blink Bonny are the ones we use with the carriage. Spider's also trained in the harness, but we only use her if one of the other two isn't feeling well."

She reached in the stall to stroke Spider's nose. as Walter started picking straw behind Spider. Lotta stopped him, saying, "Step away, Walter. You never get back of a horse like that, any horse. You're gonna get kicked."

"Thank you."

"Didn't they have horses in the camps?"

"We didn't."

"Well, you'll learn." She shifted her weight back and forth. "We'll need you to take care of the carriage as well. It's also kept in this barn. It needs to be cleaned after each use and polished weekly."

"Why don't you have a barn of your own built?" Walter asked her, as he started hauling the wheelbarrow outside. Lotta told him the compost pile was there.

"We don't take the horses on the road with us, so by renting here we get a landlord who's willing to care for them if we need him to. Also, it costs money to build a barn, more money than we can spend on these stalls in five years. And who knows where we'll be after that?"

Walter went to the other stalls and picked them the same way. Then he filled the wheelbarrow with fresh straw to replenish the bedding in all three.

The rest of Walter's day was filled with odd jobs around the Crabtree home. There was some weeding in the garden and the door to the chicken coop needed repair. Mary Ann and the boys were at the theater for most of the day, so she couldn't teach him how to make roof shingles. He would have to put off that project one more day. Just like his decision of what to do about the two ladies there. One who needed him and one who wanted him.

Chapter Ten

Dance Steps

When Walter went in to empty Tabby's chamber-pot, she asked him to fluff her pillow and to help her get into a more comfortable position. He wasn't sure she needed his help, since she managed to use the chamber-pot on her own and had walked to the door of her room without any assistance the day before. She seemed to be getting better quickly.

Tabby was wearing one of the chemises he'd brought her. It was loose and one of the straps had slipped down her arm. When he leaned over to help her, it was tempting to look down her clothes. He didn't. He stared at the ceiling and froze.

Tabby brought her hand to her chest to cover herself. "Sorry," she said in a soft voice. She pushed her strap back on her shoulder. He wasn't sure if she'd exposed herself on purpose or if it was the fault of the night clothes she was wearing.

He took a breath and leaned forward once more. Walter had to reach around Tabby to rearrange the pillow. As he did, she wrapped her arms around his shoulders and buried her face in the arch of his neck. She was using his body to hold herself up, but as he moved the pillow she whispered. "Thank you." His body stiffened a bit and she added, "You're warm." When he was done rearranging her pillow she didn't let go. Instead, she said, "Slide me a little closer to you, please." He liked the word *please*. Lotta never used it. He did as he was told, then stepped away from Tabby's bed.

When Walter left Tabby's bedroom, he discovered Lotta sitting at the table in the main room. If it wasn't for her red hair, he would have thought she was an intruder. Lotta was dressed as a man, a miner. She was wearing baggy brown pants, a loose white shirt with the sleeves rolled up, and a wide-brimmed hat. Most of her hair was pushed under the hat, but she couldn't hide it all. "I need help with a couple of dance routines," she told him. "Come out on the porch with me."

When they were back at the spot where they had danced the day before, she said, "When I dance, I usually dance alone. That's good for jigs and tap and soft-shoe, but other dances require partners. I want to learn those moves, with you. I want to glide with you, as they do in a waltz, and I want you to lift me high, as they do in classical dance."

"Do you think we can do that?"

"I'm small and you're strong. I don't think lifting me will be hard. We'll start with one of those, a simple one. Gliding may be difficult for you, but we can work on those moves later."

He nodded.

"I don't want to just be a good dancer in San Francisco. I want to be the best in the world, and I want to bring you with me."

Walter scratched his neck, then looked at her outfit. "Why are you dressed like a man? And why aren't you wearing boots?" She was barefoot, which would have been strange for a gold miner, even if he was standing in a creek.

"I can't wear a skirt for some of the routines I want to work on, but sometimes I dress like a man just because it feels free. I get tired of all the layers we women wear—chemise, petticoat, underskirt, and the worst of all, the corset. We wear so many clothes they could stand up on their own. I think if I left my dress on top of my underthings, I could disappear for a month and no one would notice I wasn't in the pile."

Walter grinned and rolled his eyes.

"I wear boots, sometimes, but not now. I can't dance in those heavy things." Lotta took Walter by his arm and moved him to the center of the porch. "Face the house," she told him. "I'll stand with my back toward yours, facing out toward the yard. I'll link my arms in yours, then I'll lean against you for support and finally lift and spread my legs as you start to spin. Just don't fall down and we'll make a pretty picture."

They were a little wobbly, but they tried a few more times until it felt right. "We'll do another," Lotta told him. "I stand in front of you, on one foot with my other leg pointed to the side and my arms up at shoulder length. You put your right arm around my waist, then slide it up my body toward my chest. Hold me firmly with that arm, then put your left arm around my thigh and pick me up."

This one was easier because Walter didn't have to twirl while he lifted her.

"The final lift is fun, but more difficult than the other two. Try not to drop me."

"I won't."

"We start in the same position as the last lift, but this time you bend down further and grab my other thigh. You keep your right arm around my waist and don't drop me."

"You said that already."

"As you pull my lower leg up, I have to spin in your right arm. Get it?"

He nodded. "I think so."

"You have to hold me up, but not tight, so I can move in your arm. Then I finish by throwing my arms out and smiling at the audience. Of everything we're doing today, this will look the best."

"If we do it right," Walter said, in a soft voice.

"Yup. If we do it right." Lotta agreed.

They had a couple of near falls, but nothing that hurt either one of them. Eventually, they got the spin/lift to work well.

"What now?" Walter asked when they both got too tired to keep practicing.

"Now we work on the waltz. I need to do this dance with a skirt and petticoats. So, you wait here. I'll be back as soon as I change."

Walter sat on the porch steps as he waited for Lotta. When she returned, she was wearing a full, red skirt with a thick black belt and a white blouse. The blouse had a large collar and puffy sleeves. She spun around, holding the skirt and her petticoats out. She had looked hard and strong when she was dressed like a man, but now she looked soft and feminine. Lotta was truly a great actress.

Lotta was right about Walter's skills. He learned the lifts quickly, but the waltz had to be gentle and smooth. Lotta hummed music she called the Prima Donna Waltz while she worked with him on the box step, the simplest Waltz step. He was awkward and clumsy, so they never got beyond it, but Lotta said she was encouraged. When they were done, she hugged Walter and kissed him on the lips, just a peck, but Walter remembered what Tabby had told him about the way a kiss connects two souls.

Lotta went back inside to change again, this time into the simple shift she wore when working around the house. Walter followed her in but went straight to the kitchen. It was time to prepare supper.

Tabby and Lotta sat next to each other at the dinner table. They whispered and joked while eating, as if they hadn't been competing earlier that day. They paid very little attention to Walter, who talked mostly to Mary Ann during the meal. She wanted him to teach Ash and George to use tools. He said he would.

"Not tomorrow," Lotta told him. "You're to meet us at the theater tomorrow morning, remember?"

"I do."

On the way home, Walter thought how strange his day had been. Lotta and Tabby had let him touch them in ways that were personal, but there was all that laughing and joking at supper, as if they were more interested in each other than in him. He wondered if they might have known he was eavesdropping when they were talking about him. It's possible the second half of the day was a great big joke. He could see Lotta organizing the prank and Tabby going along with it. He resolved to pretend anything either of them asked him to do was normal. That's what he'd done that day and it worked fairly well.

Chapter Eleven

A New Contract

Walter was looking forward to talking to Frank, but when he reached Chinatown, Frank wasn't there, again. Walter walked to the saloon and found him sitting where he'd been the previous evening, on the porch of the watch repair shop.

"So how did it go with Ru yesterday?" Walter asked, after he took a seat next to Frank.

"She's got a problem and so do I."

Walter shook his head slowly. "That's a surprise. I'm sorry to hear it."

"You don't understand. I did what you suggested. I told her I would pay for a kiss and that was all I wanted. She didn't take the money but kissed me anyway. We did the other stuff, too. I'm no longer a virgin, which I guess is a good thing, but I'm in love and it's complicated."

"You mean because Ru intends to keep working?"

"She'll give up selling pokes, if I get a better job and we get married. That's what she said. The problem is I don't think I'm ready for marriage. She's sixteen with lots of experience. I'm only thirteen and she's my first. She says the things she does with other men don't mean anything and I believe her. It's the things I haven't done that bother me."

Walter raised his eyebrows. "I guess the question is: how *much* do you love her?"

"Yup. That's the question. And there's more. This has to do with Tabby."

"Tabby?"

Frank stared away from Walter. "Yup. It seems Odell went back to Jahiel to buy a contract to replace Tabby. That was expected. But it's another friend of Ru's, which means someone else she cares about is taking the place of Tabby because of what Ru arranged. She doesn't regret what she did, of course. Tabby is Ru's best friend, but the other girl has already been beaten."

Walter pressed his fist against his mouth then spoke through it. "We can't go back to Mary Ann and ask for more money. She'd wanna know when it's gonna end? And the answer to that is—it won't."

"Ru knows that. She's got another plan. It seems Odell's gotten himself into a tight situation. He spent most of his savings on his thugs, food, and liquor. When he bought this new contract, he had to borrow. Anyway, he's now got bags of gold dust he plans to use to pay back the loan and Ru knows where they are."

Walter sat up straight, his legs tense. "I don't like where this is going," he said.

"I didn't spoze you would. Anyway, what I'm saying is, if we steal his money, he'll be in a bind that could cost him his life. He'll have to leave California. That way he can never mess with the lives of good women, at least not here."

"You gonna do this?"

"Ru and I are. We're hoping you help us."

"I promised Mary Ann and Lotta I wouldn't go after Odell."

Frank raised his eyebrows. "Break your promise."

"I won't do that without speaking with them first. They've been good to me."

"Spoze that's all right, but we can't tell too many people. Odell might find out. Only reason I told you, is we need your help."

"I don't break promises, so you're not gonna get my help unless I can talk it over with Mary Ann and Lotta."

* * *

The following morning when Walter arrived at the theater, he found two women working in the ticket office. He asked if they knew where Mary Ann and Lotta were. They told him Lotta was downstairs in the shop and Mary Ann was on the stage. Walter went through the lobby and into the stage area where he saw Mary Ann, bent over a large cloth that covered the entire stage. He went up to check in with her.

"I'm here and ready for work," Walter told her. He would wait until they were with Lotta before talking to her about Odell. No sense in going through his explanation twice.

"I'm doing the backdrop," Mary Ann said. "I've got it nailed to the stage, so it will stay flat. It's an outdoor scene: a few trees, a small pond, and the sky with clouds. Sounds easy enough, right?" Walter had no idea how to answer that, so he shrugged as Mary Ann kept talking. "I'm sketching it with charcoal. I need you to paint in the lines, starting on the parts I've finished. I'll show you which colors to use and where to use 'em." He went to step on the canvas, but she stopped him. "Take off your shoes. Either barefoot or socks doesn't matter, as long as your feet are clean."

"They are."

"Begin with light blue. Try not to go over the lines, but if you do, we can cover with other colors. It just makes everything a little harder and that's not why you're here. Understand?"

Walter worked side by side with Mary Ann. At first, he put the paint on too thick, but Mary Ann stopped him and got him going right. It was hard work, but not as hard as it was for her. He was using a brush attached to a pole. He could stand, while she had to get on her knees to complete her sketches.

"These are the base colors," she explained. "The light blue is for the sky, the green for the trees, and the darker blue for the pond. When we're done here, we have to let it dry. Tomorrow we come back and paint highlights." She finished the sketching before he was done with his part, so she helped him finish.

When they were done, they stood back to look at their work. "It doesn't look like much yet," Mary Ann said, "but it will when we finish and hang it up."

Walter tightened his fists and stood straight. "I need to talk to you and Lotta. It's important."

"It's lunch time. Why don't we go downstairs to see what Lotta's up to? We can eat and talk there. I packed a hamper."

"Thank you."

Lotta had been working on the panels for the box set. They were set up on the shop floor as they would be positioned on stage. She'd been painting them and was ready for lunch.

Walter felt his stomach tighten as he sat on a wooden crate, at a table made from a few boards lying across two sawhorses. "I have to break a promise," he blurted out. "I have a friend who needs my help," He looked down at the table then back at Lotta before adding, "Two friends."

Mary Ann folded her arms across her chest, leaned back and said, "Tell us."

Walter explained the situation then said, "Frank's a friend of mine and so is Ru. I have to be there to help them. So that's the bind. I promised you I wouldn't go after Odell, but it looks like I'm gonna help people who are doing just that. I don't like going back on my word, but I don't have a choice."

"Odell is a monster," Lotta said, throwing her arms up and clenching her fists, as if she wanted to punch someone.

"We've always wanted to do something to stop him," Mary Ann said, agreeing with her daughter. "Maybe now is our chance." she looked at Walter. "If Frank and Ru can come up with a decent plan, Lotta and I will help you."

"You sure about this?" he asked, glancing back and forth from mother to daughter.

"I'm not a thief," Lotta replied, "but I'm an actress. If you need someone to distract him while you rob him, Ma and I can figure out a way to do that."

"She's right," Mary Ann agreed. "We can do that."

* * *

They waited five days, for a cloudy evening that could provide the cover they needed.

Frank was the first to act. He climbed to the roof of Odell's brothel with a bucket and a long rope. He lowered the bucket to Walter, who passed twenty bags of dirt up to his friend. These would be put in place of twenty bags of gold. They'd decided not to take everything Odell had, just enough to force him to default on the loan. It was Mary Ann's idea to leave the bags of dirt at the bottom of the pile of real gold, so Odell might not notice anything was wrong until he had to pay his bill. "If he doesn't know when the gold was stolen," Mary Ann said, "he won't know who had the opportunity to take it. He'll assume it was a man before he thinks of a couple of thirteen-year-old boys and three women." When she made that statement, Frank glanced at Walter and rolled his eyes, but she did have a point.

Ru was the next to act. She entered the brothel alone, which was the part of the plan that scared Walter the most. Ru was to say she was there to visit Enid, the young woman who had replaced Tabby and had taken such a serious beating. Enid's room was upstairs, near the room where Odell kept the gold. Ru took a loaf of white bread with her and an apple. She would claim the food was for Enid, but she expected Odell would take some for himself, maybe all of it.

Walter counted to five hundred before he followed Ru. He was to claim he wanted to buy some time with a prostitute. Tabby had coached him, saying, "If you were older, they would expect you to be forceful and to have fun picking out the woman you want, but at your age, you're better off pretending to be nervous and a little shy. They'll probably laugh at you, but that's good. They won't think you're up to anything." Tabby was walking now and doing some of the Crabtree's housework, but none of the amateur thieves wanted her with them when they stole the gold. She'd worked Odell's brothel, so they knew her too well.

Walter walked into a foyer that opened on the left to a large room. There was a hallway in front of him and a staircase that ran alongside the hall, but he went into the room. Several women were there, some sitting in upholstered chairs, at least two lying on couches. A few of them were naked. The others were not wearing much.

Three men were also in the room, two standing and another sitting at a table. They were fully dressed. The man at the table was reading a newspaper, which he was sharing with a naked woman who was lying on one of the couches. Neither of them looked up from what they were reading.

"Looking for some pleasure?" A woman asked him. She was dressed in a society outfit – a long black skirt, a dark red bodice covered with a black capelet, and even a black hat with a bow. But when she spoke, she spread her legs, revealing she wore no drawers.

"Yup." Walter cleared his throat then spoke a little louder. "How do I do this? Do I pay you?"

"You pay me," the man at the table said, setting his newspaper down.

Walter had never met Odell, but he knew this was the man, especially since he had the apple and loaf of bread Ru had brought in. Walter pulled a small bag of gold dust out of his pants pocket. "Is this enough?" He handed it to Odell.

"You got more?"

Walter shook his head.

"This'll get you that one." The man pointed at a thin woman with lots of lines on her face, who was having trouble combing through the tangles of her hair. "Or that one." He indicated the woman who had first spoken to him. She was at least forty.

"How about her?" Walter asked, his voice cracking. He walked up to a young woman lying on her side, on a blanket, on the floor, wearing only white stockings with no garters, black shoes, a necklace, and a bracelet. She was younger than the other two and had shiny brown hair. She'd pulled a strand of it into her mouth and was chewing on it.

"If you got another bag like the first one, you can have her."

"I don't know," Walter said,

"She's young and talks too much, but she knows what to do. She's got more regulars than any other tail in the house."

"Walter!" someone yelled from across the room. Walter and Odell turned at the same time to see Lotta standing there, tapping her foot, her face the color of her hair. "What are you doing here?" she screamed.

The two men who were standing stepped toward her, but Odell raised his hand to stop them.

"Lotta Crabtree?" Odell said, as her ma followed her in from the street. "And Mary Ann? You two don't belong here."

"He's the one who don't belong here!" Lotta yelled. "He belongs to us."

"Easy, Lotta," Mary Ann said. "I've done business with Odell before. He's honest. I'm sure he'll understand our point."

"What I understand is that I sold you Tabby's contract. I treated you fair. You got her and I understand she's holed up at your place. You can do what you want with her, but I don't see how that gives you the right to mess with my customers."

"We got a contract on Walter, too," Lotta yelled at Odell. She was breathing hard. Her nostrils flaring. "He does what we tell him to do. If I say sit, he sits. If I say lie down and roll over, he does that. We own him for as long as we own Tabby."

"You're a prostitute, Walter?" The girl with the shiny hair was standing now. One of her stockings had slipped down around her ankle.

"We don't use him that way," Mary Ann said. "He does odd jobs."

"That's one way of putting it," the girl said, looking at Walter and laughing. "I don't know. Looks like a virgin to me." She circled him then leaned in and stared in his eyes. "What do you say, Walter? Are you like us? Are you really a tail?"

"Leave him alone!" Lotta yelled, this time at the nearly naked girl who was teasing Walter.

"Do as she says," Odell told her.

The girl went back to her blanket, pulled up the one stocking and straightened the other, then she sat down. "So the great Lotta Crabtree is in love with a boy whore," she said, mumbling just loud enough to be heard.

"Quiet," Odell yelled. He turned to Mary Ann. "I don't know what you two got going with this fella. It's none of my concern. I run an honest business here. He paid, so he can have either of these two tails. That one or that one." He pointed at the two older women he'd told Walter he would sell for a single bag of gold dust. "If he gives me another bag, he can have any tail in the room. That's all I care about. This is a place of business. Whatever you two got going with this fella, you better leave to talk it over."

"Now there's a good idea, Odell," Mary Ann told him. "We'll leave as soon as you give us back the gold."

"Oh no. A deal's a deal. The girls are ready. He can have his time with either one, but he can't get his money back."

"You're a thief, Odell!" Lotta screamed. "You beat Tabby near to death and now you're stealing from us!"

"None of that's true. Tabby got hit by a client who got carried away. That happens sometimes. And as for the gold, I'm only keepin' what's mine. Walter here, he paid for a poke and two of my gals are ready to give him one. The deal's done and I'm keepin' my money."

"Is that it?" Mary Ann asked, nodding at the small bag of gold dust on the table.

Odell grabbed it and put it in his pocket. "Don't get any ideas about snatching. This gold is staying here."

"A bag that small?" she said. "Keep it. It's nothing to us, but we're taking Walter now."

"Do what you like," he said, grinning.

Walter, Lotta and Mary Ann went around the building to where they could receive the gold from Frank, then they left the brothel carrying a bucket of gold dust. They walked about a quarter of a mile to the place they'd decided to meet after they were done. Frank showed up a few minutes after they arrived. "Everything worked fine," he told them. "I waited until I heard Ru open the window, then I lowered the bucket. It took her very little time to make the switch."

Ru showed up about five minutes after Frank. "It went well," she said. "The room looks exactly like it did when the gold was there. I don't see how he'll know until it's too late."

"What about Enid?" Walter asked.

"What about her?"

"Will she talk?"

"No chance of that. She's the one told me about his gold stash."

* * *

About a month after the robbery, Odell disappeared, as Frank suspected he would. No one knew where he went, and no one cared.

Even though Mary Ann and Lotta were wealthy enough to invest their take of the gold without raising suspicion, the others weren't. It was decided to bury it all on Mary Ann's property, halfway between two maple trees, and to leave it there for at least a year or two.

Walter was proud of all the friends involved in the rescue, but it was Mary Ann who surprised him the most. He knew Lotta had a kind heart and a brave nature, but her ma had always tried to act stern and at times seemed a bit selfish. He would never think of her that way again.

Enid, once she had healed, went to work for Ah Toy without a contract. She had to give a high percentage of her fees to her madam, but she couldn't be sold. She was happy, preferring a madam over a pimp.

Frank left the butcher shop for a job at the docks. He and Ru started calling themselves engaged, but Frank couldn't afford a ring, so it was unofficial. Ru continued to work at the saloon. She told everyone she planned to quit when her contract ran out, but only if she and Frank had enough money saved to buy a home. They thought they would, since by that time they would be able to safely dig up the gold.

Tabby took over the cooking and cleaning around Mary Ann's home and helped out at the theater, mostly in the box office. She said she liked building things and also helped Walter with the sets. Walter enjoyed the company of both Lotta and Tabby at the theater and at the Crabtree home. He no longer had the feeling they were competing for him, but even though there was less flirting, he grew closer to both women.

Life seemed to settle into a regular routine for more than a year until someone unexpected showed up.

Chapter Twelve

Back in their Lives

Walter's work in the garden didn't stop as the seasons changed. Mary Ann knew which vegetables to plant in cold weather and the compost always needed tending. The garden was structured with twelve raised plots containing rich soil, bordered by logs about as thick as Walter's arms. This design allowed easy access to the plots for maintaining and harvesting. The plots had been built before Walter began working with the Crabtrees, so he didn't know if Mary Ann started the garden herself or hired someone. Mary Ann continued to work with Walter and when Tabby was feeling well enough, she joined the other two. Lotta sometimes came by to watch, but other than eating the produce, she wanted nothing to do with gardening.

Each one of the squares was designated for different plantings. Walter was working on two of the areas, one for potatoes, the other for onions and cabbage. Mary Ann was working with a larger plot that had corn and beans. Tabby was weeding the area with cucumbers and lettuce.

Mary Ann got up and stood with her legs spread. Her eyes were wide and she was flexing her fingers. Walter turned to see what had caused her reaction. A tall man with a large belly, a full, salt'n pepper beard and a dark brown mustache, was approaching the farm. He was wearing a white shirt with gray stripes that matched his gray pants. He also wore wire-rimmed spectacles and a black hat with a wide brim. His clothes were clean and pressed, giving him the look of a businessman or a politician.

Walter was reminded of the day his pa had been approached by Abner Johnson, the claims officer whose arrival had led to his pa's death. Walter hoped this man wouldn't be trouble for Mary Ann. She appeared to recognize the stranger.

"Well hello, Mary Ann," the man said, grinning. "It's good to be home."

"This is NOT your home, John. You know that!" Mary Ann took a step toward him.

"That's not how the law works, but we can get into all that later. For now, all I want is a hug from you and the chance to check on the lads. How's John Junior?"

"You know we call him Ash," Mary Ann said.

Tabby slid over beside Walter, gripped his hand a little tighter than he expected, standing partially behind him. They were both breathing hard.

"I've been thinking about that," the man replied. "You call him Ash and others call him Jack. I want him to start using my name. I am the head of this family and I want to be acknowledged."

"You're the head of nothing. I've raised and provided for the children. God knows where you've been."

"I am here now and I want what's due."

"What's due? How many years have you been gone?"

"Now, now woman. You know I've always had you on my mind. Since I keep hearing about how well you and Lotta are doing, I decided to come home to make sure you are taking care of my money."

"Your money?"

"Lotta has my blood. That's why she's a star. Since she's half me, I want half her brass. That's generous. You know the laws. I can take it all if I choose to." He turned to Walter and Tabby. "Who are these two?"

"They work for us." Walter was glad Mary Ann didn't go into more detail.

"You can afford servants? You're more big-time than I thought. Let's see what's inside your lodging, see how you've been living. Hope you haven't wasted my money."

John turned to walk toward the house, but rather than following him, Mary Ann said, "I've been expecting you would return eventually, John, and have planned for this moment."

"Planned?"

"Yup. What to do about you."

Mary Ann and John walked to the porch and entered the house. When the door closed, Tabby tugged on Walter's hand, twisting him so she could look in his eyes. "What do we do now?" she asked, without releasing her grip.

Walter shook his head. "We shouldn't follow," he told her. "They need time to talk."

"Do you think they're talking about our contracts?" Tabby whispered.

"Why would they? They haven't seen each other for a long time."

"You heard him," Tabby said. "He's after money. If she tells him, he'll want to sell us. I'm sure of it."

"I don't think she'll tell," Walter reassured her, "and if he does find out somehow, he'll want to take Lotta's other money before he gets involved with something as complicated as selling our contracts."

Tabby rocked back and forth, her eyes blinking fast. "You think so?" she asked.

"I do. And I also believe John is a decent person. Lotta's as kind as anybody I know. She had to get it from somewhere. Besides, Mary Ann married the fella and she seems to be a good judge of character."

"He wants half her money."

"He thinks he has a right to the money because the law is on his side, but he knows he didn't earn it."

"That's what worries me. If he has a right to their money, he has a right to our contracts."

Walter touched her shoulder and smiled. "Mary Ann will handle it. I'm sure. We should continue our work in the garden and find out what's going on when she's ready to tell us."

Tabby pulled Walter closer and kissed him on his cheek. "Thank you," she said, "for listening to my fears."

Walter wasn't sure he deserved her thanks but was grateful for the kiss. It was the first time her lips had touched his skin since the time they'd spent together in her saloon bedroom.

When they were done in the garden it was time to prepare dinner, so they walked toward the house. They discovered Lotta sitting on the porch. Her father and Mary Ann must have passed her, yet here she was—alone.

"Are you all right?" Tabby asked as she got down on one knee. Her hands were dirty from working in the garden, but she touched Lotta's shoulder anyway and Lotta reacted by leaning forward to hug Tabby.

"They walked right by me," Lotta pulled back from Tabby. She started rocking back and forth as she spoke. "He waved as he passed. Can you believe that? After all these months he waved, didn't even stop to say hello. I think it's been more than a year since I've seen him and he didn't even ask how I'm doing." Her voice cracked. She paused to collect herself. "Now he's back in there with Ma and who knows what they're talking about. She's a strong woman, but something about Pa makes her foolish."

Tabby looked in Lotta's eyes. She nodded as she said, "I'm sure he wanted to greet you, but he couldn't because Mary Ann needed to get him alone."

"You don't know our relationship. He left when I was five when we were back in New York. He said we could come out and join him, but he wasn't there when we arrived in San Francisco. Now I'm a success and sure enough, he returns. All he wants is money."

Tabby looked up at the porch ceiling as she spoke saying, "You're not alone in this. I know what it's like to have a father who leaves. He's a man. That's what they do." She brought her gaze back to Lotta. "You want someone you can count on? Count on me. I will always be your friend."

"Me too," Walter told her, "even if I am a man." They all smiled and Lotta shook her head.

"I can't say how much you both mean to me," Lotta told them as she leaned back. "My career, it isn't enough. I need friends. I can count on Ma, but even she isn't enough. It's good you're both here. Now go inside and fix dinner. I need time to be alone."

When Walter and Tabby entered the kitchen, he asked her, "What do you think?"

"Lotta's strong," Tabby told him. "We'll see what happens at dinner, but I think she'll change the subject and move on."

"I hope you're right, but I worry about her and about the boys even more."

Tabby waved her hands and laughed. "Ash and George will be fine," she told him. "He shows up once or twice a year for a short time, then takes off again. He's never been a permanent part of their lives. Besides they're young boys. All they care about is what adventure the next day will bring."

"I hope so," Walter said, laughing with her.

Walter went outside to kill and clean a chicken that hadn't been laying, while Tabby mashed potatoes and prepared dried beans. He brought her the chicken parts so she could fry them, then went behind the house where he chopped wood until dinner time.

The table was set for seven, but there was a small controversy when the family took their seats. John wanted to sit next to his wife. Mary Ann wanted him as far away as possible. John won the argument, which Walter didn't see as a good sign. He looked at Tabby, who shrugged.

"I spoke with Adah Menken today," Lotta announced. She was sitting to the right of Walter. Tabby was on his left.

Mary Ann raised an eyebrow. "Where did you see her?"

"At the theater. She saw my show last night and wanted to speak to me."

"That's quite an honor," her pa told her.

"One she deserves," Mary Ann said, turning to Lotta, she asked, "What did she have to say?"

"She talked about the show and my singing and dancing. After that, she had a suggestion."

"Did she?" Mary Ann folded her arms across her chest.

Lotta held her head high as she announced, "Adah thinks I'm ready for New York."

"So do I," John told her. "It should help your career."

"Of course it will help her career if she's a success," Mary Ann said, speaking a little louder. "There's a lot to think about, John. You can't just stroll in here and imagine you can control everything. Especially you. All of your projects have fallen flat unless I made them work. Why should anyone take your advice?"

"I'm saying she should take Adah Menken's advice, not mine."

"Adah Menken appeared on stage naked, riding a horse like Lady Godiva. Do you really want that for your daughter?"

"From what I've read, she was wearing skin-toned clothes."

"The men in the audience thought she was naked, including the critics."

"Adah Menken makes more money than any actress alive today."

"Which brings us to what you're doing here. You said you want money. What for?"

"I said I deserve money. Lotta is my child. Everything she makes is legally mine. I'm only asking for half."

"You're not going to get it. I've invested the money. The laws may say you have some right to what we've earned, but you would have to spend years in court to get anything and any new money we take in would mean starting the cases all over." She moved closer to him and spoke in a firm voice, separating her words. "Just tell me what you want the money for. Are you having trouble affording meals? Do you have a place to live? What is life like for you, John? You're fat enough, so I assume you're eating."

"All right. I'll tell you. I wish to go back to England. It's been far too long since I've seen my mates and my family."

"So that's it?" Mary Ann said, shaking her head.

"Yes. I'll earn it if that's what it takes." John nodded toward Walter and Tabby. "You can send these two on their way. I can cook, clean, and work with my hands."

"Let me think on that," Mary Ann said as she grabbed a fork full of mashed potatoes. "There might be something we can work out."

The table conversation was limited and focused on England. Lotta tried to bring up Adah Menken and New York a few more times, but each time Mary Ann turned the subject back to John in England. After those failed attempts, Lotta looked down at her supper and stopped speaking. George whined about Ash stealing bread off his plate, but Mary Ann hushed him, so the two boys retreated into whispering to each other. Walter and Tabby were too busy listening to speak.

"London's dirty," Mary Ann told John, "but the countryside is beautiful."

John leaned back and crossed his arms. "It's the people I miss the most," he told her, "but there are still places I love. I'm tired of San Francisco."

"You were restless in New York, too."

"We should never have left England."

"We've done well here."

"You have."

The conversation went on like that during the rest of the supper. When the meal was over, John and Mary Ann went out on the porch to continue their talk while Lotta, Ash, and George began a game of dominoes, spread out on the floor. Walter helped Tabby clean up. They heated the water, then she washed the dishes while he dried and put them away.

Tabby was moving slowly, fidgeting with each dish before she handed them to Walter. "I'm more worried than before," she whispered.

"Why?" he asked, speaking in a full voice. "It sounds like Mary Ann will be sending him to England."

"Maybe, but not for long and if Lotta wants to go to New York, where does that leave us?"

Walter laughed a little and shook his head. "Mary Ann isn't going to sell our contracts no matter what John does. If Lotta goes to New York, she might set us free, but that's the worst she would do. We would find a way to make a living. You wouldn't have to go back to the saloon. I could work the docks with Frank."

"Where would we live?"

"I know people in Chinatown. I'm sure we could find a place."

Lotta stepped into the kitchen. "Is that the plan?" she said, her eyes wide.

Walter turned to her. "I'm sorr..."

She cut him off before he could apologize. "I go to New York and you two take care of each other?" Her face was almost as red as her hair.

"We're worried," Tabby told her.

"Maybe you are, but Walter sounds like he's looking forward to going his own way."

"You got it wrong, Lotta. We both love it here. I love the work at the theater, especially love watching you dance and practicing with you."

"We love your ma and your brothers, too," Tabby added. "We wouldn't want to be anywhere else. That's why we're worried."

Lotta's eyes started to water. She looked at the ceiling.

"New York sounds like a wonderful opportunity," Walter said as he stepped toward Lotta and handed her a towel. "But if you go, what happens to us?"

Lotta wiped her nose then held her head high and said, "You'd both come with me. I would never leave either of you."

"What would we do?" Walter asked. "You're not going to be building your own sets in New York."

"There are always things to do. You would take care of me!"

Walter looked at Tabby who raised her eyebrows. "I never thought of you as someone who needs anybody other than your ma."

"Then you don't know me." She turned toward Tabby. "Neither of you do." She sniffled. "Before you two came, I was lonely, real lonely. I had my ma as well as George and Ash, but they are family, not friends." She stared at Walter. "I've been telling you that since the day you and Frank took me fishing." She took a couple of steps away then turned back. "I need you both to talk about things only people our age can understand, but most of all, I need to feel you both care about me. When you talk about leaving that hurts. It hurts bad."

Lotta walked out of the kitchen.

Chapter Thirteen

A Father's Concern

When Walter arrived the next morning, he went back to the garden beside Lotta's house. Tabby was already weeding. She stood up.

"You missed an interesting night," Tabby told him. "John and Mary Ann slept in the same room."

Walter asked, "Where else is he going to sleep? You have a room. George and Ash have a room. Lotta has a room. Mary Ann's bed is the only place available. Besides, they're husband and wife."

Tabby folded her arms and tapped her foot. "That's not all. He got up in the middle of the night, stole a bag of gold dust, and disappeared. No one knows where he went."

Shortly after Tabby told Walter that John was gone, the man returned. He showed up at the garden where Walter and Tabby were busy pulling weeds. He greeted them pleasantly but was walking with a wobble and stunk of whiskey. Walter recognized the smell from when he used to deal with his own pa's drinking. He hoped Lotta and her ma could find freedom from the problems alcohol brought to a family, but not the way he had when his pa died.

John dropped to his knees and started to weed the corn plot, or at least to pretend he was weeding. After a few minutes, Walter left to go to the stable. He thought if he left Tabby alone with John, she might discover where Mary Ann's gold dust was, or at least where John had gone the night before. But shortly after Walter reached the stable and started polishing the carriage, John showed up again. It seemed it was up to him to discover John's secrets.

"What is your relationship with my daughter?" he asked, his speech soft and weak.

The question surprised Walter. He closed his mouth, paused, then answered saying, "She's a friend." He added, "I help around the house, I help at the theater, and I help with her dancing when she asks me to."

"You dance with her?" John tugged at his shirt sleeve. "How often do you dance with her?"

"Two or three times a week, for as long as she needs me. She's working on routines she can't do on her own."

"You have experience?"

"No. I grew up in one of the mining camps. The dancing there was different than what Lotta does, but I'm learning."

John looked up for a moment, as if he was studying the beams that held the barn roof up, then he turned back toward Walter and, with a grimace, said. "Having a man around the house is good for Ash and George and must make life easier for Mary Ann. It's Lotta I worry about because I'm not sure what you mean by a friend. Are you a friend of that Tabby girl, too?"

"Yup," Walter said. He bit at his lip before adding, "I like them both."

"You do? You fancy having two women when most men around here have none?"

"I don't *have* them. They're friends. That's all."

John rubbed his neck. "We're going away," he told Walter.

"I figured that, what with all the talk about England."

"I'm not making myself clear. We're all going away: Mary Ann, Lotta, the boys, and me. We're all going to New York. I figure I'll be watched every moment over there. I went out to celebrate my last night of freedom. Now everyone's miffed."

Walter noticed he and Tabby weren't on the list of people heading east. Maybe she had been right to worry. He felt his stomach turn, but said, "I'm not miffed."

John smiled. "Too busy thinking of yourself and Tabby, right?"

"Can you blame me?"

"I suppose not." John took a step away from Walter then turned and went back. "Lotta and I were arguing over you two. I say leave you here. She says bring you along. Mary Ann will make the final decision as she always does.

"But I'm talking too much about this move. I need to ask you about Lotta. She cares about you and I need to be sure you don't take advantage. I see you and Tabby as a pair and Lotta as the outsider. A young woman can get hurt when she's outside and wants to be inside. Do what you like to Tabby, but if you hurt my child, I will punish you. I promise."

Walter figured the man meant what he said, but he had weakened his threat by sneaking out late at night to drink with his friends.

* * *

Walter didn't hear any more about the trip for two and a half weeks. He didn't see much of Lotta during that time. She left the house every day, to meet Adah Menken. The two young actresses went riding together. They spent a lot of time hanging out by the ocean. Walter didn't know what they were discussing. He figured it had something to do with the opportunities in New York, but the one thing he was sure about was how Lotta had to be disappointed and embarrassed by her pa's behavior.

Lotta asked Walter to come to the theater one day, where she introduced him to a dance called a rumba. He held her the same as when they danced to a waltz, but the count for the music was different and they had to sway their hips. He had trouble concentrating when Lotta moved that way.

He continued to share chores with Tabby and once, while they were gathering eggs, they reached for the same nest and got a little too close. The walls and ceiling of the little coop seemed to swirl as he leaned in and kissed her. She pulled him closer and kissed him back, dropping an egg in the process. After that single kiss, they stepped away from each other and hardly said a word as they finished gathering eggs.

Walter hoped Tabby didn't mention the kiss to Lotta, but the next day at the theater, when they were done dancing, Lotta hugged him. She'd never done that before and the way her hair smelled made the theater sway the same way the chicken coop had when Tabby was in his arms.

"We're going to New York," Lotta told him. Before dancing with him, she had changed out of her work clothes into a beautiful white dress with red trim that matched her hair and a short, lace skirt. The outfit was probably meant for a performance, but he'd never seen her in it before.

"All of us?" Walter asked her.

"Yes, all of us. Come let's sit on the stage." She snuggled up close to him and leaned her head on his shoulder. "I told Ma Tabby can look after the boys while you look after Pa. It's not gonna be easy. When he sneaks out at night, you'll have to go with 'em, make sure he makes it back alive. He won't have his friends with him in the big city, so he may want you to come along."

So John was right about being watched in New York and Walter was to do the watching. He cleared his throat then said, "Uh...Maybe."

Lotta giggled. "It will work out. You'll see. And there's something else I'd like you to do for me."

"Tell me what."

"Talk to Tabby. It's important."

Walter felt his heart beating faster. "I talk to her every day. What do you want me to say?"

She sat up straight. "Ask her if she can get herbs to prevent pregnancy. She knows about that stuff."

What did this mean? Was Lotta seeing someone? Walter hated the idea of her with another man. He wanted to crawl under the stage and hide. "That's woman stuff," he said. "Wouldn't it be better if you asked her yourself?"

"I don't want to. That's why I'm asking you to talk to her. It's important and I need it today."

He swallowed before asking, "Today?"

"Yup. I love Ash and George, but I don't want another brother."

"It's for your ma?" He felt a little giddy at the thought.

"Of course." She smiled. "What did you think?"

"Isn't she too old to have another baby?"

Lotta leaned her head on his shoulder again. "Every woman's different."

"I didn't know that." He turned his head toward her, inhaling the aroma of her hair again. "I'll ask Tabby."

"Thank you." Lotta kissed his cheek. "I'll find some way to pay you back. I promise." She stood and went inside the house.

* * *

When Walter got back to the house, he went to the garden where he found Tabby was weeding again. He asked her to come with him to the stable. "I need to let the horses out in the pasture and I was hoping we could talk on the way over."

They started on the short walk, side by side, but not talking. She was on his right side, holding her left arm straight down. He noticed how she wasn't swinging her arm and wondered if she might have hurt it. She didn't seem to be in pain and even picked up the pace he had set. He could feel her concentrating on her arm, on her hand in particular and unintentionally he started to imitate her, holding his arm as straight, keeping it next to hers, only inches away.

Tabby slowly moved closer to him until the back of her hand brushed against the back of his. He felt a chill run up his spine and was drawn to feel the chill again. He moved to her, as she had done to him and their hands brushed once more. This time he kept his hand close to hers and felt her twist until her palm was against the back of his hand. He moved again, so they were palm to palm, then pushed his fingers between hers until they were interlinked.

They let their arms sway now, ever so gently, as they continued walking toward the stable. "I have something to ask you," Walter said.

"Something you need me to do?

"Something Lotta needs."

Tabby frowned. "Oh?"

"She wants herbs that can prevent pregnancy."

She dropped his hand, moved a step away from him, and stopped walking. "Why didn't she ask me herself?"

"She said she didn't want to. She didn't tell me anything other than that, except she wants them for her ma."

Tabby raised her eyebrows and clenched her fist. "And you believe her?"

"Why not?"

"Her pa has slept in her ma's bed for weeks now. Don't you think it's a little late for herbs?"

"Why else would Lotta want them?"

"Could it be she wants to remind you who I was before I came here? How I always had to deal with the chance I might get pregnant?"

Walter looked down, then back at Tabby. "I don't think Lotta is that sneaky."

"Then could it be she wants the herbs for herself?"

"You think she has someone at the theater?"

Tabby crossed her arms and narrowed her eyes. "You remember how I dressed up as Lotta back when I first met you, right?"

Walter nodded.

"You know how Lotta helped me with that, loaned me the dress and even had it altered."

He laughed and rolled his eyes.

"She didn't just like the idea," Tabby told him, "she was all-fired happy about it. Why do you think that was?'

Walter had no answer. He turned toward the stable and started walking again. Tabby followed, but after a few steps, Walter turned and went to her. He hugged her and spoke to her in a low, shaky voice, "I like Lotta and I don't wanna hurt her. But...But, you're the one, Tabby. You're beautiful and smart and you make me feel like I can take on the world. I don't just wanna be around you, I wanna be part of you. I wanna hold you like I'm holding you now until nothing and no one can ever pull us apart. I don't like this fix we're in. I don't know what to do."

"I do," Tabby whispered, as she hugged Walter back. "I have those herbs Lotta wants. I've been taken 'em myself, every day, just in case you might say something like you just said. So let's get to that stable and find us a place where we can forget about anything other than you and me."

Walter did forget his problems while he and Tabby were together in the loft. The feel of her naked chest against his own reawakened the memory of the first time their bodies had touched and that memory led to others—the first time he'd watched her down a glass of whiskey, the first time he'd seen her smile, the first time he'd touched and smelled her hair, and the way she'd listened to the sad story of his absent ma and turned it toward the one light in that darkness, the way the faceless woman had chosen to give him life.

They took their time as they made love and they took their time afterward. Tabby curled up next to him, resting her head on his chest. He loved that position, the way he could rock her gently, just by breathing. Yet when the time came for them to get dressed and leave their sanctuary, they still had fun, laughing as they tried to rid their bodies and clothes of all the tiny blades of hay.

When they got back to the house Tabby gave Walter the herbs, so Lotta was happy. But if Tabby was right about Lotta's intentions, the situation had gotten worse rather than better.

Chapter Fourteen

The Trip Back East

Over the next two weeks, Tabby and Walter worked together in the garden, the chicken coop, and in the kitchen, but she didn't go back with him to the stable, even though he asked her to more than once. She didn't say why, but the way she stared down when he stood close to her told him she was worried about Lotta.

Lotta kept dancing with him each day, when they were done repairing sets, checking props, and fixing costumes. They danced close, but Lotta gave no indication she wanted Walter to stay close to her when they were done dancing.

The trip to New York meant there would be no show in San Francisco following the current one, yet there was still plenty of work to do. On the day the show closed, the entire set had to be taken down.

* * *

Walter had spent very little time with Frank in the months that led up to the day they had to say goodbye. Walter had been busy with Tabby and Lotta, while Frank was with Ru, but that day their separate lives didn't keep them from the memories of the years they'd known each other. They were in the saloon where both started drinking whiskey as they laughed and shook their heads over how young and foolish they'd been. The stories went on for a while, then stopped suddenly.

"You know she's upstairs, don't you?" Frank said. He was half through his second drink. "She's with a client. Still says she won't give it up until we have enough cash for a house. Sometimes I think I should sneak over to Lotta's place late at night and dig up our part of the gold."

Walter clenched his jaw as he whispered. "We dug it up. We had to, now that we're headin' to New York. I have your portion with me—yours and Ru's. But it's still too early to be spending big amounts, especially on property. Everyone will know when you buy a house."

Frank didn't seem to be listening. He said, "I love her with all my heart, but it's hard."

Walter tapped his fingers on the table. He fidgeted with his drink, but didn't bring it to his lips. He said, "I know what you mean."

"No you don't," Frank snapped. "Tabby's given up that way of life. Besides, ya got Lotta, too. They're the ones with their hearts all twisted up. Not you—never the grand Mister Walter Cain."

Walter bit his lip, but didn't say anything.

Frank sighed and looked down at the table. "Ru thought I was bothered 'cause I'd never been with another woman. She arranged for me to spend some time with one of the other girls and let me tell ya, that did not go well." Frank laughed a little, then took a drink of whiskey. "She said those men don't mean nothing to her, that it's just physical. But they talk to her and she listens."

Walter perked up. "How do ya know that?"

"She tells me what they say."

"Well there you have it." Walter leaned back in his chair and crossed his arms. "Tabby once said she would get in serious trouble if she talked about any of her clients. If Ru tells you things about hers, she trusts you. That's something, isn't it?"

"I spoze so. Just not sure it's enough."

Walter smiled. "Make it enough. Ru's a good woman. She's worth waitin' for."

* * *

It was another two weeks before the Crabtree family and their two servants boarded the steamer to Panama. Tabby, much to Walter's dismay, had brought the Crabtree Bible to the docks. Apparently, she was asking for God's forgiveness, which did not bode well for her relationship with Walter.

Mary Ann didn't tell Walter and Tabby what to expect until they were all on the deck of the ship. When she did, her description wasn't as bad as he imagined. "When Lotta was five we came here from

New York. We took a steamer to Colon, a little town on the Atlantic side of Panama, at the foot of the Chagres River. From there we rode a long boat with native paddlers upriver, a mule train through the jungle to Panama City, and another steamer to San Francisco. Turns out there's a railroad now, all the way from the Pacific to the Atlantic. It takes three hours instead of a week and a half. We'll still have to take this ship we're on and another steamer from Panama to New York, but we'll shoot right through the bugs and diseases in the jungle. Lots of people died back then, making their way across Central America. We don't have to depend on luck this time."

Lotta put her hand on Walter's shoulder, while Tabby watched, her eyebrows raised just a little. "How about you?" Lotta asked Walter. "How'd you get to California? I figure you weren't born here, being the son of a miner."

"You're right. I was young, real young. I remember being on a boat, but that's about it."

"Maybe you sailed around the horn. Some people did that back then."

"Maybe so."

The first three or four days on the boat were miserable. Everyone other than Lotta was vomiting. It was hard to know how she avoided the problem, but Walter had a theory. He thought it had to do with her dancing. "She throws herself around the stage so much and so often," he told Tabby, "she probably can't get seasick."

The adults managed to get out of their cabins in time to throw up over the rail, or at least near it, but both Ash and George got sick in the men's cabin. Mary Ann had reserved two rooms, one for the women and one for the men. This meant the place where Walter slept stunk of vomit. It also meant, per Mary Ann's instructions, Tabby wasn't allowed to enter the men's room. So Walter was responsible for cleaning up what the boys had done even though he was as sick as they were.

On the fifth day, after Walter and Tabby were over their seasickness, Tabby suggested they find a way to have some time alone.

That night, when Walter was certain John, Ash, and George were asleep, he sneaked out to the deck. He didn't know if Tabby's second thoughts were over, but he hoped so. He missed the feel of her body and, although he talked to her every day, their talk was different when she was in his arms.

Tabby was waiting on the deck when Walter arrived. She turned to face him and he knew the night wasn't going to be as he had imagined. She was smiling but holding the Bible.

"I came here by myself last night and discovered how beautiful the sea is at night. I wanted to share it with you," she said.

Walter rubbed his cheek. "You should be careful where you go alone. We don't know everyone on this boat."

"There are people on the bridge. I waved to them last night. They would hear if I yelled, besides I'm not alone tonight. You're here."

Walter looked up but didn't see anyone.

"Come here," Tabby instructed, taking his hand and leading him to the railing. He could see her face by the light of the half-moon. Her eyes were wide. "Look up." Tabby put her arm around him and positioned her head next to his. He tried to follow her gaze toward the stars. "There's magic in the night sky out here. God's greatness is clear now that we're away from any trees or hills blocking the horizon. For me, it's even clearer than the words in the Bible. God speaks out here. He's talking to me now and He wants to speak to you, too."

Walter shuffled his feet. "He told you that?"

"Yup. You know how I once told you that a kiss can mean more than anything else we do because it's how we touch each other's soul?"

Walter nodded.

"This is the way God kisses us, under a sky like this one, with a moon that's bright, but not so bright its light blocks the stars. You have to take a deep breath then look up and all over, moving from one star to another until you're a little dizzy. You'll see it if you try. You can count them if you like, but I promise you'll lose track. There's too many.

"I went to an astrologer once. She could look at the stars and tell where I'd been and where I was going. She said I would find love with a man from the camps." Tabby looked down from the sky and into Walter's eyes. "I told her I was a whore, but she said most of the women in San Francisco were prostitutes, so she already figured I was. She said I'd find love anyway. It wasn't something I could run from. It was in the stars. I know the Bible doesn't speak well of astrology, but I think God sent that woman to me, so I'd know you were coming. Kinda like the way He sent John the Baptist to tell people about Jesus.

"Now we're here, leaning on this rail, smelling the salt water, my arm around you, standing so close I can feel you breathing, and all around us is God's love. He's like a blanket, wrapping us up and keeping us protected from the worst of the world, keeping us warm, saving us from the evil of people like Odell, from the greed like what turned your pa against Frank's pa—and then killed him. I want you to kiss me, Walter. Then, when we go back to our cabins, I want you to lie in bed and think about God and about me."

Walter turned and wrapped her in his arms, then they kissed. "I always think about you," he said when their lips parted, "but why have you been avoiding me?"

Tabby stepped back and shook her head. "I wasn't avoiding you."

"The stable was beautiful," he told her, narrowing his eyes. "Why wouldn't you go back there with me?"

"The love was beautiful, but the place was wrong, all piss and manure. I needed to be here, needed the waves, the sky, and God."

"And men watching from the bridge," he said.

Tabby crossed her arms and tapped her foot. "Don't you understand anything I am saying?" She looked up one more time, then turned and headed back to her cabin.

Walter leaned against the rail again and tried to count the stars, as she'd suggested, but couldn't reach a hundred. He decided the stars were like gold nuggets in a gentle creek, only more valuable. He took another deep breath, then thought more about what Tabby had said. He was filled with a sense of awe but confused. He wasn't sure if he was in awe of God or Tabby.

When Walter was about to enter his cabin he heard a voice saying, "Talk to me before you go in there." He turned to see John Crabtree standing behind him. The man had a whiskey flask with him. Walter wasn't sure how he'd managed to sneak that by Mary Ann. "I just saw Tabby go into her cabin. I suppose she was with you." John came right up to Walter. He didn't smell of whiskey, so Walter figured the flask was still full. "It makes sense. I can understand how a servant would rather be with another servant than a successful actress. Just be careful."

"We were talking and looking at the stars. Is that so wrong?"

Walter could hear John breathing hard. "It is if Lotta gets hurt." He waved the flask, nodded, then walked toward the bow of the boat.

Walter followed. He was destined for a strange relationship with Lotta's pa. Mary Ann wanted him to keep an eye on the old guy, but it seems the old guy had decided to keep an eye on Walter. Maybe this would make his job easier, maybe not.

"You ever try to count the stars?" Walter asked John, repeating what Tabby had said.

"Of course not. Why would I do such a foolish thing?"

"The sky makes you feel like all the mistakes you made in life don't really matter. It makes you feel small compared to everything out there." Walter leaned against the rail next to John.

"Spoken fancy, like a true servant." John nudged Walter with his elbow and laughed. "Mistakes matter, if you're trying to make something of your life. In my case, I tried too hard and missed the mark too often. While I was trying, I wasn't home as much as I should have been. I think it was my pride. Lotta and Mary Ann have done quite well, but I flopped in California and now I'm paying the price, tagging along to New York like you and that girl Tabby.

"I always thought I was meant for something bigger than getting up each morning and working with my mits. I thought I could outsmart the people around me. I could figure out what they wanted and flog it to them. Turns out, I was wrong. I see the world a little differently than other men here in California, which means they don't care about what I want. So each scheme I tried to make some money hasn't worked.

"The one thing I did right in my life was to marry Mary Ann. She understands people well enough to make a buck. And then there's Lotta, a mixture of the two of us. She's got Mary Ann's drive and instinct along with my impulsiveness and creativity. That's why she's so successful on stage." John held the flask out to Walter. "You want a swig?"

Walter took a drink. It was the first whiskey he'd had since he met Frank at the saloon. He remembered what to expect, so he didn't choke. He liked the burn and the little swirl in his head, but he wasn't going to drink too much. John was talking like a friend and Walter wasn't going to let anything get in the way of that. "What are you planning to do in New York?"

"Me? I'm going to do whatever Mary Ann tells me to do, just like you and Tabby." John stared at his hands on the rail. "I don't see anything else there for me. When we used to live in New York I had a bookstore. Mary Ann took it over when I left, then sold it when she and Lotta followed me. Now nothing is there for me except living off Lotta's brass." He took another gulp from the flask.

Walter looked up at the stars again but didn't speak. He didn't know what to say, since John's situation wasn't that different from his own, except John was a Crabtree. But New York was a big city with plenty of opportunities. Other people, including John, had survived there on nothing but their wits. If things didn't work out with the Crabtrees, he and Tabby would find a way to survive.

John stepped away from the rail and Walter. "Let's go back to the cabin," he said, "before we start pretending we're mates."

* * *

They arrived in Panama late on a Saturday afternoon and spent the night on the ship. The train was scheduled to depart the following afternoon, so that gave Walter some time in the morning to see Panama City. Since it was Sunday, Tabby wanted to attend church. She couldn't get anyone other than Walter to go with her. He was happy they were alone, but she was disappointed. "I thought Lotta and Mary Ann would enjoy seeing how the local people worshipped," she told him, but Walter knew there was more to it. Tabby wanted to share her new found religion.

They followed a number of dark-skinned, native women dressed in bright-colored, loose blouses and mismatched skirts, also bright. Many of the older women wore kerchiefs over their hair.

"All those women in such fancy clothes have to be going to church," Tabby said and she was right.

The building they were led to was large and beautiful, two stories high with elaborate stained glass windows and statues of Christ and the Virgin Mary in recesses along the front wall. Inside was also magnificent. The worship area had a ceiling as high as the one in the American Theater back in San Francisco with more gold covering the wall behind the altar than Walter had seen since the day they robbed Odell.

They took seats in the pews and listened as the reverend spoke in Spanish. Watching the congregation and the minister in such a magnificent chapel was how Walter pictured heaven, but it was impossible to know what the preacher was saying.

After the service, they went through the city toward the train station, where they were to meet Lotta and the others. Mary Ann had arranged for their luggage to be transferred.

As they walked, Walter and Tabby passed large homes and shacks, all in disrepair and all overcrowded. Women were hanging laundry, children were playing in the dirt, but most of the people Walter saw were sitting still, in their yards or on their porches, staring at the two gringos passing by. They seemed to live a boring, sad life, which was how Walter pictured Hell.

One of the houses had three tables set up in the front yard, which seemed to be a makeshift restaurant. A woman was serving what smelled like chicken and potato soup along with corn cakes, both foods were cooked on a wood grill. Tabby and Walter were hungry, so they sat at one of the tables beside two women. The cook approached them and spoke in Spanish. They couldn't understand what she said, so Walter pointed toward the food the others were eating then to his mouth.

Mary Ann had provided Tabby and Walter with some Colombian pesos, but they had no idea how much to pay. Walter put two coins on the table. The woman took one and brought them each a bowl of soup and two corn cakes. The food was good, although a little spicy for Walter's taste. They ate quickly and left.

Once they were on the train, Tabby and Walter found Lotta eating alone in the dining car. They sat at her table and ordered coffee, so they'd have something to sip on while she ate. Lotta was dressed in trousers that stopped just below her knees with white stockings underneath and a pair of heavy boots. She also wore a light green blouse with a long, white vest over it. Walter recognized the outfit as one of her costumes. He wondered why she was wearing it but didn't ask.

When her two friends sat across from her Lotta asked, "How was the church?" she spoke through a mouthful of potatoes.

Tabby leaned back. "They were speaking Spanish. We didn't know what was going on."

"That's right," Walter added, "but we could see how rich the church was and how poor all the homes around it were. Those people are in places that reminded me of the camps, but we didn't have to live in the shadow of a castle. I feel bad for them."

"They'll survive," Tabby told him. "In most ways, they're better off than we were."

"Those were hard times," Walter agreed.

Lotta looked out the train window, then back at Walter and Tabby. "We weren't rich when we first arrived in San Francisco, but we had friends and a little money left over from the sale of the bookstore in New York. We didn't have it as bad as you two did, but we still had to struggle. We couldn't depend on Pa. He hadn't even met us at the pier. If my dancing hadn't worked out, we could be as bad off as the people you saw here." She looked at Walter. "Are you asking me to do something about it?"

Walter shook his head. "There's no way anyone could help all those people and if you gave to some, the ones you left out would be mad as Hell. That's how people think."

"Still, charity is what is needed in this world," Lotta said, "but when I start to give money, I plan to choose people closer to home."

She pushed her plate away and pulled a thin cigar out of a wooden cigar box she'd been carrying in a pocket. She lit the cigar, leaned back, and started puffing, like all this talk of money had her thinking she was a banker. A few of the diners at other tables looked at them and spoke in hushed tones the ladies waving their handkerchieves in the air. One couple called over a waiter who shrugged off their complaints. The cigar smoke didn't bother Walter. He was glad to see Lotta relaxing. They still had weeks to go on the northbound steamer before they would be in New York.

Chapter Fifteen

Performing in New York

In New York, Mary Ann rented Niblo's Saloon, a small venue adjacent to the more famous Niblo's Garden. Lotta was going to perform in a short burlesque based on the opera singer Jenny Lind, called *Jenny Leatherlungs*, a short play entitled *The Mysterious Chamber*, and she would finish with a solo performance on the banjo and some clogging. Mary Ann's choices seemed a perfect way to showcase Lotta's music and comedy, which is how they wanted to introduce Lotta to her first eastern audience.

Walter had been wrong when he told Lotta they wouldn't have to build their own sets in New York. They had to hire the entire crew, including actors, musicians, a stage manager, and people to work on the set. Between carpentry, painting, and supervising the other workers, Walter had plenty to keep him occupied. Neither John nor Tabby helped. She kept busy with Ash and George, exploring the city, while John searched for his old haunts. When he couldn't find them, he looked for new places to buy whiskey.

The evening before opening day, Mary Ann visited a street vendor and bought dinner for all the workers who were staying late. The set construction was almost complete, but she had a few minor details she wanted to fix before Lotta's performance.

Lotta had not helped with the set since she had been busy with rehearsals, but she came in to see the final results.

"Are you nervous?" Walter asked her.

"Once I step on a stage, I get caught up in the jokes and the music and forget there's a world around me. I'm sure that will happen here like it did in California."

When the last-minute changes were complete, Mary Ann, Lotta, and Walter rode back to their hotel on a trolley. Tabby was there with Ash and George, but John was still out on the streets. The women went to bed in their room, while Walter waited up for John, sitting in a chair beside the sleeping boys.

John returned hours later, smelling of whiskey, but able to walk a straight line. He nodded to Walter as he entered the room, but didn't speak.

The next day Walter stayed with Tabby and the boys. They would ride the trolley together when it was time to see the show. John went his own way again but promised to be at the theater in time. Lotta kept to herself the entire day, probably thinking about the performance and running through her routines in her head. Mary Ann went to the theater early, to spend the day there. Walter had no idea what she planned to do, but he figured she'd find something to keep occupied.

When the performance was about to begin, the cast gathered backstage. Lotta and Mary Ann gave them a pep talk and told them to keep up their energy. But something was different about this performance. It was getting close to the time to start and the seats were less than a quarter full. This was particularly bad because they were performing in a small venue.

Lotta had never experienced anything like this. Walter went back to speak with her. He found her pacing. When she saw him, she turned and walked away, clearly not wanting to talk. Walter went back into the audience and sat between Tabby and John.

"What is she going to do?" Tabby asked Walter when he returned to his seat.

"She's going to perform," he told her. "There's no choice."

John leaned over and said, "We're losing money tonight."

Lotta didn't miss a beat, but Walter knew she was suffering. The advertisements had gone out, but apparently, a chance to see *San Francisco's Favorite* wasn't enough to entice New York audiences.

When the performance was over there was some light applause, but no shouting words of praise and no tossing bags of gold dust. Tabby, Walter, John, and the boys gave a standing ovation, but they were alone. The others were starting to file out of the theater.

"We need to talk to her," Walter told Tabby.

Tabby winced then nodded toward the boys. "I have to watch George and Ash."

"I'll take care of them," John told her. "Go talk to my daughter."

They went back to Lotta's dressing room. The door was closed, so they knocked.

"Go away," Lotta shouted, her voice cracking.

Walter stepped closer to the door and said, "We're here for you."

"We?" Lotta asked.

"I'm here too," Tabby told her. Lotta opened the door. As they walked in, Tabby said, "It's just a setback. It will go better tomorrow."

"If people didn't come tonight, why would they come tomorrow?"

Walter raised his eyebrows then said, "Tomorrow is Saturday. Maybe more people will be looking for something to do."

"The reviewers were here tonight. Tomorrow's too late. They saw the empty seats." Lotta paused between each sentence to take a breath.

"The show was great," Walter told her. "You were great. I think they will surprise you."

"When do you expect the reviews?" Tabby asked.

"Sunday's paper," Lotta told her.

Tabby clasped her hands in front of her chest and stared at Lotta. "When we were on our way to Panama, Walter and I stood on the deck of the steamer. It was late at night and we were staring up at the stars, admiring the heavens." Her voice trembled a bit at first, but grew strong. "Those stars are like you, Lotta. Standing in their light was beautiful, but it's also beautiful to stand in yours. Your performance was spectacular tonight, as it always is. If the reviewers can't tell you're a star, they shouldn't be reviewers. I say we celebrate before Sunday. What those guys think doesn't matter."

Lotta laughed. "You two," she said, shaking her head slowly. "You always make me feel good."

* * *

The following afternoon, John went to a tavern he'd discovered where most of the patrons had spent time in the California mines. He handed out free passes to that evening's performance. These men had memories of Lotta's shows and were eager to see her perform again. When the show opened that night, the hall was about three-quarters full. Lotta was excited and Mary Ann actually hugged John in front of everyone backstage.

However, about ten minutes into the show, another problem became apparent. The paying patrons and the free-pass ex-miners had different ideas about the way to act in a theater. The men who had seen Lotta in San Francisco stood and yelled when she came on stage. They danced alongside Lotta to the music and tossed items on stage. The New Yorkers didn't know how to handle this behavior. Most of them stared at the ex-miners more than they looked at the performance and a few exited before the show was over. It was worse than the night before.

The reviews came out on Sunday and were as bad as Lotta had feared. *The Herald* critic said, "Miss Lotta...possesses any amount of aplomb—a graceful French word for the more vulgar English word, brass..." *The Clipper* review said, "Her style is certainly not intended for a first-class audience, concert halls being her proper stamping ground."***

Lotta's show closed after one week. Fortunately, B. F. Whitman saw the show and recognized her talent. He offered her an opportunity in Chicago, performing five different roles in a show entitled *The Seven Sisters,* a show Whitman treated as a female minstrel show. One of the roles was Tartarine, a character Lotta played in blackface while she sang, played her banjo, and danced energetic numbers such as jigs and reels. Walter recalled how Lotta had once told him she didn't like working in that messy, thick makeup, but she seemed happy with the show. It ran for three weeks and made a huge profit.

After the Chicago show closed, Mary Ann scheduled a tour of the Midwest. Tabby and Walter joined the Crabtrees, but George and Ash did not. Mary Ann put the boys in a boarding school.

* * *

The tour went on for three years after the success in Chicago. The response to her show was tremendous everywhere they went. The only time they had any problems with audience reaction was when Lotta added her patriotic number. When the civil war ended, Mary Ann added southern cities to the schedule. Although the war was over, the wounds were still fresh, both physical and mental. Lotta dressed like a Union drummer boy played the snare drum and danced. She cut the routine when she was in the southern states, but in the border states, there was still a lot of sympathy for the south.

During the third year, when they were performing in Philadelphia, Walter and Tabby were eating lunch in the green room. Walter was talking to Tabby, facing her, so he didn't notice when Lotta entered the room.

Tabby raised a hand to stop him. She asked Lotta, "What's wrong?" Lotta's eyes were wet and puffy with circles underneath.

"You're not upset over last night's show, are you?" Walter asked. "I thought it went well."

"It's George." Lotta's voice cracked. She looked at Walter then back at Tabby. "He's been hurt."

Walter stood and stepped to Lotta, reaching out for her hand as Tabby cried, "Oh my God!"

Lotta stepped back from them both. She looked down as she spoke. "Ma just told me. We're going to New York, to see him in the hospital. He lost a leg."

"Wha..what happened?" Walter asked, feeling so dizzy he had to sit again.

"He did a foolish thing, ran away from the school. He tried to hop onto a moving freight train and must have slipped. He was run over by one of the wheels. He lost the one leg and toes from the other foot. The doctor says he'll live, but his life will never be the same. He'll be limping around on a fake leg for the rest of his life, maybe even using crutches. He was so active, so full of life. And now what will he be like?"

Tabby went to Lotta and hugged her as Walter asked, "What can we do?"

As soon as Tabby was done with her hug, Lotta stood straight and raised her head high. "I need you both to be here tonight. We're putting up signs announcing the cancelation of tonight's performance, but it's too late to put a note in the paper. People will be showing up at the door wanting to see a show. I need you to work the ticket booth. Give them refunds or make exchanges, but always explain how this is a family tragedy and it can't be helped. Tell them how sorry I am. Tomorrow's show will go on as scheduled. Ma's staying with him, but I'm coming home."

"You sure about that?" Tabby asked. "Everyone will understand if you need more time off."

"No, they won't," Lotta told her.

Tabby started to argue, but Walter touched her arm to stop her. The stage was Lotta's life. To other people, it might seem as if singing, telling jokes and dancing would be hard after such a disaster, but it was the way Lotta handled everything, good and bad.

The tour would go on.

* * *

Around two in the morning, when they were on tour in Cincinnati, Walter was woken by pounding on the door of the hotel room he shared with John and by Mary Ann screaming, "Crabtree! Are you in there?"

Walter glanced at John's bed and saw the blankets thrown back. He had snuck out while Walter slept. Walter got up and let Mary Ann into the room.

"He broke into my trunk, stole all the earnings from our last couple of stops. Do you have any idea where he might be?"

Walter was certain John was at a local, all night tavern, but since they hadn't been in Cincinnati very long, he had no idea where the man went to drink. "I'll go look for him," he told Mary Ann, which seemed to calm the woman a bit. "There can't be many alehouses open at this hour."

It seemed the further Walter walked from the hotel, the darker the streets became. There were still a few gaslights flickering. They helped but didn't provide enough light to see anything other than the streetlamps themselves from a distance. There was no moon out that night, which didn't help, either.

There was no way Walter could know where John had headed, so he chose a street at random, which was a mistake since it happened to be bordered by a dark park. There was enough light to see he was alone, no shadows of figures in front or behind. Overall this was good, although if an attacker did appear there would be no one to hear his cry for help.

Walter cut back on a street where there seemed to be a little more light and saw what appeared to be an open tavern. That would be a place where John might go. Yet when he got there and stepped inside, he didn't see Lotta's pa. He did discover a number of young women who hiked their skirts and tried to get him to stay. The scene reminded Walter of the first time he met Tabby, but his thoughts quickly shifted to the other woman he met that day, Ru.

He hadn't heard from Ru or Frank in more than a month and the few letters he had received in New York and Chicago had been brief. Frank's skill at writing was less than his own and Ru was as illiterate as Tabby had been when the Crabtree's first took her in. Yet Walter hoped for some limited news or at least a note saying they were fine. He received a couple of letters in Chicago, but since then there'd been nothing, even though he had sent his friends a copy of Lotta's schedule.

Walter left the tavern and decided to head back to the hotel, returning by the way he had come. He started to pass the park again, but this time he decided to take a closer look. He could see the streetlamps on the other side, so it wasn't a big area. Still, there were benches where someone might lie down and shrubs where a person might hide. If John decided against drinking in a saloon, this would be a perfect place to down a bottle of whiskey alone.

There was a man lying on his belly. When Walter saw him, he thought this might be John, but when he turned the body over, he was greeted with a volley of curses and then, "Leave a man in peace, you asswipe."

It was not John, just a different drunk, one who clearly did not want assistance. Walter walked away but continued the full length of the park. If one person was spending the night there, another might be hiding a short distance away. When he was done searching the park, Walter started down side streets. Even though he was close to the hotel, he would weave around a bit before returning. When Walter finally entered the room it was half past three and John still wasn't there. There didn't seem to be much else Walter could do, so he went to bed. In the morning, Mary Ann reported the theft.

Although a few days passed, the tour was still in Cincinnati when Tabby told Walter, John had been caught. "He was in New York. The police recognized him coming off a train. Apparently, all the publicity helped, although Lotta's still not happy about that. She and Mary Ann have been arguing about the next step. Since Lotta's no longer a child, he has no claim to her money and can go to jail. That's what Mary Ann thinks should happen. Lotta wants to say he didn't steal anything and should go free."

Walter whistled. "Sounds like Lotta's gonna win this one. Even though Mary Ann controls their finances, the money is Lotta's. If she doesn't want to say it's stolen, she doesn't have to."

"Maybe you're right. I don't know. Lotta and her ma are at the Western Union now, sending telegrams back and forth, trying to settle things."

The show went on that night and was great, as always. The compromise they reached was to send John to England. They'd been talking about sending him there for so long, Walter had thought it would never happen. This mess had forced the issue.

John wanted to go back, to see his friends and family. Now he was going to get to do that, but with a major difference. He wasn't allowed to return. Mary Ann was arranging this by providing him with a monthly pension. If he came back to the States, he'd lose the income and wouldn't have anything to live on.

Turned out John had gone to New York to see the boys. Mary Ann thought his reason showed he had something good going on inside. She agreed to send Ash and George along to England with him. They could finish their education in a boarding school over there. George's wounds had healed, but he was maimed. Mary Ann wanted to get him away from whatever had pushed him into trying something so foolish. This solution seemed to help all around. Although Lotta told Walter she would miss her pa.

The tour continued.

Chapter Sixteen

Triumphant Return

After three years on the road, it was time for Lotta to return to New York. Her reputation had not only recovered from the disastrous performance at Niblo's Saloon but was greater than it had ever been. She'd performed in large cities across the country including Boston and Chicago, all to tremendous acclaim. Clifton Tayleure, a Broadway producer, contacted Mary Ann and offered Lotta a role in two short plays to be performed together: *The Pet of the Petticoats* and *Family Jars*. Only fourteen performances were scheduled, but if the show was successful there would be other offers.

Lotta played Paul in the first show, which gave her the opportunity to dress in men's clothing, something she'd been doing more of, both on and off stage. In *The Pet*, she wore a fancy white suit with a matching stovepipe hat, an outfit that helped her appear debonaire. She played to a full house on opening night and gave as fine a performance as she ever had.

When the show ended Walter was certain Lotta's return to New York would be a victory. The reviews would come out the following day and he'd been around long enough to know they'd be good. There had been wonderful energy in the show, not just from Lotta, but also from all the supporting actors. And the audience reactions had been tremendous. This time Lotta had conquered New York.

Walter went to Lotta's dressing room to congratulate her, but he also had something important to discuss. He had waited for the perfect time and he figured this was it. She would be in a great mood after everything had gone so well.

He knocked on the door.

"Who's there?" Lotta called out.

"Walter," he replied.

"Good. Come in."

She was dressed in a white chemise. It was an undergarment, but one she slept in as well. He'd been living with her family long enough to have seen her like this more often than he could remember.

"I'm glad you're here. I need help dressing."

"You're wearing a dress?"

"Ma says I have to since the reception will be formal."

"Can we talk while I help you?"

"Of course."

Walter picked up her corset and wrapped it around her midsection. He started to tighten the laces in the back. "I've grown very close to Tabby over these last few years."

Lotta's arms hung loosely at her side. "I know," she said. "I've seen you two together. I'm very glad for you both." Walter pulled tighter and she said, "Ouch. That's a bit too much."

"Sorry." He loosened her laces a little.

Lotta had stopped dancing with Walter when the tour started keeping her busy almost every night. He hadn't known if her schedule was the only reason or if the end of the dance practices also had to do with the way he and Tabby acted around each other. Her comment hinted at an answer to that question and made what he had to discuss a little easier.

He finished with the corset laces and reached for her petticoat. He slipped it over her head then tied that as well. He took a step back from her and rubbed his hands on his trouser legs. "I'm planning to ask for her hand in marriage."

Lotta spun and faced Walter. "Oh!" she said, her hands going to her chest. "Why are you telling me? Do you want my blessing?"

"I guess I do."

"Why? You do know those silly contracts are done. You have no need to ask me first."

"But I work for you. So does Tabby. I didn't want you to hear this from someone else."

Lotta smiled and sighed. "And I hope you will continue to work with me, both of you. You have my blessing and my good wishes, but you're free to do whatever you want to do. Now hand me my corset cover and help me straighten my bustle. I don't need your help for the rest. Go ask her and don't tell anyone else. Tabby's the one who shouldn't hear this from anyone but you."

Walter was surprised Lotta was so accepting of his intentions toward Tabby. In the back of his mind, he thought she had still been competing for his attention. Truth was, Lotta was a career woman. Nothing would ever come between her and her time on stage.

Walter found Tabby waiting in the theater seats. Other than her and a couple of stagehands straightening the set for the next day, the theater was empty.

She had dressed for the theater and the reception in an outfit Mary Ann had bought her. It was the prettiest dress Walter had ever seen on her, blue-green with tan trim, The top was sleeveless, but she wore it over a beige bodice with long sleeves. The skirt puffed out a bit, but not too much for her to have trouble sitting. She probably had a few petticoats underneath, but no crinoline and only a small bustle. It had a short train that extended about two feet behind her. She was also wearing a matching hat.

"Hello," Walter said, as he sat next to Tabby. "Mind if I wait here with you?"

"Please do," she told him. "It was a wonderful show. Is Lotta happy?"

"She seemed to be, but I imagine she's still worried about the reviews."

"I'm sure they'll be good."

A young man yelled to the two stagehands from offstage. "Miss Lotta needs to see you in her dressing room"

That was nice of her, Walter thought, as the men left him alone with Tabby.

Walter took a couple of quick breaths, bit his lip gently, then said, "Tabby?"

She cocked her head a bit.

"We've been together a long time now."

"Years," she said, "but I don't think that's too long. Do you?"

"No. You don't understand what I'm trying to say. I don't think I could have survived everything we've gone through without your help and your advice."

"No. It's me. I couldn't have survived without *your* help. Odell would have killed me if you hadn't done what you did and you know it."

Walter shook his head. "But there's more to it than just me being there at the right time. Something about you made me do whatever I could to help. But what I'm trying to say is everything we did together turned out right. Look where we are. Look how good life is. Before you, my pa was my family and everything back then was all twisted and messed up. That is—until he led me to you and life changed. That's what I mean. It isn't just circumstances. It's a feeling, a connection that draws the best out of me and out of you, too—I hope. I never want to give that connection up."

"Why do you think you have to?"

"I don't think I do, but who knows—if we don't make something more permanent."

"Permanent?"

"Yes. I just think the more time we spend beside each other the better off we are, both of us."

"I agree with that. I never want to lose your friendship."

"Yes and I never want to lose yours. And more than that, I never want to lose you. If that makes sense. It's something I've given a lot of thought to."

Walter squirmed about in his seat, so he could reach in his pocket.

"I want to show you something I bought. I saved a long time to get this and I hope you like it."

Walter stood, stepped into the aisle, then got down on one knee. Tabby's mouth was open. She was starting to say something, but it was apparent she couldn't think of the right words. Walter spoke, "Will you marry me, Tabby?"

"Oh! Oh!" Tabby leaned to Walter and kissed him. She brought her hands to his face and ran her fingers through his hair as she held the kiss. When they finally broke she said, "Of course I will. I can't imagine life without you."

Walter gave her the ring, a small diamond set in a gold mount. "The gold will always remind us of San Francisco," he said. She kissed him again.

They both wanted to marry as soon as they could with as simple a ceremony as possible, so they tied the knot at a justice of the peace with Mary Ann and Lotta as the witnesses. There was a party after that night's performance with all the actors, stagehands, and everyone else involved in the show invited, including John Brougham, the famous playwright who wrote *Little Nell and the Marchioness*, the show they'd opened the day after *The Pet of the Petticoats!* closed.

The Pet was a success, but *Little Nell*, a play based on *The Old Curiosity Shop* by Charles Dickens, was a huge hit. Lotta was a star rising higher every day.

Walter thought the time had come to move on from his job working with Lotta and Mary Ann. There wasn't much for him to do since Mary Ann wasn't producing the shows. The New York producers had their own crews building sets. When he combined that fact with Mary Ann and Lotta living in a hotel with maintenance people, Walter was left with a useless feeling.

"I'm not earning my keep," he told Lotta one afternoon, a couple of weeks after the wedding. "I want to move on, but I need your help."

Lotta sighed, then said, "I'll miss you."

"We'll still visit, but we're married now. We can't go on living off your goodwill forever."

"I understand, but you're welcome to stay with us as long as you want."

Walter stood straight and cocked his head slightly. "We need to leave."

"Then how can I help?"

"The thing I know best is working on sets. I was hoping you could put in a word for me with one of the local crews."

Lotta shrugged then smiled. "I'll miss you," she told him, "but I'll speak to John Brougham and we'll see what happens."

A week later Walter was working on *Little Boy Blue* at the Bowery and scheduled to work on *Columbus Reconstructed* at the Olympic and *The Demon, the Doctor and the Devil's Draught* at the Worrell Sisters' New York Theatre. He was earning enough money to afford an apartment in a small tenement in Harlem, above two stores. Harlem was a perfect place to live, with a small downtown area surrounded by farms and country homes. Yet it was close enough to the city to commute.

Their apartment took up half of the third floor, with two bedrooms, a kitchen, and a sitting room. Below them, the second floor was laid out in the same manner and the ground floor had a bakery and a dress shop. This Harlem flat was not like the overcrowded tenements often mentioned in the newspapers, the dark and dirty ones in downtown Manhattan where he was born. Each of these homes had only one couple residing there, although a family on the second floor had a couple of children, two boys.

A privy and a water pump stood in the yard behind their building, separated by enough distance to keep the well water clean. This was a step back from what they'd experienced in the hotels, where there was always at least one water-closet on each floor. Walter and Tabby would have to take turns carrying water up to their kitchen and bringing their chamber-pots down. But having a place of their own would be well worth those daily tasks.

There were always shows in New York, so building sets kept Walter busy and provided a decent income for them both. Tabby, however, wanted to contribute. She found a job as a seamstress through the woman who ran the dress shop in their building.

"You won't make much money," Walter told her when she mentioned her plans.

"I know, but I can work out of our house. It will be perfect when we have children."

"Children?" It was the first time he'd thought of being a pa. It made sense, now that they were married, but he felt his heart beating faster. His pa hadn't been a decent role model, and wasn't around long enough, so how would he know what to do?

"I haven't stopped taking the herbs yet," Tabby said. She smiled then added, "but I'm thinking about it. Wouldn't it be nice to have a little Walter?"

Walter laughed. "Or a little Tabby."

"That's right. Our first could be a girl."

"First?" He said, his voice rising a pitch higher.

"Sorry. Too far in the future. Still, there's something we have to talk about if we're thinking about having a child." Tabby cleared her throat. "A couple of the girls I worked with in Jahiel's saloon had kids who got picked on because their mothers were prostitutes. It will be much harder on our children here in the east, where women have choices we didn't have."

"Are you saying you're ashamed of what you did?"

"I survived and earned enough to help my ma save her farm, but I don't think New York people will want their children to have a friend who is the child of a whore."

"Don't use that word."

"Other people will—if they know." She wiped her hands on her skirt. "We have to think of our child's life."

Walter hesitated before saying. "You want to keep your life a secret? I'm not sure that's possible. People here know what things were like out west for single women without money."

Tabby started to rub her hands, but Walter reached over and stopped her. He held her hands and stared in her eyes for a moment before speaking. "So what do we say?" he asked. "Do we just not bring it up? Do we lie to everyone, even our own child? How far do we go?"

Tabby pulled her hands from Walter and balled them in fists. "As far as we have to," she told him.

Chapter Seventeen

Goddaughter

In late summer of 1868, more than a year and a half after Tabby and Walter first discussed having a child, Charlotte Cain was born. Their child was named after Lotta, who was also to be named the godmother at Charlotte's baptism. Tabby and Walter had attended St. James' Methodist Episcopal Church since their move to Harlem.

During the birth, Walter waited in the apartment across the hall with his neighbor, Adamo Grisi, while the midwife attended to Tabby. She was helped by Teresa Grisi, Adamo's wife. Lotta could not be with Tabby at the birth because she had to be on stage for a performance of *The Firefly*, but she came to visit the next day and many days after that.

Adamo and Teresa had met Lotta a few times prior to Charlotte's birth and were quite impressed that their neighbors had such a famous and wealthy friend.

"She's easy to talk to," Teresa told Tabby and Walter one day after Lotta left, "not at all what we expected her to be like."

"You're right," Tabby said. "Lotta hasn't forgotten her beginnings. But her ma is different. Mary Ann is concerned with what society people think about her and her family. She likes to visit with us when we go to their hotel or the theater, but I doubt she'll ever come here."

After Charlotte's birth, Lotta started coming to the apartment at least three times a week, which meant Tabby and Walter spent more time with her than they had since the tour. It also meant Lotta saw Teresa a lot since Tabby's neighbor also worked in her home as a seamstress and spent a lot of time sewing in Tabby's apartment.

The time had come for Tabby to talk to Lotta. Walter suggested they all talk at the theater since Teresa and Adamo wouldn't be there. He and Tabby arrived when Lotta's performance was drawing to a close. They entered through the stage door and waited for Lotta in her dressing room.

"There's a favor I need to ask you," Tabby told Lotta when their friend arrived.

"Anything for the mother of my godchild."

"The people in this city can't possibly understand what life was like in San Francisco and they might look down on our daughter if they knew what I did for money. Walter and I have talked this over and we don't intend to tell anyone I was a prostitute. We don't intend to tell Charlotte until she's old enough to understand and we don't intend to tell our friends, like Teresa and Adamo, ever. I don't want kids to tease Charlotte."

"I understand and I can keep a secret, but my ma could be a problem."

"Why's that?"

"She's proud of how we helped you and brags about it to her society friends. She calls your story *charity work* and hopes it will help her get in their groups. She says she's never mentioned your name, but rumors could still start. No other women have traveled with us."

Tabby straightened her skirt then said, "I didn't realize she did that."

Walter brought his right hand to his forehead. "There's not much we can do. We can't challenge her, after everything she did for us. Our only choice is to go about our day to day lives and respond the best we can if our secret comes out."

Tabby grabbed hold of Lotta's make-up table. "If it does, life will be rough for Charlotte."

"True," Walter said, speaking in a steady voice, "but Charlotte isn't going to have to go through anything close to what you went through. For one thing, I won't abandon her, like your pa did to you and your ma. You came through a life that was harder than hers will ever be, yet you got closer to Ru over the years, made a good friend. And you met me."

Tabby smiled. "That was a great thing."

Walter pressed his lips together then spoke again. "And what about me? My life was also hard. Children are always going to have hardships because the world is not perfect."

Tabby tugged at her hair before saying, "So we do nothing?"

Walter cocked his head and looked in Tabby's eyes. "The only other thing we could do is bring it out now. If we talk to Teresa and Adamo, we may find our friends are more understanding than we thought. If we do that, we control the rumors rather than letting the rumors control us."

They were all quiet until Tabby said, "Those are our only choices?"

"I can't think of another." Walter stood, walked behind Tabby, and rubbed her shoulders. "Maybe honesty is better than dealing with rumors and suspicion."

They said goodbye to Lotta, then headed home, with a lot to think about. If Adamo and Teresa were friends worth having, they would understand. That same rule would apply to Charlotte's friends, as she grew older. As far as Walter was concerned, anyone who couldn't accept Tabby for the woman she was, could go to Hell!

* * *

Teresa pushed her chair from the kitchen table, leaned back, and touched her belly. "That plum cake was wonderful, Tabby. You are a fabulous cook."

"You are much better than I am, Teresa. The liver pudding you served us last week was delicious. What did you call it?"

"Crostini di fegatini. It's a Tuscan dish."

"Tuscan?" Walter asked.

"Tuscany is the region of Italy we come from," Teresa told him. "It's my mother's recipe."

"The Chianti is excellent," Adamo said. "Is it from Italy?"

Tabby smiled. "Probably. It was a gift from Lotta."

"So kind of her," Teresa said, "and kind of you to share with us. But you said there was something you needed to tell us."

Tabby looked at the window then took in a breath before speaking. "We know you are thinking of having a family."

Adamo laughed. "I don't know if *thinking* is the right word. We are just doing what is in our nature. Bella natura!" he exclaimed, slapping his hands together.

Teresa winced but smiled slyly. "Adamo! Per favore. That's personal."

"Perdonami. Sometimes I talk too much."

Walter smiled. "You're fine. We want you to be honest with us and we want to be honest with you. That is why we need to speak to you."

"Did we do something wrong?" Teresa asked.

"No," Walter answered. "Tabby and I have talked. We want our families to always be close. We want our children to play together. We want them to grow up best friends. But, as we said, we want to be honest."

Adamo spoke. "You're not ashamed of us are you?"

"No."

"You don't think less of us because we're immigrants, do you?"

"This is about us, not you."

"How can it be about you? You were both born in this country. You are friends of Lotta Crabtree. What do you have that might make us doubt you?"

Tabby shook her head. "Let me tell the story, Walter." She hunched over, leaning her elbows on the table. "We are doing well now, but this was not always the case. I grew up in Montana, with my ma and pa who were good to me—until my pa left. Walter was raised in the gold camps near San Francisco, living in a bunkhouse. He and his pa lived day to day. On the days when his pa didn't bring any gold home and Walter didn't have luck fishing, they didn't eat. That's how bad off they were."

"You've told us this before," Adamo said.

"But I didn't tell you everything. After my pa left, my mother had trouble working the farm alone. She needed help, which cost money and she needed to pay the mortgage, which cost more money. A friend of mine, an orphan, lived with us. She and I tried to help with the farm, but we didn't succeed and, like everyone else, we had to eat. Ma would never have kicked us out, but we knew we cost more than we were worth. All three of us would probably have died if a man hadn't shown up with an offer to solve our problems. It seemed like a gift from God, but was more like Satan's work."

Tabby stood and turned from her friends. She wrapped her hands around her stomach, bent her neck, and spoke in a soft voice while facing the wall. "His name was Jahiel and he ran a saloon in San Francisco. The saloon was also a brothel. Jahiel was in Montana because times were hard there, making it a good place to look for desperate young women. That's what we were, desperate. We both signed contracts. We gave my ma enough money to save her farm, then went to the west coast with Jahiel."

Adamo gasped. "You were a whore!"

"Don't use that word!" Walter pounded his fist on the table.

"Calm down," Tabby told them both, then she sat back at the table. When Walter also sat down she continued. "I was a prostitute, but whatever word you use it's still true I sold myself to survive."

Teresa reached forward and stroked Tabby's arm. "You've changed your life, haven't you? You found God?"

"I have."

"That's what counts."

"And what about you?" Adamo asked, staring coldly at Walter. "Have you changed?"

"What…"

Tabby cut Walter off with a wave of her hand. "He has changed also. He goes to church with me and he found God there."

"I love our church," Walter told Teresa and Walter, "but it was Tabby alone who brought me to God."

"Did you know Tabby when she worked at this brothel?" Adamo asked.

Walter held his head high. "That's where I met her."

Adamo looked down and hid his face with his hands, while Teresa squeezed her eyes shut. Neither of them responded to what Walter had told them.

Tabby attempted to turn the conversation away from the subject of her history, but Teresa and Adamo were unable to comment on anything else. They finished their wine, then said goodbye and walked across the hall to their apartment.

In the weeks that followed, Walter and Tabby saw very little of Adamo and Teresa. When they passed in the hall or on the street below, they nodded but didn't smile or speak. Tabby noticed Teresa talking with Clara Mameli, the baker in the shop below the apartments, and when Tabby stepped into the shop to purchase bread, the woman seemed nervous. Tabby asked how her day had been, but Clara said she was too busy to chat.

Less than a month after their conversation, Adamo and Teresa moved out of the tenement, without saying where they were going.

* * *

Two days after the Grisis left, Clara Mameli knocked on the door of Walter and Tabby's apartment. Clara was a short, Italian woman in her mid-fifties with salt and pepper hair and the energy of someone half her age.

"I bought this building," the smiling baker told them as she stood at their door, holding a plate with three pastries on it. "I'm your landlord now."

"Come in," Walter said, stepping aside and gesturing toward the kitchen table.

Tabby, who was standing behind Walter and holding Charlotte, also stepped to the side so Clara could pass. "May I offer you coffee?"

"That would be nice. I take mine with a little sugar. These are cannoli siciliani. I brought them to share with you."

Tabby moved to hand Charlotte to Walter, but Clara stopped her. "May I hold the baby?"

Clara seemed to be approaching them in friendship, but Walter was wary. Tabby had told him how she'd seen her talking with Teresa.

"I wish to assure you that your rent will not be going up for at least a year," Clara said as she sat at the table then took the baby from Tabby. Walter joined Clara, taking a seat beside her. Normally, Walter would not have been happy thinking about any rent increase, even one a year away. But he'd been worried she might kick them out, so the idea that she expected them to be living there for at least a year thrilled him.

"So this is a social call?" Tabby asked as she bent to light the fire in the stove. While she waited for the fire to get going, she added water to the coffee pot from the bucket on the counter.

"You've been my neighbors for a long time, but now you're my tenants as well. I'd like to get to know you better. I've never held your baby before now. I love children, but never had any."

"Her name is Charlotte. She's four months old, born on April 4th."

"Charlotte is a lovely name."

"Thank you. She's named after her godmother."

"Are you Catholic?"

"No, Methodist Episcopal, but we named a godmother anyway."

The conversation went on as the coffee started to perk, moving from how beautiful Charlotte was to the recent hot weather. Clara was smiling and talking, but not saying much of substance. They didn't eat the pastries until the coffee was ready. That's when the conversation changed, as well.

"I've rented the Grisi apartment to another Italian couple, Alina and Francesco Solera," Clara told them. "They'll move in sometime next week. He's a house painter, but couldn't get much work downtown. He thinks he'll do well out here where there are farmhouses and barns."

"That will be nice," Tabby said. "We miss having a couple living next door."

Walter nodded in agreement.

"Now, this isn't easy and might be none of my business, but I have to say something to you both." Clara held Charlotte with her right hand as she scratched her forehead with her left. "I lost my husband on the boat when we were traveling from Italy. He was stabbed. They never knew who did it, but I suppose Gino was in a fight over something that didn't matter. He was like that."

"We're sorry," Tabby said.

"Thank you," Clara replied. "We were newly married, headed to America to make our fortune. I woke up that morning a married woman and by that night I was single with little money and no way to make more."

"Couldn't you bake?" Walter asked.

"I didn't know how—not back then. And in the downtown tenements, nobody baked anything fancy. I had nothing, no place to live and no food. I had to beg. I was on the streets for about a week when a man took me in and gave me a place to stay, a single room with three other young women. It was crowded, but I had a bed, food, clean clothes, access to a cooking stove, and a place where I could take a bath. To me, it was luxury. We were all young. I was eighteen and only one of the girls was over twenty. He would take us out at night to meet men on the street."

"Oh," Tabby said. "Did they hurt you?"

"He protected us from the violent ones," Clara told her. "In that way, I guess I was lucky. He also paid us a little more than the room and board, which was better than the other men who kept girls. I saved my money, made friends with someone who taught me to bake, and ended up with this shop, way up here, away from downtown." She paused for a moment then looked straight at Tabby. "What I'm trying to say is that it was fortunate the Grisis left. I don't like gossips and Teresa gossiped like a wash woman. I don't know if the Soleras will be more discreet, so I'm asking you to keep your secret, as I've kept mine. Honesty is nice, but I don't want trouble. There are things that should stay private."

The cannolis were delicious, a smooth, sweet filling wrapped in crisp fried dough. Walter had never tasted a dessert he liked more. He nodded to Clara as she handed Charlotte back to Tabby. "Thank you for bringing these," he said before he popped the last bite in his mouth. He wanted to tell her they would keep the secret, but his mouth was full of pastry.

"I'm not ashamed of how I lived out there," Tabby said to Clara.

"Neither am I," she responded, "but we're living with many people who've just arrived from Italy or Ireland, with old country ideas. We have to adapt to circumstances."

"We worried people would learn about me even if I didn't tell them." Tabby explained. "We didn't want to seem like we were hiding something."

"I understand," Clara said as she took her empty plate and headed for the door. "Trust is a good thing, but knowing who and when to trust is better." She stepped into the hall and Walter closed the door behind her.

"I like her," Tabby told Walter as soon as Clara was gone.

"I do, too. She's a strong woman and has done well for herself."

"In some ways," Tabby replied, her voice breaking slightly, "but she has no children. I wonder if that is a result of her time on the streets."

Chapter Eighteen
The Return Tour

In 1869 the transcontinental railroad was completed, which meant a trip from New York to California would now take ten days, instead of a month and a half. To Lotta, this meant a homecoming was possible.

Mary Ann would go with her, of course, but Lotta hoped for someone younger, someone she could do things with during the long days. She went to Tabby and Walter's home and asked them to go, but Charlotte was an issue. The girl was too young to travel.

"I went from camp to camp when I was not much older than she is," Lotta argued, "on horseback."

"She's a year old," Tabby said, "not six like you were. Even if she was five years older, I'd still think she was too young to cross the country. I worry about train robbers, among other things. San Francisco is a long way and you're not coming straight back."

"Then would you like to come, Walter?" Lotta asked. She turned to Tabby and added, "I promise I won't lure him into my bed."

Walter laughed, while Tabby offered only a weak smile.

"I have to work," Walter told her.

"Then how about you, Tabby?" Lotta suggested. "I'll pay you much more than you can make sewing and I'm sure your employer will welcome you back when we return."

"I have to take care of Charlotte."

"Walter can handle her when he's not working and I'll pay Alina to take her the rest of the time. You trust her and Francesco, right?"

"I do."

"I'll also pay them to make Walter's meals." Lotta leaned back in her chair and shrugged her shoulders. "They would get money, you would get much more than you're used to earning, and I would get a companion. Everyone wins."

"Not having Tabby at home with me would break my heart," Walter said quickly.

Tabby nodded, then said, "And I'd have to leave both Walter and Charlotte."

"You could come with us to San Francisco, then skip the rest of the tour," Lotta suggested.

"How long will you be there?"

"We're stopping by Salt Lake City for a performance, then we'll finish the ride out to Sacramento. After that, we take a river steamer down the Sacramento to the San Francisco Bay. Once in the city, we're booked for a six-week performance, but you don't have to stay for the entire run. You could come with me and be back in four to six weeks. Charlotte won't forget you in that short time."

Tabby looked at Walter. Her eyebrows were raised and she was biting at the inside of her cheek. Walter wanted to tell her no, but he could see she was thinking about the offer. Her life was secure, but it lacked excitement. He knew she'd feel some regrets if she didn't go.

"We can work this out," Walter told her, feeling a breath catch in his chest as he spoke the words. "It would give you a chance to see Ru again."

"That's true. I do miss her."

Lotta looked back and forth between Tabby and Walter. "You can write him," she told Tabby, a pleased expression on her face.

Tabby took Walter's hand. "I promise I'll be back as soon as I can."

* * *

Walter received the first letter from Tabby more than two weeks after the day she was expected to arrive at Salt Lake City. Thanks to years of Bible lessons, Tabby could read and write ably and she had worked with Walter to help him improve his skills.

Since Lotta was paying Alina to cook for Walter, she and Francesco shared their company as well. He and Charlotte ate their suppers in their neighbors flat and Clara also joined them. Alina provided the main meal and ale, Clara brought bread and sometimes cake, and Walter brought along the letters from Tabby.

Walter read the letters aloud. When he first thought of sharing Tabby's notes, he decided he would omit any sections he considered too personal. He changed his mind as he read them the first letter because he found that his friends cared about his wife and Lotta too much to skip any sections.

My Darling Walter,

The train ride was fun at first, but long. I slept in a Pullman Car, in a compartment in the same car as Mary Ann and Lotta. There were beds on one side and plush chairs on the other, so with the exception of our meals in the dining car, we spent all our time in the car where we slept. The car did not have bunk beds as I was expecting, so there was a good amount of privacy, although only a curtain separated me from the aisle and the other passengers. It took a while to get used to the rocking of the train, but once I did, I slept well.

Lotta has a performance scheduled for the night after we arrive in Salt Lake City. The following day they intend to catch a train and head on to Sacramento. I'm looking forward to getting there, transferring to the paddle boat, and riding down to San Francisco Bay. I wrote Ru to let her know I will be in town, but I doubt my letter will get there before I do. Your letter will also be delayed. I expect you might be reading this after we've been in San Francisco for a couple of days.

There is a reason why I am glad I came on this trip with Lotta. Although we've seen a lot of her since Charlotte was born, this is the first time in years we've had a chance to sit alone. The Pullman car we are in has enough length for us to find a place where we can talk without Mary Ann hearing us.

Lotta has had a chance to express a problem to me. She is lonely, very lonely. I don't know if she ever mentioned Bolton Hulme to you. She met him in New York after he attended her performances more than anyone else, even Mary Ann. He followed her when she was on one of her tours. I believe Lotta liked him, but Mary Ann didn't approve. He was a member of a rich family, but didn't have either status or money of his own. He just passed away and Lotta is grieving. She wishes she hadn't listened to her ma and had allowed her relationship with him to go further. So there's regret there, too.

The life of a star isn't as easy as some think it is. People recognize her on the street, so she can't go many places she wants to go. When she meets people, she can't be sure if they like her for herself or if they have hopes she can help their careers.

Her mother is her best friend. They spend a lot of time alone in their hotel room in whatever city they're performing, playing cards and other games. That's why she was so intent on one of us coming with her. The only time she has ever had close friends was when you and I were working at her home in San Francisco. When she was young she was alone, moving from camp to camp and after we moved to New York, she was too busy for any friends, even us.

She's tried to get to know some of the other actors and stagehands, but as you know theater people stay in their own groups. Stars spend their time with other stars, while chorus people stay among their own. Relationships with men are even more difficult for her. Mary Ann is still very particular about who she will allow Lotta to see, because of her desire to make friends in New York society. Lotta has become a loner, but I don't think she wants to be alone.

We think of our problems, of how hard we have to work to put food on the table, but famous people have their issues, too. I'll write more about this after I've talked with her again.

Your loving wife,

Tabby

Before sending this letter, I wish to add this.

We drove through Salt Lake City on our way from the train station to our hotel. The city reminds me of other small cities, not nearly as busy as New York or Chicago. There is a huge Mormon church known as Temple Square, which is twice as tall as any of the other buildings near it. The theater is near Temple Square, but we won't see it until tomorrow. I will write more about the city after I've had a chance to see other parts.

I hope things are going well with you and with Charlotte and Alina is careful with our daughter. I miss you every day.

Again, your loving wife,

Tabby

Clara wrinkled her nose. "That's a surprise," she said.

Alina agreed. "I've only met Lotta a few times, but she seemed happy."

"You only see her when she comes to visit Charlotte. She's away from the stress of her career and her mother," Walter said. He paused for a moment then added in a softer voice, "And she loves her goddaughter. It makes sense she's happy here."

"She's an actress. How can you know what she's feeling?" Clara asked.

"She's not on stage," Walter responded.

"What does that mean?"

Alina leaned in toward the others around her table. "I believe Walter is saying actresses make up their feelings when they are on stage, but off stage they are like everyone else. They feel their own joys and sorrows."

"How would you know?"

"I don't, not for certain, but it makes sense, doesn't it?" Alina said. "Even though Lotta is rich, she has her problems. Money isn't everything."

"Maybe you're right," Clara told her, "but not having enough can make life hard."

* * *

Two letters had arrived at the same time, but Walter decided to wait until the next day to read the second.

My Darling Walter,

We've just arrived in Sacramento. The train ride was pleasant. We rode in a rail car as plush as the one we rode in on our way from New York to Salt Lake City.

Lotta was as fabulous as ever during her performance in the Prophet's theater. The theater is impressive, as big as a courthouse with pillars in the front. Inside, it looks a bit like a church because the audience sits on long benches that resembled pews, although the best seat in the house is an upholstered rocking chair, set right in the middle. It's reserved for the Prophet himself, Brother Brigham Young.

The stage is large, tall, and deep, with two levels of box seats on both sides. They used prepainted backdrops for Lotta's performance, but they were nice. I sat toward the back because I've seen Lotta dance many times. This time I wanted to see the reaction of the audience.

She was a hit, but I was glad when we left Salt Lake City. A reception was held after her performance where she got to meet Brigham Young. He was enthralled with her, which seemed a little awkward. He's much older than she is and has multiple wives. A practice that is allowed in this city.

I believe Lotta could have stayed there and married President Young, if she'd wanted to be another one on the list. I did get a chance to talk to Lotta during the train ride. She had been pleased to meet President Young (he is the second president of their church). She was impressed with what he had done in the city, the making of Temple Square and of course, the theater. She was also quite impressed with the man himself. I asked her what she thought of the many wives and she said she would rather share a man with other women than not have one at all. I couldn't tell if she was joking, but I thought the comment was sad.

Your loving wife,

Tabby

Clara raised an eyebrow then said, "We're back on Lotta's loneliness again."

Walter nodded. "I was expecting to hear more about Tabby's feelings and less about Lotta's. But that is typical of my wife. She puts others before herself."

Alina placed a hand on her chest. "That is so sweet of you to talk about your wife that way. Why don't you ever say things like that, Francesco?"

"You make me look bad," Francesco told Walter. He laughed a little when he spoke, so it was clear he wasn't angry. "Some people are good with words, others with actions."

"That's you," Alina said, rolling her eyes, "a man of action."

It seemed as if an argument might be starting, so Walter switched the subject back to Lotta. "Most of Lotta's problems come from her mother. If Mary Ann wasn't so protective and such a social climber, Lotta could meet normal people."

Clara sat up straight, then asked, "You think normal people are nicer than rich people? Are you sure? Seems to me poor people would be after her money more than the rich would."

"Everyone wants money," Francesco said, "even the ones who have too much."

Walter clenched his jaw. "I need to write Tabby back. I should suggest something for Lotta and I don't know what to say."

"Tell her to take Lotta out once they arrive in San Francisco," Alina suggested. "She needs to get away from her mother."

* * *

That evening Walter wrote the following:

Tabby my love,

Charlotte and I are both doing fine, but we miss you. I wish I could be traveling with you and I am sure Charlotte feels the same. She cries out for her "Mama" often.

It sounds from your letters that you are having quite an adventure. Salt Lake City seems an unusual place. I can't imagine why a man would want multiple wives, especially a wealthy man, like Brigham Young, rather than a poor man who might need help on a farm or in a shop. For me you are everything I need and everything I've ever wanted.

I am concerned for Lotta after reading your letters. I had no idea she was feeling sad. Although I know I was not truly happy before I had my family, I thought Lotta's career was enough for her. She always seems so happy on stage and, when the performance goes well, she seems happy off stage as well. Yet it makes sense that a sensitive woman like her would want someone to share her happiness.

Charlotte and I are having our suppers with Clara, Alina, and Francesco. This daily meal has turned into quite a social event. Recently, we've been discussing your letters and your conversations with Lotta. I hope that is all right with you. Our friends are all helpful and kind people.

Alina suggested that you take Lotta out to places around San Francisco. I realize she will have a full schedule and that you wish to visit with Ru. But if you can find time to take Lotta to places she might enjoy, we all believe it would lighten her mood. Alina also feels that getting her away from her mother would be helpful.

I've told you the story of the day Lotta went fishing with Frank and me. She expressed her loneliness way back then, but I thought she'd overcome those feelings during the time we all worked together in San Francisco. I'm saddened to hear they've come back. You might take her for a trip to the old house. Perhaps some happy memories would help.

Please keep your letters coming. They are such a joy to receive.

With all my love. Your husband,

Walter

It seemed a bit foolish to be sending advice to Tabby when the delay between sending mail and receiving it across the country could be weeks, but Walter felt satisfaction in sharing suggestions even if Tabby wouldn't get them on time. Two days later Walter received another letter from Tabby.

My Darling Walter,

We have arrived and settled at our hotel in San Francisco. Lotta is scheduled for a six-week run. Her first performance was last night and went exceptionally well. She opened with "Little Nell," but her schedule includes many other shows, The "Pet of the Petticoats" and "Firefly" among others. Last night's performance competed with a show at the brand new California Theater starring John Brougham in "Shylock." Lotta's show was sold out. Brougham's was not. She doesn't like to talk about it since the manager there is an old friend, but I can brag about her.

She performed exceptionally well, which I believe was because she was back in San Francisco. Everyone loves her here and she loves the city.

I went by the saloon to find Ru, but she no longer works there. It seems she and Frank have married and are living on a wheat farm outside the city. I found their home and we had a great visit. Frank was in the fields, but Ru called him back to visit.

Ru reminded me how she once told you she'd be selling pokes for as long as men would have her. Those words turned out to be empty when she found love. She and Frank are perfect for each other and, best news of all, Ru is pregnant.

Frank asked about you. I told him you were building sets for shows in New York. I said you were a carpenter, a painter, and a general handyman. He was impressed. He said to say "hi" and here I made the only mistake of my visit. I suggested he write to you. It seems Frank and Ru have only learned enough reading and writing to be sure they're not cheated at the grain mills.

Frank was surprised when I told him you can read most anything now. I said I learned by studying the Bible and suggested they might find a church in town that would help them the same way Lotta helped me. He didn't seem interested. He said he knew as much about reading as he needed to know and as for religion, he found God in the wheat fields, the forests that surrounded those fields, and the sky that brought the sun and rain. I wish they could find God the way we have, but they understand the beauty and magic of planting a seed and watching it grow. That's important.

Your loving wife,

Tabby

Walter did not bring this letter to supper, to read to the others. Instead, he talked about parts of what she'd written and kept other parts to himself. Everyone at the table accepted his decision to keep some of her words private. Still, they didn't hesitate to ask questions.

"She didn't bring up Lotta's problems this time?" Clara asked.

"Lotta's starting a six-week run. At this time her mind is too occupied to think about anything else and Tabby had other things to do. Remember, San Francisco was her home for many years."

"So she visited friends," Clara said, smiling. "I've always dreamed of going back to Italy one day, to see the friends I knew as a child."

Alina looked straight at Walter. "Did you send our suggestions?" she asked, changing the subject back to Tabby.

Walter fidgeted with the cup of beer she had given him. "I did, but Tabby hasn't read them yet. The mail takes weeks even if the conditions are perfect."

"Lotta needs a man," Francesco said, spitting out his words. "Tabby taking her around town won't help with that."

Walter could tell Francesco had given this some thought and was eager to express his own view, especially to his wife.

Alina tilted her head and looked at her husband. "She's not going to meet anyone if she stays in her hotel room."

"She has money. Why doesn't she hire a matchmaker?" Francesco asked.

It was a surprise how suddenly the subject had jumped back to Lotta's loneliness, but Walter was glad it had. "Arrangements can be made in society," Walter told Francesco. "The problem is the Crabtrees aren't accepted by society, so Lotta could find a husband, just not one her mother would approve of. Society is made up of people whose families have been wealthy for generations. They look down on anyone self-made, especially if the money came from acting."

"Snobs!" Francesco said his lip curling.

"Exactly," Walter agreed. "But there's also the problem that Lotta probably wants to find her own husband. She's very different from her mother."

Clara sighed. "Not every woman needs a husband, you know?" she told Walter. "Mine managed to get himself killed and I'm still alive."

"But Lotta is lonely," Alina said, reaching out to Clara and touching her arm.

"There are other ways to find people to talk to."

Alina looked toward Francesco. "True, but it is not so easy to find someone who will listen."

Francesco turned his eyes down. "Tell us about the friend of Tabby's," he said, changing the subject. "Did you know her?"

"Her name is Ru," Walter said. "She worked with Tabby."

Clara sat up straight and brought her hand to her chest.

Walter ignored Clara's reaction and continued speaking. "Ru married my best friend, Frank."

Alina grinned. "Best friends who married best friends. How sweet."

"Spoze so," Walter told her. "Frank and I grew up together in the gold camps. Our fathers were friends for a long time, then they weren't. That's another story." Walter's voice broke. He paused, then continued in full voice. "They were engaged when we left California, but we hadn't heard anything about them since we came east. Tabby tells me they've bought a wheat farm and are doing well. They're expecting a child."

"Wonderful news," Alina said, looking at Francesco again. This time he smiled and stared back. "When is the baby due?" she asked.

"Tabby didn't say."

Chapter Nineteen

New Orleans

At supper the next evening, Clara told Walter she had a telegram for him. "It's from Tabby. I convinced the man from Western Union to leave it with me since you weren't home." She handed him the paper sheet.

Walter Cain

Will be returning a month later than expected. Going to New Orleans with Lotta. Will explain further in mail. Give my blessing to Alina, Francesco, and Clara. Give Charlotte love and kisses from her ma.

Your loving wife, Tabby

"I'm sorry," Clara told him. "I know how much you miss her."

Walter stared at the telegram. "I do miss her," he said, shaking his head slowly. "I know it's only a while longer, but Charlotte and I want her home." He looked at Alina, who was holding Charlotte on her lap. It was hard to believe his little girl was a little more than a year old now.

"Lotta must have convinced her," Francesco said. "Do you think she offered more money?"

"She must have," Walter answered, "but Tabby would only agree if she thought Lotta needed her more than we do. I know Lotta is lonely, but so am I. I want my wife at home. I want her beside me when I sleep. I want to see her holding her daughter."

The conversation at supper was awkward with long gaps of silence. Walter and Charlotte went across the hall to their own flat as soon as they were done eating.

* * *

The following day a letter arrived from Tabby. Apparently, it was sent prior to her decision to stay on the tour through New Orleans.

My Darling Walter,

Lotta and I attended an art show featuring the work of Thomas Hill, who is an English artist who settled in Massachusetts but came west to paint landscapes.

Mary Ann was thrilled we were attending his exhibition. It was set up in the house of a couple who are members of San Francisco's Society. Although Mary Ann wished to impress them, they certainly didn't impress us. I don't remember either the woman's name or the name of her husband and Lotta doesn't either. Still, the show was fascinating and the paintings so beautiful I felt I could walk right in them. The show will be displayed for a month, by invitation only. This was a party to celebrate the first day the paintings could be viewed together.

Thomas Hill knew Lotta from her stage work and was pleased she had taken the time to see his paintings. There were many society people at the art show, all in fancy dresses and suits. I thought this might be an opportunity for her to connect with someone, but Mr. Hill took a great deal of her time, showing her each painting individually and explaining what he was trying to accomplish with each brush stroke. Lotta was thrilled, but I didn't think this was good. He is married and much older than she is, so he is not a potential suitor. Mary Ann also spoke with Mr. Hill for a good length of time. She seems to like him because, like her, he came to America from England and found success.

Perhaps at another art show, God will touch Lotta with a blessing that can solve her loneliness. She says that as long as she has me she isn't lonely, but when she speaks that way, I wonder if I am helping or hurting. As you know, good friends are wonderful, but no substitute for someone who matches your mind, body, and soul. I encouraged her to keep trying.

During the carriage ride back to our hotel, Lotta spoke of nothing but the artwork, of the form and the colors and how a landscape can bring someone into a different world. She said she is jealous of Thomas Hill because his paintings will last for years while her dancing is over when each show ends.

Ru and Frank have invited me to have dinner with them tonight while Lotta is performing. I caught up with much of the news yesterday, but there's is so much Ru and I need to tell each other. I've told her about Charlotte, but I didn't get into many details. With her expecting her own baby, I think it will be nice to tell her of some of the problems as well as the joys.

Ru did tell me of one rumor she heard, that I want to pass on to you. It seems Odell was killed, shot by a woman, which seems appropriate. I know he was in Nevada when it happened, but I don't know anything else.

I am looking forward to the day when I will see you again. I can't tell you how much I miss your smile and your strong arms.

Your loving wife,

Tabby

Alina, Francesco, and Clara lost interest in Tabby's letters when the content Walter shared moved from Lotta's loneliness to her interest in art. (Lotta and Tabby went to three more art shows after Thomas Hill's.) Of Walter's three friends, Alina seemed most interested in other people's problems. She loved to solve them, or at least to feel as if they would have been solved had people taken her advice.

Walter considered Alina to be a bit of a busybody, but he understood the argument that she was interested because she cared. He didn't know why she cared so much about Lotta. The two had met a number of times when Lotta came over to see Charlotte, but they'd never talked one-on-one, at least not to his knowledge. For this reason, Walter thought Alina's interest in Lotta's problems might be a tendency to gossip, especially since Lotta was well-known.

Tabby also wrote of her desire to get back to New York, to see Walter and Charlotte. Walter wanted to believe his wife missed him and their daughter, but the telegram he'd received confused him. Finally, a letter arrived explaining why Tabby decided to go to New Orleans.

My Darling Walter,

I will be returning to New York a month later than expected. I know you will receive my telegram before you read this letter, so this shouldn't be a surprise to you.

Mary Ann approached me and offered me $2,000 to stay in San Francisco until Lotta's show closed, then to follow them to New Orleans and, while there, to help convince Lotta to spend time with various gentlemen she intends to introduce to her daughter. Mary Ann wanted me to stay the entire time they are in New Orleans. I managed to convince her to limit my time there to three weeks.

Including the extra week in San Francisco, I will be away from you for a month more than we expected and possibly a few days beyond that. I will be returning after the three weeks in New Orleans, even though the show will still be running. She has promised me that much.

I feel awful about this arrangement for a number of reasons. Of course, the extra month of missing you and Charlotte will be hard. Coming on this tour has already been the most difficult decision of my life, far outweighing the hard decision to leave Montana to work with Jahiel.

I once told you I sold my body, but not my soul. Now, I am accepting money to break a promise I made to you and to help convince a friend of something that could affect the rest of her life. These betrayals make me feel I have crossed the line and sold my soul.

I do want to say one thing in my defense. Although I will be accepting money to help convince Lotta to consider the men her mother has picked, I will not be doing this only for the money. Some people are meant to be on their own. Lotta is not one of those. I believe in Mary Ann's plan.

I already regretted traveling while you two were left behind, managing on your own. I hope you can understand my decision and forgive me. Remember, with the extra $2,000, Charlotte's future will be secure.

Please arrange for Alina and Francesco to continue to watch Charlotte when you are unavailable. Mary Ann promises to pay them twice as much for their time during this extra month.

I miss you now. I will miss you when I'm in New Orleans. And for the rest of my life, whenever I am apart from you, I will always miss you.

Your loving wife,

Tabby

Walter needed to talk about Tabby's latest letter at the supper table because it confirmed that he would need Alina and Francesco's assistance with Charlotte for an extra month. Fortunately, Alina who spent the most time with Walter's daughter was happy to continue working for Mary Ann, which she'd already told him when Tabby's telegram arrived.

"We appreciate the extra money," Francesco told Walter, nodding at Alina. "We've already paid a few debts with what Alina has earned and this double pay will help even more."

The conversation quickly turned to the idea that Mary Ann would be arranging for Lotta to meet some potential suitors. Walter told them Tabby was staying the extra time because her presence made Lotta comfortable. He did not tell them about the rest of the arrangement between Tabby and Mary Ann, because it was a secret. He didn't want to accidentally interfere with the relationship between his wife and one of his best friends.

Walter received a few more letters from Tabby, only one short letter from New Orleans.

My Darling Walter,

We've been in New Orleans for most of the day. We came by rail and steamboat, went to the St. Charles Hotel to settle, then took a tour of the city. It's a busy place with lots of people, trolleys, tall buildings, churches, and parks. It is closer in size to San Francisco than New York, but it feels like a bigger city.

Lotta has decided to be baptized while she's here. She's joining the Episcopal Church in a couple of days, but the ceremony will be in her hotel room. I guess scheduling a baptism in a public place for a woman as famous as Lotta would cause too much of a stir. I brought up her beliefs a few times when we were alone, but she didn't want to talk about God. I think the baptism may be another of Mary Ann's attempts to raise Lotta's status in society. Hopefully, I'm wrong about that.

I miss you more each day and I'm looking forward to getting back to New York and my family. I promise there will be no more delays.

Your loving wife,

Tabby

Tabby returned home the day after that letter arrived. That evening, she and Walter had supper with their friends. Tabby brought a check from Mary Ann to pay Alina for taking care of Walter and Charlotte. Alina turned it around a few times in her hands and stared at it, before handing it to Francesco.

"This is the first check I've seen," Francesco told her. "We were expecting cash."

"People are using checks now," Walter told him. "It's common. About half of the production crews I work on pay that way. I've never had any trouble."

Francesco pursed his lips. "I don't trust banks."

"I see," Walter said, smiling. "We'll go together to the one I use. They'll exchange your check for cash. I use the same bank as Mary Ann, so they won't have any trouble."

"Thank you," Alina said.

"Enough of that," Tabby said, her eyes sparkling. "I have some news you'll all want to hear." She laughed then said, "A man is courting Lotta"

"Finally," Alina shouted, then she stepped forward and hugged Tabby.

"Who is he?" Francesco asked.

Tabby stepped back from Alina. "He's the Grand Duke Alexis of Russia, a very important person."

"Which means Mary Ann is happy," Walter added.

Tabby continued. "Yes, very happy. He saw Lotta perform and I guess he was in the mood for romance because he contacted her the next day. He took her out on his yacht."

"Yacht?" Alina said, surprised. "Sounds like a fairy tale."

"Spoze it does," Tabby told her. "Turned out it wasn't his own boat, but this is even better. It was loaned to him by the United States government. Mary Ann is thrilled, but I worry this will be short lived. Lotta has a schedule she has to adhere to. She was still planning to go to Memphis when I left to come home. I imagine the Grand Duke has to go back to Russia, so we'll see what will happen."

"I've been following the articles about her tour," Walter told Tabby. "She told a reporter the trip to Memphis was still scheduled. She said she was looking forward to it."

Tabby sighed. "Then I guess her personal life didn't go so well, but there's still hope. Mary Ann is planning a tour of Europe. Maybe the Grand Duke will meet her there."

That night Walter went to bed first, so he was already lying on his back when Tabby joined him. They had a double, wood frame bed with a cotton stuffed mattress that Lotta had bought for them as a wedding present. It had been a long time since Tabby was beside him and for a moment he just enjoyed the small stirrings of the woman he loved.

She was on her side, facing away. He could see her in the moonlight shining through the window. He reached over and touched her at the place where her waist became her hips. He moved his fingers a little to enjoy the smooth feel of her skin.

"I missed you," Tabby rolled to face him. "I hope we never have to separate again."

Walter lifted his body slightly with one arm braced against the mattress and leaned to kiss her. Her lips were soft and wet. He loved the way she moved her mouth when she kissed. He placed his free arm over her and pulled her closer. She was dressed in the cotton chemise she had worn under her dress that day. He caressed her chest through the material, moving from one breast to the other.

"I m...missed you, too," Walter told her speaking softly. He felt awkward as if this woman he was holding was a part of his soul, yet, at the same time, a stranger. He always understood her so well, but this night he wasn't sure. He knew what he wanted, but Tabby had been traveling just that morning. He knew she was tired, but didn't know if she wanted to sleep.

When she reached over and pulled his body close, he had the answer. She missed him enough to want him more than she wanted rest. He kissed her again.

"When you were in San Francisco, you looked for men for Lotta?" he asked even though he already knew the answer.

"I did. She and I went to art shows and other events in the city during the afternoons when she wasn't performing. Although I looked, she wasn't interested in meeting a man that way and after Mary Ann asked me to go to New Orleans with them, I realized why. Mary Ann wasn't thinking about her daughter's loneliness, she was trying to move the family up in San Francisco's society, the mine owners, politicians, and other powerful families. Anybody Lotta might find with me wouldn't have her mother's approval, so why bother?"

Walter spoke in a dull, even voice. "Did you think any of those men were handsome?"

Tabby squeezed him a little tighter after he spoke, then said, "They couldn't compare with you, Walter. I don't need anyone else and if I ever lose you, I'll spend the rest of my life alone. I know that because there is no one else as wonderful as you."

"I want you to be happy," Walter told her, "so I'm not going anywhere."

Tabby laughed. "Come here," she said, then they kissed again. It was a long kiss and when they broke apart she wiggled a bit, sat up, pulled off her chemise, then lay still, the moonlight reflecting on her skin. "Every part of me missed you," she told him.

He reached for her again and began kissing her from her head to her toes, listening as her breath grew faster, deeper and finally into gasps that matched the combined shivers of her body and his. He now knew for certain, she had missed him as much as he had missed her.

Chapter Twenty

To Europe and Back

With Tabby home, Walter thought there would be no more letters, but one came. It was from Lotta who had begun a tour of Europe. It was addressed to Tabby. She called him into their sitting room to share it with him. He took a seat on the old sofa, while she stood by the window to read in the light.

Tabby,

I wish you were with us. The first London performance didn't go well. It would have been nice to have you to talk to.

We decided to perform Musette since it is set in England and was well received in America. However, the English took offense from the beginning. I guess they knew the play and were prepared to express their displeasure. The worst moment was when the nobleman was chasing Little Bright Eyes (my character) through the countryside. The English must really love their noblemen because they shouted insults and encouraged the villain.

To compound the problem with the choice of Musette, Minnie Palmer has been over here for a while. I don't know if you've heard of her, but she is a thief who imitates me. She does my material and copies my style of acting, singing, and dancing. Of course, stealing doesn't work for her in America, where people are used to seeing my performances, but here in England the people seem to think she's the original and I'm the imitator. Even some of the reviewers called my show a copy of hers and it doesn't help that she's younger than I am. I can't tell you how mad it makes me, thinking of her using my ideas to sell herself.

We had to close the show after the first act and cancel the future performances, but Ma and I put our heads together and came up with a plan. We switched from Musette to Little Nell and the Marchioness and where I played the banjo, I switched to the mandolin. The changes worked. The audience and the critics loved this show, so like back with our first New York performance, we managed to overcome.

So there, Minnie Palmer!

I hope things are going well for you and Walter. I miss you both and I'm eager to return home to see my darling goddaughter.

Love,

Lotta

Tabby collapsed next to Walter on the sofa. "What do you think?" she asked.

Walter turned on the sofa to face Tabby. "I know *Little Nell* is not a new show for Lotta, but it's still amazing they were able to put together a different performance so quickly. Think about the minor roles. They're using local actors for those, aren't they?" He paused, shaking his head. "I guess professionals can do things quickly when they have to."

Tabby narrowed her eyes. "That's not what I meant. She didn't mention the Grand Duke."

"You're right." He shrugged. "Is that important?"

"If you'd been in San Francisco with Lotta, if you'd heard her grief when Bolton died, then you'd know how important it was when she met the Duke. If he didn't show up, Lotta must be heartbroken."

"She certainly sounded happy," he told her. He looked around the room then back at Tabby before adding, "If solving show problems keeps her mind off her loneliness, thats a good thing."

"Maybe—for a day or two, but Lotta needs more than that. She needs someone other than her ma to share her life. Everybody needs that."

"I don't believe you. Some people like being alone. What's right for us isn't right for everybody."

Tabby opened her mouth to speak but didn't say anything. She sighed, then stared down at her hands. Walter knew how much she loved Lotta, but he also knew that sometimes people had to solve their own problems and sometimes the solutions were found in unexpected ways.

Lotta's tour went from England to Italy, Switzerland, and Germany. She continued to receive critical acclaim, but there was no mention of the Grand Duke Alexis in either the papers or Lotta's letters.

Tabby repeated her worries to Walter.

"Lotta's a strong woman," Walter reassured Tabby each time she brought the subject up. "She'll be all right."

When Lotta returned to New York, she started visiting Charlotte often. She talked with Tabby and Alina while she was there. When she didn't have a performance, she would join them for supper and be able to visit Walter, Francesco, and Clara, who were all out earning money during the day.

She talked about the problems she had in Europe, but mostly about how she solved them, rather than her anger with Minnie Palmer or the arrogance of the English noblemen. She also wanted to talk about other people's problems, specifically about the poor in America. There was a change in Lotta Walter hadn't expected.

Lotta was interested in Clara's story, especially about the time when she lived in a downtown tenement. "This was before the Tenement-House Act," Clara said. "I was in a room with no windows and no air-shaft and three other girls. It was hard to breathe."

"But you made your way out of there," Walter pointed out. "Now you've got the bakery and you own this building. You've got your own flat downstairs and rent from us each month." He used both his hands to indicate Alina and Francesco. "You should be proud."

"I am," Clara told him, "but people shouldn't have to suffer so much to have a decent life."

"That's my point exactly," Lotta said. "I want to be doing something to help people who need charity. The characters I play on stage are often young boys." Walter knew this to be true. She could get away with the illusion, because of her height and her childlike spunk. Lotta continued, "Each time I perform, I gain an appreciation for the struggling young. I've thought about the newsboys, the ones who make a penny or two peddling newspapers. They work hard, but most of them are homeless. They need shelter and food like anybody else and I've decided this will be my calling."

"You mean God is telling you to help them?" Tabby asked.

Lotta narrowed her eyes. "Spoze so, but I'm hearing it through people like Clara, who have lived it."

Clara shook her head. "I wasn't homeless for long. Once I was in the tenement I had a roof to keep the rain off."

"See," Lotta said, winking at Clara. "Those boys are even worse off than you were."

Later, when their guests had left and they'd put Charlotte to bed, Tabby touched Walter's shoulder. He was kneeling, cleaning ashes out of the kitchen stove. He stood and she said, "Lotta's been blessed by God and deserves everything she has. She's a great person."

"True," he said, wrapping his arms around her. "But it doesn't hurt that so many newsboys are already her fans. Anything Lotta gives them will be a thank you as well as charity." He felt Tabby tense a bit at his words, so he held her until she relaxed into his hug.

* * *

During the years that followed, Lotta's performances continued to succeed, her audiences grew and most reviews flattered her talent. Minnie Palmer was forgotten as Lotta was celebrated. Also, to Tabby's delight, the number of Lotta's suitors increased.

There was still a problem with a breach between her ma's preferences and her own. Lotta seemed to fall for men who hung by the stage door to meet her after a performance, while Mary Ann wanted to connect her daughter with the sons of wealthy families.

Alina took over from Tabby as the person most interested in Lotta's relationships. She followed the actress' escapades in the newspaper and asked questions when they were together.

The weekly suppers in Walter and Tabby's flat continued with Lotta attending when she was in town and not scheduled to perform. "Didn't someone save you when you were swimming?" Alina asked, sitting up straight and gazing at Lotta. "And didn't you fall in love with him?"

"Really?" Charlotte asked, setting her fork down. "He saved your life?" She was fifteen now and thinking about her own future. She was also pretty. Almost every time Walter looked at Charlotte, he was surprised by the way she'd grown into such a lovely woman. Her hair was thick and darker brown than her mother's, with some red mixed in. Walter had no idea where that color came from. He thought it might be God's way of acknowledging Lotta as Charlotte's godmother, but he never mentioned his idea to Tabby.

"That's personal," Walter scolded his daughter, but as he spoke he kept thinking of her appearance. Like her hair, her eyes were dark, darker than either his or Tabby's, while her skin was light, like Tabby's. The contrast of Charlotte's hair and eyes against her skin was lovely. He knew he shouldn't take pride in her appearance, but he did. She was beautiful, although he still thought Tabby more stunning. The gray strands in his wife's hair and the few wrinkles near her eyes seemed elegant.

"You read about that?" Lotta asked Alina, who nodded. "They never get things exactly right in the papers, but yes, I had some trouble with a leg cramp. A friend who was on the pier used a pole to reach out to me. I grabbed it and he pulled me in. Even if you think you're a strong swimmer, you never know what's going to happen. Our bodies can be weak at times and I sometimes get cramps from dancing. I don't think I would have drowned, but you never know."

Alina poked at her squash, then looked up at Lotta. "Have you kept in touch with this man?"

Charlotte tilted her head and seemed to hold her breath.

"There's not a lot to tell," Lotta said, glancing at Charlotte then back at Alina. "He likes me or at least he likes my performances, he's engaged to someone else and very much in love. He's not interested in anything from me other than my gratitude and I think he feels I've already expressed more than I should."

"But wasn't there another man?" Alina asked, refusing to give up on the subject, "someone you met after he attended so many of your performances you began to recognize him? And wasn't he the son of a wealthy family? And someone your ma liked?"

"If you mean the man from Philadelphia," Lotta said, wincing a little. "He died."

"Are you talking about Bolton Hulme?" Charlotte asked.

"No, not Bolton," Lotta told her. "Although Bolton is another one who came to so many shows, I had to speak with him." Lotta looked up at the ceiling then back at Charlotte and finally Alina. She continued speaking in a soft voice. "This is someone else who also died. My ma liked him, loved his family, and I was taken with him. His family wasn't thrilled with me being an actress and they couldn't stand my pa, but he convinced them I was the woman he wanted. We even set a wedding date, then he had a moment of weakness. We'd put him in charge of handling the money from ticket sales, which turned out to be a mistake. He wasn't getting as much cash from his family as he wanted and saw an easy way to get some more. He stole a good sum and went off on a drinking and gambling binge. Lost it all. His family paid the money back, but I never spoke to him again. When I heard he'd died, I went to Philadelphia to visit his grave, but it was too late for forgiveness."

"That's so sad," Charlotte said, wiping her eyes and her nose.

"Let's talk about something else," Walter suggested. He turned to Francesco. "You've got a new job. Why don't you tell Lotta about that?"

Francesco rubbed his mouth with his right fist. "They don't want to hear about me."

"Yes we do," Lotta told him. "You've given up house painting?"

"I wouldn't say I've given it up. I might go back." He shook his head slowly.

"I was painting a house a few miles north of here, a tall one." He spoke to Lotta but glanced around to look at the others. Alina's eyebrows were raised and she seemed to be holding her breath. Francesco continued. "I had to climb to the third story to do some work under the eaves, had to lean out from the ladder. The owner saw me up there and noticed I don't fear heights the way most people do.

So he tells me I can make a lot of money working on the new East River Bridge, the one they call the New York - Brooklyn Bridge. It seems he works for the company building it and can get me on there. So, I sign up, but when I get there I find the problem isn't going too high, it's going too low." He paused for effect here and Alina shook her head.

"They're working under the river to secure the giant towers that are going to hold the cables," he said. "This is a suspension bridge so there's all these wire cables that are going to support the bridge as well as the carriages and people crossing it. Anyway, we need to work underwater, so they've designed these giant boxes open at the bottom. They're called caissons. The company pumps so much air in them, the water can't come in. That all sounds good until you try it. People have gotten sick from the pressure. They call it caisson's disease. I've been one of the lucky ones, but Washington Roebling, the man in charge, he has the disease so bad he's now an invalid."

"I read about this," Walter said, "didn't his pa have his foot crushed between a pier and ferry?"

"That's right, but it was before I was there. The wound infected and he died, so his son took over. Now the son is sick."

"Oh my God," Tabby exclaimed.

"Roebling is still working on the engineering with his wife carrying the information back and forth. She's one smart lady. She had to study math to understand the messages she was bringing, so she can answer questions from him and from the people on site. She's smart for how quickly she learned things and also because she doesn't go down in the caissons."

"There's still using them?" Lotta asked.

"No choice is what they say," Alina muttered.

"I can get you a job at a theater, if you want it," Lotta told him.

"Thank you, but no. I can go back to painting if I want to. It's just they pay so much more at the bridge."

"Money doesn't do you any good if you're dead," Alina said.

"It would help you after I was gone," he told his wife.

Alina held her hands up. Her nostrils were flaring. "That's blood money," she shouted.

Francesco answered in a soft voice. "Most of us don't get sick and many of the ones who do, come back to work in a few days."

"Still," she told him, clearly trying to control her anger. "I don't want that kind of help."

* * *

Francesco never suffered from caisson disease and continued working on the bridge until it was completed in 1883. When the underwater work was done, his job shifted to the heights of the towers, painting the cables. Alina then feared he would fall to his death, which also didn't happen. When the work was done, Francesco went back to house and barn painting, with quite a bit of money saved.

From what Walter could tell, life for Alina and Francesco returned to the way they'd lived before the work on the bridge began. But one evening, while the group of friends was sharing another supper in Walter and Tabby's flat, Alina began to push for a move to the country.

"Life is dull," she said. Walter was surprised by her comment. They seemed comfortable. Their home was dry and warm and Clara kept the rent low, as she did for Walter and Tabby.

"We've never had children," Alina continued, tugging on the neck of her dress. Turning to Tabby she continued, "There's life in this flat. Charlotte has grown into a fine young woman. We've had the joy of watching that happen, but not in our own home. I want to move to the country where there's life around us."

Charlotte froze, her ears turning red as she stared at Alina. She didn't like to be the center of attention, especially in a group of adults. Walter had no idea where she got her shyness. Tabby and he were anything but bashful.

"Life?" Francesco asked, shaking his head. "There's plenty of life here, too much at times." He cleared his throat. "I don't mean our friends," he said, indicating the others at the table with a wave of his hand. "But we always hear the people down at the street shouting, laughing, and sometimes fighting."

Alina shifted in her seat. "I'd like to have a barn with a horse, maybe some goats and chickens," she said. "I've missed out on taking care of a child, so I'd like to care for animals. I don't think that's unreasonable. We could sell eggs for an extra income."

"I didn't have children," Lotta told her, tilting her head, "and my life was never dull."

"That's not a fair comparison. You had a career on stage and traveled all over. I stayed in my little flat, sewing and cooking."

"But in the beginning, Ma ran a book shop, then out west, a boarding house."

"Exactly. Your life wasn't dull because you and your ma didn't take the easy path."

"We don't need extra rooms and a backyard," Francesco shrugged, then scratched his temple. "I work at those houses all day. I've seen how life is no better there. Besides, wouldn't you miss our friends?"

"We could still come by to visit like Lotta does."

"I have a suggestion," Lotta said, leaning forward. "Ma and I have a cottage in the mountains of New Jersey we've named *Attol Tryst*. We go there on weekends and more often in the summer when the theaters are dark. Why don't all of you come out there for a week or so, maybe in July? You can see if you like country living."

"I've read about your cottage," Francesco told her. "It's a mansion. We can't afford a place like that."

Lotta looked at Francesco and smiled. "There's plenty of smaller homes in the area and you can paint for a living as easily in New Jersey as you do here. There's also a number of hotels around the lake, a huge one right next to our house. They need maintenance help, especially in the summer. In the winter there are jobs to be had cutting and pulling slabs of ice from the lake surface to be stored at the ice houses. They pay well if you don't mind heavy lifting."

"How would we get to your house?" Walter asked.

"You take a train to the lake, then a boat to the Hotel Breslin. That's the one by our home. The trip's half the fun."

"What about me?" Charlotte asked. "Would I have fun?"

"There are social events at the hotel. We could even plan a party at our house and invite lots of young people. You'll make friends."

Chapter Twenty-One

Lake Hopatcong

Alina, Francesco, Walter, Tabby, and Charlotte rode on a train through northern Jersey on the Monday morning of the second week of July. They were heading toward Lake Hopatcong, Lotta's enormous house, and the lakeside party promised to Charlotte. Clara had to keep the bakery open, so she decided not to go with them.

Walter's work had slowed down for the same reason Lotta's had stopped, fewer New York shows in the summer. However, summer was Francesco's busiest time of the year. It had taken a good deal of convincing by Alina to get him to agree to spend a week in the country.

Charlotte took a window seat with her pa beside her. They were both quietly watching the trees pass by at a speed Walter wasn't used to. In addition to the wooded areas, they passed fields, farmhouses, and Morristown, a town Walter knew from one of Charlotte's school books. It had been Washington's headquarters during a critical period of the revolutionary war.

As he looked out the window, Walter imagined himself running along the small dirt road that followed the tracks and wondered if Charlotte had the same daydream. He had to admit traveling this fast was fun.

When they reached Hopatcong, they got off the train at a stone building not far from the lake. They took their trucks to the pier where a large ferry was tied. It was a sunny day, but not too warm. There was a cool breeze blowing across the clean, blue-gray water. Walter loved the smell, so different from the salty, dirty water of the rivers surrounding New York.

They boarded the boat, deciding to go to the upper deck because it was open and the weather was so nice. The ferry stayed at the pier for a while, but no one in their group seemed hurried. Walter leaned back in the deck chair he'd chosen and watched as the other passengers boarded. This was a lot like watching people come to the theater. These were the same class of wealthy Americans, mostly from New York, but their dress wasn't as formal or as dark. The women were wearing hats and long dresses, mostly white or pink with floral patterns. The men also wore hats and long coats, white or blue. Some had ties, but most did not.

Once they left the dock, Walter enjoyed watching the birds swooping over them. They were gliders, unlike the songbirds he'd seen on the shore. They would swoop through the air, then dive to the water, often coming up with small fish in their beaks.

Lotta and Mary Ann met them at the pier in front of the hotel. There were two men with them, who took the trunks and placed them in wheelbarrows. As the men worked, Walter looked at the hotel, which was five stories tall and must have had thirty rooms on each floor, twice that, counting the ones facing away from the lake. The enormous yard was decorated with carefully trimmed bushes, flowering plants in large clusters, and potted plants on pillars bordering the paved path to the main entrance. The building was magnificent, but at this time their group wasn't going inside. They were walking around the Breslin toward Lotta's house.

Lotta put her arm around Charlotte and started crossing the lawn toward the side of the hotel. Walter picked up a light bag he'd brought to carry their money and Tabby's Bible then followed Lotta and his daughter, close enough to hear their conversation. Tabby hurried to walk beside Walter, with Alina and Francesco behind them, and finally, Mary Ann alongside the men with the wheelbarrows.

Lotta pulled Charlotte closer. "Tell me, goddaughter, do you have a suitor?"

Charlotte turned her head briefly, to glance back at her mother before answering. "Not yet, Aunt Lotta, but I'm still young. There's plenty of time, at least that's what Ma says."

Walter glanced at Tabby. She seemed to smile, but the look faded quickly.

"You're not as young as you think," Lotta told Charlotte. "But don't worry. I don't have a suitor either and I'm old."

"Are you—unhappy?" Charlotte seemed to struggle to find the right word. Walter knew his daughter rarely spoke about relationships.

"Not at all," Lotta said. "Right now there's more to life than men and when I have to retire there will be lots of prospects, after my money I'm certain. But let's talk about you. Do you know any boys?"

"There are some at our church, but I don't like the ones who seem to like me."

"Ah! It's funny how that works."

"When we go to church, we sit in the pew, sing the hymns, and go home. The boys do the same with their families. I only meet the ones who come to me—and they usually tease me. Sometimes, I think the boys who keep away become the ones I like, because I don't know how silly they are. If they ever spoke to me, I'd probably see they're as foolish as the others."

"You, my darling, are wise beyond your years. Do you meet boys anywhere else? At your school, perhaps?"

"My school's all girls and I only go on Saturdays. I help my ma with sewing the rest of the week. She says it's as important for a girl to have a skill as it is for a boy. I guess that's in case I never marry, but I want to—someday."

"Well, we'll see what we can do here," Lotta told her. "People come to the lake to have fun, not to worship God. Although, sitting by the lake in the evening can be spiritual." Lotta paused, then added, "The party I promised is going to take place. Do you swim?"

Charlotte shook her head.

"We'll get you a bathing dress anyway and you will meet friends. You're a pretty girl, Charlotte, all you have to do is reach out and not be shy."

Walter slowed his pace a little, as he thought about the conversation he'd just heard. He remembered how difficult it was to be young and was worried about Charlotte. Life wasn't as hard for her as it had been for him and Tabby, but it wasn't perfect and that's what he wanted for his daughter. He was glad Lotta was there to help.

Lotta's cottage was almost as impressive as the hotel, more when Walter considered how it was a single-family residence. It stood three stories high, with gray shingles on the outside walls and brown on the roof. The windows were trimmed in brown, slightly lighter than the roof, and those windows were everywhere, on gables, verandas, and bay windows as well as the flat walls. There was also a circular drive that would allow carriages to pull up under an awning, so wealthy guests would not have to get out in the rain.

Inside was just as remarkable. There was a library with books by both classic and modern authors, alongside books on stagecraft and history of the theater. Walter was certain Lotta had pages dedicated to her in that last group. They continued on to a number of rooms dedicated to entertaining, with windows that were more splendid from inside than they appeared from outside, all offering a lovely view of the lake. They went upstairs and through some narrow halls to bring the luggage to the bedrooms where the guests would be staying. Along the way, they passed artwork and shelves of memorabilia from Lotta's many productions.

The plan was to eat dinner at the Breslin around two. Later, in the evening, a light supper would be served at Lotta's cottage. The dinner would be formal, but Walter, Tabby, and Charlotte did not have formal attire and neither did the Soleras. At first, Francesco resisted the suggestion to "mix with the millionaires," as he put it. Yet Lotta was insistent. She had provided clothing for her guests and told Walter and Francesco, "Your wives will not want these dresses to go to waste." Walter looked at the two women then at Francesco. His friend replied by shaking his head and shrugging, which is how Tabby and Walter ended up going to their bedroom to change into the outfits Lotta had left them.

Spread out on the bed, for Tabby, was a white bodice and a long, skirt with a pink, green, and light brown floral pattern over a black base. There was also a large black sash she would wear on her waist and tie at her back. She would keep her own chemise on, but Lotta had provided other underthings to make the outfit perfect. There was a corset, corset cover, and a crinoline petticoat, to hold the skirt out as if she was constantly twirling. Tabby hadn't dressed this well since years earlier, in the saloon, when she had dressed like Lotta to impress young Walter.

Next to Tabby's clothes, Lotta had left Walter a black dinner jacket, gray slacks, white shirt, and an off-white vest. He also had a pair of black shoes at the foot of the bed, next to a pair for Tabby, also black. The shoes were shined so well, their surface reflected like a frozen lake at night.

They started to change out of the clothes they had worn for the journey, but when Tabby was down to her chemise and Walter was wearing only his drawers and an undershirt, the conversation somehow switched to what they'd heard Lotta and Charlotte talking about on their walk from the boat to the cottage.

Tabby pushed the clothes on the bed over and took a seat between what she was going to wear and Walter's outfit. She ran her fingers through her hair then looked at Walter, who had taken a seat in an upholstered chair with a walnut frame. "You heard Lotta talking about suitors for Charlotte, didn't you?" she asked.

"Yes," Walter told her, leaning toward Tabby as he spoke. "Do you think she's too young?"

"I don't. Fifteen is old enough for the boys to come courting. It just makes me wonder if we've done something wrong. Why does her godmother have to find her a beau? Shouldn't it be our responsibility?"

Walter leaned back and crossed his arms. "We take her to church. She could meet young men there."

Tabby blew out a breath. "I haven't given much thought to suitors. What was always on my mind, was making sure our daughter didn't face the hardships we suffered. And we did that. She's always had a roof over her head and food in her belly." Tabby raised her voice slightly. "I taught her to sew. If I'd had a skill like that, I might have stayed in Montana and saved Ma's farm without going to San Francisco and the saloon."

Walter noticed a tear in the old, yellowed chemise Tabby was wearing. Her flesh was poking through on her right side, just under her ribs. She sewed all day but didn't have time to repair her own undergarment. He glanced at the expensive skirt Lotta had provided, then back at his wife, her eyes a little wet. "Charlotte needs to know how to be as much like her beautiful mother as possible," he said, his voice cracking. "Everything else will take care of itself."

She smiled, but said, "No it won't. That's why I wanted her sewing with me. It gives her a skill she can fall back on if times get tight." Tabby sat up straight, her shoulders pushed back. "But that's not all she needs. Maybe we did shelter her more than we should have. The best part of my life has been sharing it with you, so Lotta has a point. Charlotte needs to find her own Walter." She glanced at the expensive outfit beside her on the bed. "I'm just not sure throwing a party for rich young people is the best way to do it."

Walter frowned. "Are you saying a good man can't be found among the rich?"

"Maybe I am, a least I'm saying there's a lot of difference between those people and us."

"Lotta is rich and she's been the best friend we could have hoped for."

"Lotta wasn't born rich."

Walter got out of his chair and went to Tabby. He dropped to one knee and took her hand. "Charlotte's not going to come away from this party with a husband. She's just going to have a good time with people her own age. After this week, when we're back in New York, we'll see what else we can do for her." He leaned in toward her and spoke softly. "Now tell me, what's this about? After all these years, are you jealous of Lotta?"

"Jealous of Lotta?" she said, then she swallowed and added, "Maybe a little—of her ability to give Charlotte things we can't give her."

Walter squeezed her hand. "Everybody Charlotte knows gives her something different, but nobody gives her as much as her mother does. Never knowing my own mother has made it easier to see how special your relationship is."

"You didn't know your mother and mine sold me to save her farm."

Walter stood, took in a breath, then looked down at Tabby. "Is that what this is about? *Your* mother?"

"I don't want to be like her," Tabby told him, fingering the collar of her chemise. "I want to be everything to my daughter, everything my mother wasn't."

"Did your mother know your plans when you left Montana?"

"I'm not sure she knew what the work was, but she knew I was leaving." Tabby paused and looked down as she gathered her thoughts. She raised her head and looked at Walter. "I want Charlotte to be near me always. I don't want to lose her the way my mother lost me. But she's growing up and that's what scares me."

"It will work out," Walter told her. "It's part of life, but for now we better get dressed and head downstairs. The others will be waiting."

Walter and Tabby were the last to reach the library, where the others were gathering, all except Mary Ann who decided to eat at the cottage. Everyone was wearing the formal attire Lotta had given them. Francesco, who was wearing a blue jacket with tails over tan slacks, seemed the most out of place. He was pacing about as he tugged at his shirt collar and pulled at his coat sleeves.

Alina had on an off-white dress with pale pink and purple patterns, dots on the blouse and stripes mixed with dots on the skirt. She would have some issues getting through doorways since her outfit had even more crinoline than Tabby's.

Walter was most surprised by his daughter, jerking his head back when he saw her. She was wearing a royal-blue, off-the-shoulder dress that glimmered with the shine of silk and, like Alina's and her mother's, had crinoline underneath, puffing the full-length skirt out like a pedestal. The top was tight around her chest and midsection and shaped with a V pointing down into the loose material of her skirt. There were also frilled short sleeves, appearing more like upper arm bracelets than parts of the dress. Along with the gown she wore gold dangling earrings, a matching gold choker, and long, black gloves.

Charlotte's hair was braided and pulled up on her head, emphasizing her smooth neck. and making her look older—fully grown. As hard as it was for Walter to admit it to himself, Charlotte was as beautiful as her mother.

Tabby had grabbed onto Walter's arm when they'd entered the room and was now gripping him as if she was trying not to fall over. He turned and looked in her wide-open eyes, but she didn't look back. Her gaze was focused on their daughter. Lotta knew show business and it now appeared she was using her staging knowledge to introduce Charlotte into the social world surrounding the Hopatcong resort. Tabby had been right about their friend's ability to give Charlotte opportunities they couldn't offer. Only time would tell if those paths would lead to happiness. The party Lotta was organizing in a few days would give a good sense of what was in store.

The temperature had risen slightly since their boat ride from the southern tip of the lake, but it was still comfortable. When they left the house, they walked to the hotel, following the same path they had used to come up from the shore that morning.

When they arrived at the hotel, they were greeted by the concierge, who suggested they eat on the second-floor balcony.

"I wanted to show my guests the dining hall," Lotta told him.

"We are set up for you in both places. The dining hall is good if that's what you would like," he replied. "It's just so lovely out here and a little warm inside."

Walter noticed Lotta looking up at the balcony, where other diners had gathered. She tapped a finger against her lip, then turned to the others. "What do you think?" she asked.

"It is pretty out here," Alina said.

"Yes," Lotta agreed. She turned back to the concierge. "The balcony will be fine."

They followed the hotel greeter up the stairs and turned to their right, passing a number of diners as they walked to their table. Everyone seemed to be staring at them, smiling and raising their eyebrows, while quite a few women nodded at Lotta. However, the wide-eyed, young boys seemed more interested in Charlotte than the famous actress. Walter felt a mixture of pride and worry.

The group seemed a little nervous as they sat and listened to Lotta ordering two bottles of wine, but when Alina said "It's a shame Clara couldn't close her shop and enjoy this with us," everyone seemed to wake up to the fact that they were the same group of friends who had been sharing weekly meals for years.

The talk turned to plans for the next day, when Lotta would take Alina and Francesco around the lake to look at homes in their price range.

"Ma will come with us," Lotta told Alina. "She's the real estate expert."

* * *

They crossed the lake the next day in a steam launch owned by The Breslin. Lotta had a sailboat, but it wouldn't hold seven people comfortably and would be unreliable if the wind calmed. They went to Sperry Springs on the southern side of a large bay, across the lake from Lotta's house. The homes there were rentals, but Mary Ann knew of a few homes for sale, a short distance from the camp. They found a small log cabin close to the dirt road. It had two bedrooms, a tiny kitchen, and a larger room for a table and some extra chairs.

"It's perfect," Alina told Francesco. "We're in the quiet of the woods, but not too far from the lake. We could use a boat to get to a general store or to Lotta's."

"We can't get everywhere by boat," Francesco warned her.

Mary Ann walked around the cabin slowly. "You're right," she told him, then she turned to Alina and added, "You'll have to buy a horse to get to places without lakefront and a wagon or carriage to carry both of you. But you won't need a boat. A ferry like the one you took to our house runs along the west side of the lake and stops at

Sperry Springs. You can use it to get back to the train station or to our cottage.

"The bigger problem is getting anywhere during the winter. Snow will cover the ground from mid-November to mid-March, sometimes longer. You might need a sleigh instead of a carriage during that season. The lake will freeze to a point where you can walk across it, but you don't want to test it early or late in the season when the ice isn't thick enough. You could die if you broke through. Lake life may seem easy at this time of the year, but you have to think about the winter." She leaned on the potbelly stove near the wall furthest from the front door.

"We're tough," Alina said, holding her head high. "We can make it." She reached out to grab Francesco's hand.

Lotta took a step toward a window that looked out over the road, then she turned back. "Our house is next to the Breslin," she said, "so we have a place to go if we're here when the weather is rough. We also have people working for us who will keep the woodpile stocked for cold times. I wonder if you might not be better looking on the east shore, near our home."

"They can't afford a house in our area," Mary Ann told her daughter.

"Your ma's right," Alina said. "This is the place for us."

Chapter Twenty-Two

The Party

Charlotte's party was scheduled for the following afternoon, which turned out to be as pretty a day as anyone could hope for. It was sunny, but not unbearably hot. Lotta had arranged for tables to be set up on her front yard, along with chairs, benches, and canopy tents, for the guests to seek shelter from either rain or too much sun. The breeze over the lake was soft but constant and the trees around Lotta's cottage provided additional shade.

Everyone was to come dressed in their swim attire. Lotta had made arrangements to use the Breslin lakefront. They could also dive off the dock surrounding the boathouse where Lotta kept her sailboat.

In front of her house, she had set up a couple of fire pits to cook using the wood cut from fallen trees in the forest around her home. The plan was for the aroma of burning wood to mix with sizzling pork, beef, chicken, and fish, creating an enticing smell that would make mouths water.

Lotta's plan was also to have her goddaughter appeal to another type of hunger common among young men. Charlotte was wearing a navy blue swim dress, with light blue trim. The outfit had a short skirt that was worn over bloomers. The bloomers reached below her knees. The top of the outfit had a large square collar that reached down her back like a cape but just below her shoulders. The front had a modest v-shaped neckline with a bow. She looked beautiful.

Walter and Tabby attended the party but sat at a distance to watch Charlotte meet the young people Lotta had described. They were also apart from Lotta, who sat alone where she could enjoy a cigar in peace.

Walter wondered if all fathers felt mixed emotions as they watched their daughters grow. He was proud of her beauty but wary of the way the boys were talking to her, while the girls were not.

One of the boys took a particular interest in Charlotte. He seemed to spend all his time as close to her as possible. Walter leaned over to Tabby and asked her if she knew who the boy was. She didn't, but she crossed the yard and asked Lotta.

When Tabby returned, she told Walter he was the son of a woman who had worked for Macy's department store. "*Worked for* is the wrong way of saying what she did," Tabby said. "She was the store superintendent until she married well and left to raise a family. Lotta admires her because she did so well in a man's world. I believe Lotta sees a little of herself in the woman, but she doesn't know much about the boy. She said most of the young people in this area are honorable, so there shouldn't be a problem."

"Shouldn't be?" Walter asked. He pressed his lips together.

"That's what she said."

After Walter and Tabby watched Charlotte and the boy for a while, they noticed the two young people starting to walk toward the lake. Walter stood. He took Tabby's hand and together they followed their daughter.

They kept their distance but were close enough to see Charlotte and the boy reach the lake. It seemed they were only interested in taking a dip. After they were wading in the shallow area for a minute or so, the boy suddenly turned to Charlotte, picked her up and dropped her back into the lake, on her backside. She was soaked.

Walter jumped, but Tabby grabbed his arm before he could run to protect his daughter.

"They're just playing," Tabby told him. "Look at her. She's laughing. She's splashing water at him now."

Walter saw his wife was right and sat back down.

"That's the way young people flirt. God knows why," Tabby said. "But if Charlotte likes this boy, she'll enjoy his teasing."

The boy and Charlotte splashed their way to the shore, then stood on dry land, laughing. Apparently, Tabby was right about Charlotte enjoying the soaking. *The day is not cold,* Walter told himself, *The sun will dry her.* But then the boy hugged her as if he was trying to dry her with the heat of his body rather than waiting for the sun. Walter didn't like that.

Tabby's hand was on Walter's thigh. He felt her grip tighten as she said, "This is the process young men and women have been going through since the days of Adam and Eve." She cleared her throat. "If Charlotte wants to know this boy she needs to do more than talk, she needs to touch him. Some would say I'm a bad mother for thinking that way, but I know how words alone can deceive."

"Is that how you felt when I first met you?" he asked.

"Yes." Tabby brought her hand to her heart. "Your spirit reached out to mine in a way different from any of the other men I'd known. Why do you think I let you kiss me? I felt something special."

Walter smiled, but when he turned away from Tabby he saw Charlotte break from the boy for a moment. The boy then took her hand as they began to walk toward the boathouse. "Is that a problem?" he asked his wife.

"Definitely," Tabby told him, her brow wrinkling. "We want them to know each other, but not too well."

This time Tabby was the first to stand. She headed toward the boathouse with Walter beside her. They followed their daughter and the boy who was taking her to a place where they could be alone. When Walter and Tabby stepped into the boathouse, they found the boy and Charlotte in a deep embrace, kissing with passion. Walter had never seen his child in the midst of such a kiss. They hadn't had enough time to move past the first step, but it was clear what their intentions were.

Walter pulled the boy from his daughter, causing Charlotte to shout, "What are you doing?" She looked from the boy to Tabby and finally glared at Walter. "You are horrible! You ruined everything! Both of you!" She paced away from her parents then clenched her jaw and turned back. "You always treat me like this! When I want to have fun, no matter what it is, you step in and prevent it. What's wrong with you?" She was waving her arms, crying. "Why...why don't you let me become the woman you say you want me to be?" She was shouting the words, separating each word. "Finally, Aunt Lotta gives me a chance and you ruin my day. My party! I wish you weren't my parents! I wish Aunt Lotta was my ma!" She spun around, away from her parents, and ran out of the boathouse.

Walter looked at the door his daughter had just slammed, but he didn't follow her. He released the young man. "Explain yourself," he said.

"We were just having fun," the boy replied, his face pale white.

Walter's eyes grew wide as he glared at this boy. But he'd listened to what Charlotte said, so he tried to control his anger. "If you like my daughter," he said in a steady voice, "you court her properly. Understand?"

The young man nodded and breathed out as Walter's tone changed.

"Now, get out of here," Walter told him. "Go home. I don't want to see you around Charlotte for the rest of the afternoon."

The boy spun so quickly he almost fell into the lake, but he kept his balance and left the boathouse, running as fast as Charlotte had.

Tabby smiled at Walter. "This process, the one I said young men and women have always gone through, we are part of it. You protected your daughter the way fathers have been doing since time began, but one day you won't be there for her. Charlotte will have to learn to handle herself better. She's upset now, but I'll speak with her after the party is over. We've given her a good life so far. She needs to know how to keep it good."

"You're right," Walter said in a quiet voice, "but maybe we've been too strict."

* * *

Two months later, as the weather started to cool and the leaves began to change colors, Walter heard a knock on the door of the flat. He opened it and was surprised to discover the boy who had been with Charlotte at the party.

He said, "I would like to court your daughter as you suggested."

Walter almost slammed the door, but the young man's use of the word "court" stopped him. It was the old fashioned word Walter had used when he had confronted them in the boathouse. Young people used the word "date" now. There was no respect in that word.

Walter opened the door wide and gestured for him to come inside.

Tabby and Charlotte we're both sewing, as they did every day to supplement Walter's income. Walter was only home because his shop had just finished a project and was about to start a new one. The supervisors were reorganizing the workspace in preparation for a set that needed a larger staging area.

Charlotte wasn't prepared for company. She wasn't wearing a corset or petticoats and had on a spotted blue dress that was old and a bit tattered. She also wore a yellow apron and had her hair covered with a white scarf. A flush crossed her cheeks as she fidgeted in her chair and looked down.

"Hello Charlotte," the young man said.

"Hello." She spoke weakly. She reached to touch her scarf but didn't pull it off.

"I remembered you saying you lived in Harlem," he told her, "but I didn't know where. I had to contact Miss Crabtree to get your address. She was obliging, but her schedule made her difficult to contact. That's why it took me so long to get here." He turned to Walter. "This summer I found your daughter enchanting and I would like to get to know her better. I hope my wish meets with your approval." He turned back to Charlotte. "And yours, as well."

Walter was impressed with the young man's efforts. He hadn't expected anything after he'd broken them apart, most certainly not an appearance at the door of his modest flat. "May I ask your name?" he said.

"I apologize. I thought you knew. My name is Paul Darville. My family lives in New York, south of here. We have a summer cottage near Miss Crabtree's, which is why I was invited to Charlotte's party." He looked again at Walter's daughter before adding, "On a day I mark as the most important of my life."

Walter looked at Tabby. She wore a wide-eyed expression, which told him she was as surprised as he was.

* * *

It seemed that Lotta's success extended to her ability as a matchmaker and by the spring of 1887, Charlotte and Tabby were planning a wedding.

Walter thought Paul was perfect for Charlotte. He was intimidated by the wealthy Darville family, but understood what his daughter needed and hid his own issues. His years with Lotta had proven to him that wonderful people can also have financial success.

Meanwhile, Lotta had moved on from matchmaking to her next challenge—horses. She told Walter that after so many years of performing, she'd begun to grow bored. The ten-minute call before each show no longer filled her with anticipation. The laughter and applause after her routines brought less satisfaction than they once had. And she'd begun to dread traveling on tour.

"So what's next? He asked her.

"Horses!" She was looking up at him, smiling and even trembling a bit. "I've set Ash up as the manager of my stable. He's already bought six: Roberta, The Outlaw, Nut Boy, Sonoma Girl, Lady Thistle, and My Star. They're all beautiful, but Nut Boy and Sonoma Girl have the most potential."

Walter remembered the three he'd taken care of for the Crabtrees when he first started working for them: Spider, Vespa, and Blink Bonny. They were a lot of work, but lovely animals, pleasure horses named after racers. Now that she had the money, Lotta had bought real racehorses.

Later, when Walter told Tabby about his conversation with Lotta, she said, "Lotta always needs something to keep her going. I suppose we all do, but most of us find our excitement in our marriages, the way we have. I still worry about Lotta. I think she's lonely and now that Charlotte is engaged, she's jumping into horse racing to keep her mind off her one failure."

As Charlotte began to spend more time with Paul, Lotta showed up at fewer of the dinners hosted by Tabby and Walter. Perhaps her absence had to do with the horses, but Tabby surmised Lotta didn't want to be reminded that her goddaughter was getting married while she was still alone. Walter was almost convinced, when Lotta surprised him and Tabby with a generous offer to host the wedding in July, a garden wedding at her lake house, one year after the couple met. Walter and Tabby had argued for a home wedding, a long-standing tradition among families with modest incomes, but Lotta insisted she should throw a wedding everyone would talk about in the society pages and remember for the rest of their lives.

* * *

Three days shy of a year after their last trip to Lotta's country home, Tabby and Walter were back on Lotta's lawn, sitting on the same bench, waiting for the wedding to start. Lotta was off to the side, where she had been the year before, smoking her cigar, but this time she wore a light pink, formal dress with an off-the-shoulder neckline and a dark pink hem on the long skirt. At last year's party, she'd worn men's trousers since it was a casual event.

"She looks lonely over there," Tabby said to Walter, nodding in Lotta's direction.

"She looks that way often," he replied. "She did last year, but back then she was thinking about the party and Charlotte. Now she's bound to be thinking about the wedding. She isn't lonely when her mind is working—and it always is."

The wedding took place in front of Lotta's house. It was an outdoor wedding because her house had no room large enough to hold all the guests. She did have a back-up plan arranged with the Breslin in case of rain, but that wouldn't be necessary. The weather was perfect, identical to what they had experienced a year earlier.

Walter grinned and stood tall, as he walked his beautiful daughter down the aisle and presented her to Paul Darville in front of an Episcopalian minister. Charlotte was wearing an elegant wedding gown with white lace covering a sheer dress over a pink slip the color of cherry blossoms. The dress had a small train, also trimmed with lace.

The ceremony was beautiful and well-attended with society people from New York, as well as wealthy residences of Mount Arlington and other communities surrounding Lake Hopatcong.

Mary Ann was there, along with Lotta's brothers, Ash and George, so it was a family affair for the Crabtrees. Although Tabby and Walter had no family to invite, Clara, Alina, and Francesco attended. Lotta was the maid of honor and also sang a love song. Her performance was followed by a rather lengthy message from the minister on the importance of marriage and family. When the ceremony ended, Charlotte and Paul walked down the aisle as the guests threw rice and some, who hadn't given up the strange old tradition, tossed shoes.

The guests followed Lotta down to the lawn of the Breslin where the reception was to be held. Tables were set up near the lake and a string quartet was performing music, as the guests arrived. The waiters served cocktails with whiskey, gin, rye, or bourbon, but most of the guests drank wine or beer. The feast started with soup, a choice of pea, clam, oyster, beef, or veal, then moved on to the entrees with a wide menu including ham, turkey, venison, duck or for those who preferred seafood, cod, halibut, shad, or mackerel, all served with sides. After the dinner dessert was served with choices ranging from fruit pies, cheesecake, and spice cake to puddings and custards & creams. Charlotte and Paul walked from table to table, greeting each guest.

Lotta had reserved one of the ferries for the day, the same one used for bringing the guests from the pier beside the train station to the Breslin. The boat was large enough to hold everyone invited, so it was perfect for a tour of the lake. There was a bar on board and drinks were served again, as the people enjoyed the smell of the water, the feel of the cooling breeze, and the magnificent scenery.

The tour went across the widest section of the lake. They passed two islands, which Walter knew were Halsey and Raccoon, then they cruised into the cove near where Alina and Francesco had purchased their home. They had bought the cabin Mary Ann had shown them and were now residents of Sussex county, but they kept their Harlem flat through the winter. They decided to skip the cold and snow the first year and have time to prepare for the next winter. Walter and Tabby had been glad to keep their neighbors for an extra few months.

The boat circled around the cove, then came out, turned left and passed the other side of Raccoon Island to go into another cove. They turned around there, took time to admire the woods surrounding the water, then headed back toward the Breslin.

"Our daughter's grown," Tabby said to Walter, as they sat in deck chairs near the boat's railing. "I had thought she might live with us a few more years, but she's married money and has no need for our support."

Walter noticed Tabby was slumped in her chair, looking down at the water as the boat broke through the surface. "She'll always need your advice," he told her, "and I believe Paul loves her. You know our daughter well enough to know that's more important to her than his money."

"Spoze so," she replied. She paused before adding. "Paul seems a caring, sweet person. Charlotte is lucky to have found him." She sighed, "I think this is hard on Lotta."

"Are you worried about her, again?"

"Charlotte is so much younger, yet Lotta found her a husband. She must wonder why she can't find one for herself."

Walter took a deep breath then said, "I don't know if finding a husband is important to Lotta. She has a successful career and many friends, as well as her family—her ma and brothers. Everyone goes to her for advice, because she's a giving person."

"That's right," Tabby told him. "Everyone takes her advice and her money, as we did for this wedding." She bent forward and shook her head slowly.

"That bothered me, too," Walter said, crossing his legs. "But if we had refused Lotta's gift, we would have hurt our friend as well as our daughter."

Chapter Twenty-Three

Retirement

In 1891 Lotta was forty-four and had been performing since she was six, still predominantly in the roles of children. She loved losing herself in the characters she portrayed and in her singing and dancing, but lately, *Attol Tryst*, the cottage by Lake Hopatcong had increased its pull on her.

Lotta wrote to Walter, telling him how much she loved the peace she felt by the water's edge and the joy of catching the wind when she went out on the lake in her sailboat. "I've been considering leaving the stage," her letter read. "I've taken up painting and I can't begin to describe the wonder of capturing a lakeside scene on a canvas. Yet, I'm confused. There could be some good years remaining for me on the stage. I don't know if I should give up on those. I am hoping you and Tabby will do me a favor. Come down to see my tour, then meet me afterward for drinks at my hotel. I need to talk to you both, my best friends, to get your opinion about my show and to have you tell me, honestly, if you believe I have anything fresh to offer my fans."

The train ride from New York to Wilmington, Delaware was long, but after everything Lotta had done for them, Walter and Tabby were thrilled to give something in return. They watched the show from the orchestra seats Lotta had reserved.

Walter leaned into Tabby and whispered, "She can't have the same energy she had when she was in her twenties, but it's hard to tell."

"Maybe the changes have been too slow for us to notice, like when we were watching Charlotte grow. She never seemed to change from day to day, but somehow she stopped being a baby and became a child, then a young girl, then a woman."

A man in a seat behind them leaned forward and hushed them.

Walter stopped speaking but kept studying Lotta's routine. As always, the theater lit up when Lotta stepped on the stage. She danced and sang to the same music, but always changed her routine. Walter had heard many of the actors complain because they had to spend so much time worrying about what Lotta would do next, they couldn't perfect their own performances. Her improvisations brought life to the show, but also presented a risk.

Before the show started, the theater manager had announced a couple of understudies who would be taking over some roles. These included one of Lotta's dance partners.

Walter thought how the dance partners were one of the slow changes Tabby had been talking about. Back in the camps, when Lotta first started performing, she rarely danced with a partner. Her feet would fly so fast, no one could keep up with her. In San Francisco, after Walter went to work for the Crabtrees, he would practice routines with Lotta, but they were to help her grow as a dancer. She rarely used them on stage. Now, Lotta was often dancing in the arms of a man or, in this case, *falling* into the arms of a man.

Halfway through the first act, Lotta crossed into view with the same energy and enthusiasm she always brought to her shows. The understudy was waiting for her toward the center-front of the stage. She circled him, sneaking a glance toward the audience and laughing as she danced, the way she always did. Lotta had the ability to treat audiences as if they were her confidants as if they were into the secret jokes of the show as much as she was.

Lotta leaned on the understudy's right shoulder, which was funny by itself because Lotta was much shorter than the dancer. She had to reach up with both hands, fingers interlocked, to put any pressure on her partner. He did not seem to understand what she was doing, which the audience found hysterically funny.

She released that hold, circled around him, then leaned on his left shoulder in the same manner. She was getting a great response from the audience, even a shout or two. Walter made a mental note to comment about the reactions she was able to pull from her fans. This acknowledgment was different from the days when drunken miners had thrown gold at her, more sober, but not any less enthusiastic.

Lotta released the man's left shoulder, danced around him again, then jumped up on a bench. The move seemed dangerous to Walter, because, unlike other scenes where she played a young boy,

Lotta was wearing a dress, one with a skirt long enough to trip her. Yet she did fine, didn't even have to regain her balance.

She spun around on the bench then threw herself backward, toward her dance partner. Instead of raising his arms to catch her, the confused understudy took a step away. Lotta fell flat on her back, with a slapping sound as loud as a falling tree.

Lotta screamed when she hit the stage, then lay still.

Walter stood. He forced his way to the aisle, pushing past others, then started to run up on stage. Members of the backstage crew as well as the cast had circled her, but Walter kept moving forward. "I'm her friend," he shouted. "Let me through!" But when a voice behind him shouted "I'm a doctor!" as loudly as he was shouting. Walter stepped to the side.

Lotta was taken to a hospital, which is where Walter and Tabby were finally able to see her. Mary Ann was in the room when they arrived. She was standing near Lotta's bed, looking down at her daughter. She rubbed the back of her neck as she turned toward Walter and Tabby. "They've got her on morphine," Mary Ann told them. "She's asleep."

"Do they know how badly she was hurt?" Walter asked.

"They believe she's broken her back in a couple of places, but they aren't sure. She was in pain before they gave her the drugs, but she had good movement in her feet and toes."

"Oh my God!" Tabby said. "They thought she might be paralyzed?"

"It was a serious fall," Mary Ann said. She was nervously fingering the collar of her bodice.

Walter's voice broke as he said, "We know. We were watching from the audience." He rocked from one foot to the other, then asked, "Now what?"

"We spend a few days here before we can move her to a train then back to New Jersey. I'm canceling the rest of her tour. We'll recuperate at Hopatcong."

"Sounds like a good plan," Walter said.

Tabby sniffled then wiped a tear from her right eye. "Let us know if we can do anything."

"You've been good friends for Lotta," Mary Ann told them, "and friends are what she needs most now."

"We'll do anything you think will help," Tabby offered. "When she wakes we can talk with her, read to her, pray with her, or just sit by her bed and hold her hand if that's what she needs."

Mary Ann looked back and forth between them. "Come stay at Hopatcong for a while," she suggested, pushing her shoulders back as she spoke. "Lotta won't be able to get around, so having friends to talk to could be important. Besides your friends, Alina and Francesco are living by the lake now. It'll give you and Lotta a chance to visit them as well."

Walter would have to give up his job to stay at the lake. Also, the men who brought the material and patterns for Tabby's sewing would move on to other women who wanted to work from home. They knew this decision would be a permanent change for them. They would have to start over, even if they returned to Harlem.

"Mary Ann and Lotta have helped us so much over the years," Walter told Tabby. "I don't see how we have a choice."

She shrugged and replied, "You're right and I'm glad we don't. It will feel good to give something back for once."

Lotta's recovery went well and, as the summer approached, she was able to take on a few roles in New York productions. However, she was still in pain and not at all enthusiastic about performing.

Meanwhile, Mary Ann offered to hire Walter and Tabby to do the same type of work they had done for her years earlier. They would stay in the Hopatcong house, in the guest quarters, and would work on maintenance, cooking, and other projects around the home. They would be there to watch over the house if Lotta went on tour. Walter and Tabby said their goodbyes to Clara and moved their stuff from Harlem to Northern New Jersey.

That's when the next tragedy occurred.

Tabby came running outside, where Walter was raking leaves. She was sobbing as she ran and when she stopped he could see her jaw was clenched. She had trouble speaking and when she finally did get the words out her voice cracked. "It's horrible, Walter! I just heard from Lotta. Her brother George has died. She's heartbroken."

Walter dropped the rake, clutched his hands, and brought his fists to his mouth. "George?" he said. He started to shake. "How?"

"She didn't say much and was too upset for me to ask her more. But I know this, he was on an ocean liner, crossing from Europe to America. I suppose he couldn't get the best medical care on a boat, but I don't know if he was sick or drunk or something else happened."

Walter knew George hadn't been the same since he'd lost his leg, years earlier. The youngest Crabtree boy had followed in his pa's footsteps when it came to alcohol, so Walter imagined drinking probably caused his death somehow. None of that mattered now. "Where's Lotta?" he asked.

"I left her with Mary Ann. They need some time alone."

"Lotta and Mary Ann gave George many opportunities," Walter said. "Maybe too many. I wonder if he might not have turned to alcohol if he'd had to struggle more."

"Don't ever say that to Lotta," Tabby told him, frowning slightly.

"Of course not."

"And remember, he's in a better place now. I'm sure he's looking down on Lotta, thanking her for all she did, rather than blaming her."

* * *

Lotta retired from the stage. The tragedy of George's death combined with the pain she still suffered from her fall caused her to finally make the move. She left New York and settled in her New Jersey home year-round.

"I hope she can be happy here," Tabby told Walter after they heard of Lotta's decision.

Walter grinned. "Give her time," he said.

"You're right," Tabby replied, grinning back. "Lotta always finds a way to be happy. That's her greatest blessing."

The transition didn't take long because Lotta had discovered art. She told the newspapers, "It is so delightful to wander about at will and record with my brush the many beautiful spots I find." Painting took the place of the stage.

"I want to share the experience with you," Lotta said to Tabby and Walter on a spring afternoon when the three friends were eating dinner together. "Come hiking with me. We'll find scenes to paint. Then I'll remember where they are and come back another day with my paints."

"I have to clean the upstairs bedrooms," Tabby argued.

"And I have to trim the Holly trees," Walter added.

"Forget those things for now. I want to wander along the lake's edge with you both. I want to discover new beauty. We'll work up a sweat then go for a swim together."

Tabby shook her head. "But the water's frigid this time of the year."

"You're not going to let a little cold stop you. Not after everything we've been through together."

Walter looked at Tabby who held her arms out, palms up. There was no way they could turn Lotta down. "Guess we're going hiking," he said.

The day was beautiful for a walk in the woods, sunny, but cool enough to wear jackets. They stuck by the shore. Tabby found a few scenes Lotta liked. Walter had a tendency to look down at the small waves and ripples breaking against places where grass-covered land touched the water. He suggested Lotta paint scenes from close up, but she wanted to step back. She settled on a few places she liked, one which Tabby discovered. Lotta's favorite had some trees near low bushes and tall grasses. The blue-green lake lay behind, like a smooth carpet over a wide floor and in back of the water, there was a distant shoreline with small hills reaching up toward a few clouds in a light blue sky.

"If there's a heaven," Walter said, "this is it."

"If?" Tabby scolded. But she was smiling, so Walter knew she understood his meaning.

"This is what I needed to see," Lotta said. "Now back to the house and our chilly swim to remember the day."

Lotta enjoyed many days as sweet as that one during the next fourteen years at her Hopatcong cottage. When Mary Ann passed, she found her grief was too strong to remain in the home they had shared, so Lotta moved up to Gloucester, Massachusetts, outside of Boston. She continued to paint and to enjoy the horses she owned.

Lotta spent her last years giving away much of the money she had earned as an actress. After she died, at age 76, what remained she left to various charities: disabled veterans, animal welfare, farm relief, and others. A few people challenged her will, including Ida May Blankenburg who claimed she was Lotta's child by a secret marriage. But Lotta's wishes held. Her money went where it was needed.

Tabby and Walter moved to a small house in Sperry Springs near the home of Alina and Francesco, where they resumed their old tradition of eating suppers together and, when the weather was nice, were joined by Charlotte, Paul, and the grandchildren: Harry, Emma, and Anna.

They waited a while before they showed their family and friends one unusual feature of their new house in Sperry Springs, a bedroom with its wall covered with pictures, daguerreotypes as well as photographs, of Lotta's career. Walter took Tabby's hand as he told them. "She deserves to be remembered. From the time she was dancing in the camps to her greatest Broadway successes, she brought joy to the hearts of everyone who saw her."

Walter looked at Tabby, who smiled back and added, "We never want those memories to die."

Author's Note

My goal in writing *Living in a Star's Light* was to mix real and fictional characters while creating an intriguing narrative and remaining faithful to the history of Lotta Crabtree. Historical fiction can be more accurate in portraying past events than non-fiction because all people are greater than a listing of their accomplishments. Their thoughts and feelings are presented as they come to life, but always have to fit with the actions of the real characters.

A good example of this is Lotta's friendship with Tabby, a fictional character. During the gold rush, the population of San Francisco grew rapidly and changed in demographics. The number of Native Americans decreased, while the number of men of European descent increased. These men were mostly prospectors who were either single or had left their families to search for gold. There were many more men than women. It's also true that the women who came on their own were mostly sex workers and the brothels where those women worked were often in saloons. Although there is no evidence Lotta Crabtree had a friend who was a prostitute, it is reasonable to assume Lotta, who often sang at saloons, met women who worked there.

It is also true that Lotta never forgot the struggles of her early years and not only felt compassion toward the poor but identified with them. Throughout her career she played the waif, sometimes a boy, sometimes a girl. She was short, so it was easy for her to carry off those roles even in the latter part of her career. She also gave money to charities that helped the poor, especially young boys who made meager salaries delivering newspapers. In addition to her benevolence during her life, she included the same charities in her will. It is not unreasonable to think she would help her "friend" Tabby if it was in her power to do so.

Chapter One introduces Walter, Oliver, and Frank, who are fictional characters. Lotta, a very real person, was introduced in the first paragraph of the novel. Mary Ann, Lotta's mother, was introduced later in the same chapter. The way young Lotta danced was based on fact, as were the descriptions of the bunkhouse, the temporary stage built for Lotta, and the influence of alcohol on the lifestyles of the miners.

In Chapter Two, Cyrus is introduced as are Tabby and Ru. These are all fictional characters, but the greed of the miners and the flirtations of the prostitutes were as close to real as I could conceive.

The rules concerning claims and the role of a claims officer are based on fact, as are the contracts for prostitutes. There were some male prostitutes during that time, but the idea that they would also have contracts is not based on fact. However, researching Mary Ann's life led me to believe she had some feminist beliefs that were ahead of their time, and fit well with a desire to have the same contract for Walter as the one Tabby had signed.

There were butcher shops, watch repair shops, and other stores in San Francisco in the mid-nineteenth century. There were also canvas houses, some with makeshift restaurants outside, where people who could not afford permanent homes would live.

My description of Chinatown and the hotel where Walter and Frank had their bunks was based on fact. The prostitute/madam, Ah Toy, was a real woman whose husband died on the ship during their trip to California. She turned to sex work to survive, but eventually earned a fortune and became a prominent member of San Francisco society. Guan Wu was a fictional character as were the brothel owners Jahiel and Odell.

Lola Montez was a real performer and also a neighbor of the Crabtrees when Lotta was young. Lola was known for *The Spider Dance*, which I describe in Chapter Five. She was one of Lotta's first dance instructors, teaching her specifically how to "sell" her routines on stage.

The American Theatre was a real theater during Lotta's time. It burned down in 1868. St. Mary's Cathedral with its clock tower and the slogan "Son, Observe the Time and Fly from Evil" existed when Lotta lived in San Francisco and still exists today. The local brothels were the reason the slogan was chosen.

George and Ash, Lotta's younger brothers, were introduced in Chapter Seven. George led a troubled life with two major tragedies. Both of those are mentioned in the book and are true to life. Ash, who was two years older than George, was also an interesting character. He worked in the theaters and also, later in life, helped Lotta managed her horse stable. His name is actually John Ashworth Crabtree, same as his father. Some sources called him Jack, while others referred to him as Ash or Ashworth. This is a case where I had to pick one. I settled on the latter. John Ashworth Crabtree, the father, had some character flaws which I've tried to cover honestly. However, I do believe he had good intentions and have mentioned those as well.

Adah Menken was a real performer who knew Lotta. She did appear in a show riding a horse across the stage while wearing a bodysuit that made her appear naked. It was a scandal at that time. It's also true that Adah Menken was a friend of Lotta's and often went riding with her, fully dressed, of course. The other theater personalities I mentioned are all real: Jenny Lind, Clifton Tayleure and John Brougham, among others. Minnie Palmer was also real and did try to become the European Lotta, by copying Lotta's routines.

Lotta's plays, which I mentioned in the story, were all real including *The Pet of the Petticoats, Family Jars, The Firefly, Musette, Little Nell* and *the Marchioness,* and any others I listed. Lotta's performance at Temple Square in Salt Lake City was real and she did meet Brigham Young. Some sources reported that he was interested in marrying her, but I can't confirm that this was true.

Thomas Hill was a real artist who lived in Massachusetts and went to San Francisco to paint landscapes. I did not find a record that Lotta ever met him or saw his work, but her interest in art is a fact.

Lotta never married but had many suitors. Bolton Hulme and the Grand Duke Alexis of Russia were among them. The facts, including Bolton's death and the time Lotta spent on the yacht provided to the Grand Duke by the American government, are real.

Charlotte Cain is a fictional character and there is no record that Lotta had a goddaughter. Paul Darville, Charlotte's husband, is also fictional. I thought their family would fit well with the society in the Lake Hopatcong area during the late nineteenth and early twentieth centuries.

      Lotta Crabtree spent her childhood moving from mining camp to mining camp with a troupe of actors. With no friends her own age, Lotta must have been lonely. But she was a strong child and grew into a strong woman. She found happiness in dance and music, loving the stage and loving her mother. Her life was important to the people around her and to the people who followed in her footsteps. I hope I've done justice to her memory.

Endnotes

* *Believe Me, if All Those Endearing Young Charms* written in 1808 by Irish poet Thomas Moore

** *Book of Common Prayer* written in 1549 by Thomas Cranmer

*** The quotes from *The Herald* and *The Clipper* were listed on page 148 of *The Triumphs and Trials of Lotta Crabtree*, by David Dempsey with Raymond P. Baldwin, published by William Morrow & Company, 1968

Acknowledgements:

I would like to thank:

- My wife, who is my most dedicated critic.

- My children, who are always willing test readers.

- The members of my writers' critique group: Robert Shar, Ray Morrison, and Joni Carter, a wonderful group of writers who have become like family.

- My editor, Andrea Roche, whose corrections and suggestions have helped produce a novel of which I am very proud.

Source Materials:

Books

The Triumphs and Trials of Lotta Crabtree, by David Dempsey with Raymond P. Baldwin, published by William Morrow & Company, 1968

Troupers of the Gold Coast: The Rise of Lotta Crabtree, by Constance Rourke, published by Skyhorse Publishing, 2016

Lotta Crabtree: Gold Rush Fairy Star, by Lois V. Harris, published by Pelican Publishing Company, Inc., 2017

Gold Rush Girl: The Story of Lotta Crabtree, by Sharon Elwell, published by Sharon Elwell, 2013

What Was the Gold Rush?, by Joan Holub, published by The Penguin Group, 2013

How the Other Half Lives, by Jacob A. Riis, published by Digireads.com Publishing, 2017

Apron Full of Gold: The Letters of Mary Jane Megquier from San Francisco 1849-1856, edited by Polly Welts Kaufman, published by University of New Mexico Press, 1994

Luzena Stanley Wilson '49er: Her Memoirs as Taken Down by her Daughter in 1881, by Correnah Wilson Wright, published by Dodo Press, 2018

Loan Sharks: The Birth of Predatory Lending, by Charles R. Geisst, Brookings Institution Press, April 4 2017

Women of the Frontier : 16 Tales of Trailblazing Homesteaders, Entrepreneurs, and Rabble-Rousers, by Brandon Marie Miller, published by Chicago Review Press, 2013

History of the Theatre, by Oscar G. Brockett, published by Allyn and Bacon, Inc., 1974

Daughter of Fortune, by Isabel Allende, Translated from the Spanish by Margaret Sayers Peden, published by HarperCollins Publishers Inc., 2014

Magazines

Building the Brooklyn Bridge, by Lyle R, Shelton, published in *Sea Classics; Canoga Park Vol. 47*, Feb 2014: 50-54,56,58.

Newspapers

He Married; She Not, *Alton Telegraph*, Jul 12 1883, Page 3

Lotta's Romance, *Atlantic Daily Telegraph*, Jun 20 1883, Page 1

Lotta Crabtree Now an Enthusiastic Painter Tells of Her Interest in Birth Control and Movies, *Boston Sunday Post*, August 13 1916, Page 29

The Woes of Sprightly Actresses, *Brooklyn Daily Eagle*, Dec 11 1879, Page 2

Chinatown (The Opium Joint, Chinese Theatre, and a Chinese Feast), *Terre Haute Weekly Gazette*, Jul 29 1886, Page 1

Scenes in Chinatown, San Francisco, *Marshall Clark County Herald*, Oct 12, 1880, Page 12

Frederic J. Haskin, Answers to Questions, *Albuquerque Journal*, Mar 12 1931, Page 7

Gossip About Women, *Daily Iowa Capital*, Jul 1 1896, Page 3

Loss of the Central America, *Terre Haute Daily Union*, Sep 28 1857, Page 4

Love at First Sight, *Fort Wayne Daily Sentinel*, Nov 16, 1880, Page 1

Lotta's Luck, *Lincoln Daily Nebraska State Journal*, Mar 29 1885, Page 6

Lotta's Romance, *Atlantic Daily Telegraph*, Jun 20 1883, Page 1

Lotta's Lost Baby, *Sarasota Herald*, Nov 24 1925, Page 12

Going Across the Ocean, *New York Times*, Jun 7 1883, Page 8

Lotta's Latest, *Monmouth Evening Gazette*, Jul 6 1883, Page 2

Yet Without a Peer, *Olean Democrat*, Aug 15 1893, Page 16

The Stage, Toulon Stark County News, Jan 24 1884, Page 5

Two Left in Fight over Crabtree Estate, *Lubbock Morning Avalanche*, Sun, Jul 5 1925, Page 3

Websites
Lotta Crabtree
https://en.wikipedia.org/wiki/Lotta_Crabtree

Lotta Crabtree American Actress
https://www.britannica.com/biography/Lotta-Crabtree

Lotta Crabtree and Lola Montez
http://www.standingstones.com/crabtree.html

Lotta Crabtree ; John McCullough
https://archive.org/stream/sanfranciscothea19386sanf/sanfrancisc
othea19386sanf_djvu.txt

Rebel Girls From Bay Area History: Lotta Crabtree, "The San Francisco Favorite"
https://www.kqed.org/pop/110017/rebel-girls-from-bay-area-
history-lotta-crabtree-the-san-francisco-favorite

Lotta's Legacy, by Trudy Tynan, Associated Press, 1998
http://articles.latimes.com/1998/feb/15/local/me-19312

History of American Women - Women in Theater - Lotta Crabtree
http://www.womenhistoryblog.com/2013/12/lotta-crabtree.html

San Francisco History Index – Lotta Crabtree
http://www.zpub.com/sf/history/crab.html

The Strychnine Banjo: Jake Wallace & Lotta Crabtree
https://banjogathering.weebly.com/blog/the-strychnine-banjo-jake-
wallace-lotta-crabtree

Internet Broadway Database – Charlotte Crabtree
https://www.ibdb.com/broadway-cast-staff/charlotte-crabtree-
85586

Gold-Rush Era Prostitutes
http://www.foundsf.org/index.php?title=Gold-
Rush_Era_Prostitutes

Vice's Angels: Notable Harlots in San Francisco History

http://joecontent.net/vices-angels-notable-harlots-in-san-francisco-history/

Life inside American brothel Intimate photos reveal working girls 19th Century Pennsylvania
https://www.dailymail.co.uk/news/article-6130379/Life-inside-American-brothel-Intimate-photos-reveal-working-girls-19th-Century-Pennsylvania.html

19th Century San Francisco
http://ushistoryscene.com/century/19/topic/san-francisco/

A Journey from New York to San Francisco in 1850
https://www.jstor.org/stable/1834222?seq=1#metadata_info_tab_contents

An Ounce Short - Full Movie
https://www.youtube.com/watch?v=BG3RRd-e8MU

Be It Ever So Humble... - Gold Rush Housing
https://www.sierrafoothillmagazine.com/housegr.html

History of Chinese Americans in San Francisco
https://en.wikipedia.org/wiki/History_of_Chinese_Americans_in_San_Francisco

Old St. Mary's Cathedral
https://en.wikipedia.org/wiki/Old_St._Mary%27s_Cathedral

Restaurant-ing through history
https://restaurant-ingthroughhistory.com/

San Francisco Theatrical Memories
http://www.sfmuseum.org/hist/theatres.html

19th century American foodways
http://www.foodtimeline.org/foodpioneer.html

Caisson disease during the construction of the Eads and Brooklyn Bridges: A review, National Center for Biotechnology Information, U.S. National Library of Medicine, 2004
https://www.ncbi.nlm.nih.gov/pubmed/15686275

The Bizarre Ritual of the 19th Century Wedding Photo
https://time.com/4825507/bizarre-wedding-photos/

History of Weddings in America
https://davincibridal.com/blog/history-of-weddings-in-america/
Weddings in the United States
https://en.wikipedia.org/wiki/Weddings_in_the_United_States

The Wedding "Whirl and Vortex:" Mid-19th Century Wedding Preparations
http://merchantshouse.org/blog/wedding-preparations/

Famous Names, Famous Homes on Lake Hopatcong, by Jane Primerano
https://patch.com/new-jersey/hopatcong-sparta/looking-back-famous-names-famous-homes-on-lake-hopatcong-2

Hotel Breslin & Alamac Hotel at Mount Arlington, NJ
http://www.mountarlington.org/breslin.htm

Then and Now: Breslin Hotel
https://lakehopatcongnews.com/c79-history/then-and-now-breslin-hotel/

A Look Back, Nov. 5: Sperry Springs -- A locale on Lake Hopatcong
https://www.njherald.com/20171105/a-look-back-nov-5-sperry-springs----a-locale-on-lake-hopatcong

New Jersey, NJ Lake Hopatcong, Houses on Sperry Springs 1907 Real Photo Postcard
https://www.worthpoint.com/worthopedia/jersey-nj-lake-hopatcong-houses-1802346672

Lake Hopatcong -Ye Olde Lake
http://www.njskylands.com/history-lake-hopatcong

Lake Hopatcong Historical Museum
https://lakehopatconghistory.com/somewhere-in-time/

Lake Hopatcong's Most Famous, Part 2: Miss Lotta
https://lakehopatcongnews.com/c79-history/lake-hopatcongs-most-famous-part-2-miss-lotta/

Dressing the Late 19th Century Woman
https://www.knowlesville.com/vintage/getting-dressed-12.html

Craig Hadley, A Nineteenth Century Slang Dictionary,
https://mess1.homestead.com/nineteenth_century_slang_dictionary.pdf

About Steve Lindahl

Living in a Star's Light is Steve Lindahl's fifth novel. His first three, *Motherless Soul* , *White Horse Regressions*, and *Hopatcong Vision Quest* are historical fictions wrapped in modern mysteries. In these books the characters must look into their past life memories to find clues concerning crimes in the present. His fourth novel, *Under a Warped Cross*, is also historical fiction, but without the regression twist. It is set in the tenth century, in Scandinavia, Ireland, and Britannia. His short fiction has appeared in *Space and Time, The Alaska Quarterly, The Wisconsin Review, Eclipse, Ellipsis* and *Red Wheelbarrow*. He served for five years as an associate editor on the staff of *The Crescent Review*, a literary magazine he co-founded and he is currently the Managing Editor of *Flying South*, a literary magazine sponsored by Winston-Salem Writers. He loves to read as much as he loves to write and has posted hundreds of reviews on Amazon, Goodreads, Librarything, and his blog (www.stevelindahl.blogspot.com).

Steve is married to Toni Lindahl, a pastel artist. They currently reside in North Carolina, but still spend time each summer at Lake Hopatcong, NJ. They have two adult children, Nicole and Erik.

Other novels by Steve Lindahl:

Motherless Soul

White Horse Regressions

Hopatcong Vision Quest

Under a Warped Cross

Social Media Links:

Website: http://www.stevelindahl.com/

Blog: www.stevelindahl.blogspot.com

Facebook: https://www.facebook.com/steve.lindahl.3

Amazon author page: https://www.amazon.com/Steve-Lindahl/e/B0031GLA5Y?ref=sr_ntt_srch_lnk_1&qid=1563058097&sr=8-1

Goodreads author page: https://www.goodreads.com/author/show/3117087.Steve_Lindahl

www.ingramcontent.com/pod-product-compliance
Lightning Source LLC
Chambersburg PA
CBHW070601120726
47909CB00007B/2402